Train from Marietta

DOROTHY GARLOCK

Train from Marietta

WARNER BOOKS

NEW YORK   BOSTON

Warner Books

Time Warner Book Group
1271 Avenue of the Americas, New York, NY 10020
Visit our Web site at www.twbookmark.com.

Printed in the United States of America

First Edition: March 2006
10 9 8 7 6 5 4 3 2 1

Library of Congress Cataloging-in-Publication Data

Garlock, Dorothy.
  Train from Marietta / Dorothy Garlock.— 1st ed.
    p.   cm.
  ISBN 0-446-57790-1 — ISBN 0-446-69531-9 (pbk.)
    1. Kidnapping victims—Fiction. 2. Children with disabilities—Fiction. 3.
Ranch life—Fiction. 4. Cowboys—Fiction. 5. Texas—Fiction. I. Title.

  PS3557.A71645T73 2006
  813'.6—dc22   2005049942

This book is lovingly dedicated to my dear friends
Michelle and Doug Klein.
Also to Matt and Kelli.

KIDNAPPED!

"Stay aboard! This stop's for water!"
Katherine Tyler hears the shout.
As the train from Marietta stops,
She quietly slips out.

She is tall and blond and weary.
Just wants a breath of air.
An independent woman,
Unaware of danger there.

Unaware there is another
Who has followed in her wake,
Who will seize upon the moment,
Who will use this lucky break.

Abducted! In this nowhere place
She is hidden far from sight
As the train from Marietta
Goes on, hurtling through the night.

—F.S.I.

Train from Marietta

Prologue

New York City, 1933

THE DOOR OPENED SUDDENLY. Startled, Eddy reared up out of the chair, a glass of brandy in his hand. "Oh, it's you. Come in, Uncle William."

"Drinking alone?" The portly silver-haired man was dressed all in gray from his ten-dollar hat to the custom-made shoes on his feet. Light from the streetlamp on the corner penetrated the blinds that covered the large windows. It was a man's room: heavy furniture, unadorned tabletops, everything in brown and tan tones. The lingering smell of cigarette smoke filled the air.

"Occasionally I drink alone, don't you?" Eddy took another swallow from his glass as he settled back into his seat. "What brings you out this time of night?"

William Jacobs closed the door, then carefully removed his hat and hung it on the hat rack. "I wanted to catch you when you didn't have a woman here."

Eddy set his glass down on the table by the chair. "I'm

not the womanizer you think I am. I spend an evening alone once in a while," he said with indignation in his voice.

"You're an easy mark for the little gold-digging flappers who hang out at your favorite speakeasy."

"You know a thing or two about flappers, don't you, Uncle?"

"You'd do well to remember, Edwin, which side of the bread your butter is on," William said menacingly, one thick finger pointed at his nephew.

"Why don't you remind me, dear Uncle?" Eddy said, his voice dripping with sarcasm.

"Don't get smart with me, you little bastard!"

"Don't call me that!"

"You are one, you know."

"How could I forget when you remind me day in and day out?" Eddy glared at his uncle.

"Well, I know that my sister slept with every Tom, Dick, and Harry that came along. You could be nothing else."

"And don't talk about my mother like that either."

"I took care of her all her life. I'll talk about her any way I want to."

At this, the two men glared at one another in silence. They'd had this argument many times before, neither one willing to back down.

"What's on your mind?" Eddy finally growled. "I'm sure it's something, or you'd be with your lady love."

"You'll know soon enough what's on my mind, and you'd better listen. If you know what's good for you, you'll forget about my lady love." William paused and then went to stand beside his nephew's chair. "We're in deep trouble. I've got to get some cash, and soon."

"I'll do what I can, short of robbing a bank." Eddy chuckled.

"What I've got in mind is easier than that and carries no risk to you—"

"What you mean is, no risk to *you*. Who do you want me to kill?"

"I wouldn't trust you to kill a grasshopper. You'd be sure to mess it up."

"Then what do you want me to do?"

"I want you to help me get some money out of John Tyler. He's got plenty of it. John's daughter, Kate, is leaving to go to California in a few days. The train will pass through some pretty rough country. If she was abducted from the train, my dear partner would fork over any amount to get her back."

"You mean kidnap her?"

"I mean hold her until John pays the ransom."

"Why do you want me involved in this?"

"I need you because you have a cool head. I don't want her hurt. She needs you to protect her." William did not look at him when he made the statement.

For the next several minutes, Eddy listened with increasing shock as his uncle laid out his plan. He could scarcely believe what he was hearing! Finally he shot to his feet. "I will not do it!"

"You *will* do it, or you'll be out of this fancy apartment on your ass, and not get another dime from me. Look at the easy life you've had all these years. You owe me. Don't forget that I'm the one who makes it possible for you to pay for this apartment and the clothes on your back. I'm responsible for you being accepted by the Tylers to court their daughter Susie. If you had half the sense you were born with, you'd get her pregnant, marry her, and you'd have it made, even if she's not her father's favorite daughter. If I don't get one hundred thousand dollars soon, we could both land in prison. If I go, I've got enough on you to take you with me."

"What will happen to me and Kate when we come back?" Eddy looked at his uncle as if he had never seen him before. "I just can't do what you're asking. I like her."

"If you like her, you'll go and see to it that she's not harmed. Besides, you don't have to do it alone. When Kate gets back, she won't want it known that she spent a week alone in the wild with three men, so she won't say anything."

"Three men? Who's going beside me?"

"Squirrelly."

"You can't be serious!" Eddy yelled in disbelief.

"He's going. He's loyal and I can trust him."

"You can't trust me?"

"Keep your voice down, you fool. I've contacted a man in Texas who's put me in touch with someone who knows every stick and stone in the territory. He'll be a big help."

"You know that Squirrelly has about as many brains as a bedbug."

"I'll give him his orders. Besides, I owe his father, old Felerri, a favor."

"That crook!"

"I'll use whoever I need to. Preacher or crook, it doesn't matter to me. With Squirrelly along, Kate will be convinced that you are there to protect her and bring her home."

Eddy looked down at the floor as he pushed a hand through his curly blond hair. "I haven't said I was going to do it. I've got to think about it." *You old son of a bitch! You don't know it, but you're giving me a way to get out from under your thumb and to protect Kate at the same time. I've been wondering how I could manage to get away from you, and your selfish plan falls right into my lap.*

His anger boiling over, William snatched the brandy glass from the table and hurled it against the wall behind Eddy. Broken glass and brandy flew in all directions.

"Here's something for you to think about, you ungrateful little pup. Neither one of us will go to prison if we pay the money back. Which do you prefer? Who do you think will take the brunt of an investigation? A young whippersnapper like you or a respected businessman like me?"

"But—"

"Don't be stupid! This is as much for your benefit as it is for mine. I know that you're fond of the girl. I also know the type of man Squirrelly is. If you don't go, what do you think he'll do with Kate while they're all alone in the wilderness? Yes or no?"

Eddy's shoulders slumped before he quietly said, "I'll do it."

"I thought you would."

Eddy hated the gloating look on his uncle's face. "Does your lady love know about this scheme?"

"She knows."

William walked to the door, picked up his hat, and slammed it down on his head. He took a cigar from his coat pocket, bit off the end, and spat it out on the Oriental carpet.

"I'll be back tomorrow night to give you all the details. Get ready to leave by Sunday."

William went out and slammed the door.

All was quiet in the room. Eddy went to the sideboard for a bottle of brandy and poured himself another drink. He carried it across the room and dropped back into his chair.

Confusion mixed with hope in Eddy's mind. This could be his big chance. He had to play his cards right. He'd saved up money, tucking it here and there so no one would notice. It would be easy to slip across the border into Mexico from Texas. He'd be able to live like a king on the money he'd saved. He would make sure that Kate was on her way home before he left her. If Squirrelly was in on this, he was probably hired to kill both him and Kate after his uncle got the money. Eddy couldn't let that happen. When it was all over, he would take off for Mexico and not look back. He had faith that, once back in New York, Kate would expose his uncle's plan to the authorities.

One thought filled Eddy's mind. His big chance had come at last. He would foil the hit man, cover his tracks, and be far away by the time his uncle realized he had escaped his would-be killers. Then let old William worry that someday, some way, he might be coming back . . .

Chapter 1

Tate didn't know much about style, but he knew that the woman standing beside the rough board wall of the small depot was fashionably dressed. He had glanced at her when he left the ticket counter and had wondered what she was doing in this rugged Texas town. She was obviously a city woman and as out of place as a rose in a cactus patch. Light blond hair fell to her shoulders. She wore a small blue felt hat that matched her princess-style coat, which came down over slim hips. The flared blue skirt that floated down around her calves was edged with a blue satin ribbon. Her matching shoes, with slender heels, were planted firmly beside an expensive leather valise.

What a silly hat, Tate thought, chuckling to himself. It'd offer no shade at all. Within ten minutes, her face would be cooked in the West Texas sun.

Worried about her trunk, Kate had stepped down from the train to make sure it was in the baggage car. When the railroad agent told her it had been left at the last stop and was being picked up by the train from Marietta, she had decided to wait and go on to California on the same train as her belongings. She wondered now at the wisdom of her decision. Shortly after she'd spoken with him, the agent had locked up and left. Now all who remained on the platform with her were a lone cowboy and the button salesman who had been on the train since New Orleans.

The sun was setting in the western sky. Purple shadows were sliding down from the hills. It would be dark soon. A slight chill had entered the air with the disappearance of the hot summer sun. The depot was far from town; only a sprinkling of lights shone from the houses. The train from Marietta wasn't due for another hour. It would be pitch-dark by then.

She was glad for the presence of the cowboy at the end of the platform. She'd first glanced at him when he left the ticket counter; her eyes had met his even though she knew that she shouldn't make eye contact with the strange man in dusty boots and well-worn jeans. His hair was black, and he wore a battered, wide-brimmed hat. His mouth was set in a thin line as if he somehow disapproved of her. What was he doing here at this time of night? Regardless of his appearance, she was glad he was here; she didn't want to be alone with the other man.

The salesman, dressed in a striped suit and a derby hat, paced back and forth near his sample case. She'd had the misfortune to take the same route to California that he had chosen. When they first boarded the train in New Orleans, he'd prattled on and on about buttons and snaps for hours. His twitchy, talkative nature and the way he looked at her gave her the creeps.

As the three stood waiting for the train, it seemed to her that they were the only people in all this vast and desolate land.

A door in the side of the depot opened on squeaky hinges. An old man pushed a trolley down to the end of the platform and left it so that its bundles could be loaded into the baggage car when the train arrived. Then he disappeared around the corner of the depot.

The button salesman coughed and took a step toward her. She turned to see that the cowboy was looking in their direction, but she wasn't sure who he was looking at. She pushed herself away from the wall and walked over to him.

"Is this train usually on time?"

"Sometimes," he said. "This isn't Grand Central Station, you know."

"Well, what do you know? I thought it was." She smiled up at him. But he didn't smile back.

What did she expect? He couldn't take a joke. He'd probably only heard of Grand Central Station and had never been there.

"Thanks for that valuable information." She turned and walked back to take her place against the rough boards. At least the salesman had taken the hint and moved back to his case. She looked at her watch but couldn't see the time in the dim light. She nudged the leather valise at her feet; if her trunk never arrived, at least she had clean underwear and her cosmetics.

Then, in the distance, she heard the familiar sounds of a train approaching. Could the thing be earlier than the agent predicted, or had an hour passed already? She looked at the cowboy and saw that he was peering down the track toward the east. She looked in that direction too, and soon she saw the billows of smoke rising up above the huge engine. The piercing whistle was loud enough to wake everybody for miles. The engineer was making a grand entrance into the station. Too bad only she, the cowboy, and the button sales-man were there to appreciate the effort.

The train rolled slowly past her before coming to a stop. Two cars were brightly lit and filled with passengers, most of whom appeared to be sleeping. Katherine picked up her valise, walked to the edge of the platform, and waited for the conductor to step down from the train. He smiled, took her ticket, and helped her up the steps and into the car.

The cowboy was right behind her and edged past the conductor. Katherine turned to the right and entered the car. Most of the seats were filled, but halfway down she saw what she thought was an empty seat. Carrying her valise, she made her way down the aisle and set it on the floor.

When she turned, the cowboy was still right behind her. With a grunt, she attempted to lift the heavy bag up and put it in the rack above the seat. Quick as a whistle, the cow-boy snatched it out of her hand, and as he slung it upward, the latch opened and her personal belongings spilled out over the seat and onto the floor. She looked down in horror to see a pair of her lace panties covering a pair of dusty cowboy boots.

"Sorry," he said.

Katherine was more embarrassed than she'd ever been

in her entire life. All she could do was grunt in reply, "I bet you are."

The cowboy pulled her valise from the rack and set it on the seat beside her. He reached down and grabbed a handful of lavender lace panties, silk slips, and lacy bras and stuffed them back into the case. As he did, a jar of face cream fell onto his foot and opened. Katherine looked down to see the white cream running down over the cowboy's boot. The smell of gardenias filled the air in the passenger car. All around the car, people were stretching their necks to look.

She thought the cowboy said something under his breath. It sounded like "Oh, hell!" but she wasn't sure.

Fearing that he would wipe the face cream off his boot with her lavender panties, she pulled a big handkerchief out of her pocket and handed it to him. He jerked it out of her hand with a disgusted look and proceeded to wipe the cream off his boot. After glancing up and down the aisle to make sure he had picked up everything that had fallen from her bag, he tipped his hat toward Katherine and moved on to the front of the car in search of an empty seat. Fuming at the cowboy's back as he walked away, Katherine sat down and moved over next to the window. He'd made her look stupid in front of everyone! She was certain that her face was beet red with embarrassment. What a grouch, she thought. It wasn't her fault he was so clumsy. Were all the men in the West clods like him?

A cough that came from the aisle caused her to turn. The button salesman stood with his hand stretched out toward her. There, swinging from his fingers, was one of her bras. She snatched it from his hand, pushed it into the pocket of her coat, and looked back out the window. The salesman chuckled before walking on.

Until now, the first part of the trip had been uneventful. What more might happen before she reached California?

Tate Castle moved on to the next car in the train in search of an empty seat. Finding one, he threw himself into it.

He never wanted to see that woman again! All he was trying to do was help her lift that damned bag. How was he supposed to know that it was going to fly apart? Did women actually wear that kind of thing? Holding a handful of those undergarments was like holding a handful of air!

He was glad finally to be heading home. It seemed like forever since he'd seen his ranch, his friends, and, most important, his daughter. He'd missed her terribly and knew that she'd missed him too.

It was still a couple of hours to Muddy Creek, where he would get off the train. He was bone-tired. Tipping his hat down over his eyes, Tate tried to sleep as the scent of flowers drifted up from his boot.

The sound of the steel wheels screeching against the tracks wakened Katherine. The train came to a stop at the next depot, a darkened little town called Los Rios. A new group of passengers came on board. A heavyset woman carrying bundles of clothing under her arms came down the aisle and plunked herself in the seat beside Katherine. The woman looked over at her and grinned, showing snuff-stained teeth. Katherine smiled, then quickly turned away; it was obvious that the woman had not bathed in quite a while.

"Hello, dearie, where are you goin'?"

Katherine acted as if she hadn't heard, and kept her face turned toward the window.

"I'm going to St. Elena to see my brother and sister," the woman offered. "I've not seen them in two years."

Katherine turned briefly and said, "How nice for you." The woman's odor was sickening.

"My brother's been sick," the woman continued, "and my sister lost her husband not long ago. Between you and me, it was no great loss. He wasn't worth diddly-squat! Too lazy to come in out of the rain, you know?"

"Too bad."

The train lurched and then moved smoothly down the track. The smelly woman kept talking, not seeming to care that her audience wasn't listening.

Katherine leaned her head against the window, her thoughts wandering.

A year ago she had received her nursing degree, fulfilling a lifelong dream. After she had worked for a couple of years in a clinic in New York City, her uncle in California made an offer that she couldn't refuse. He was a doctor at a large hospital in San Francisco and wanted her to come out and assist him. Jumping at the chance, Katherine packed up her belongings and headed West. She was looking forward to seeing new things and meeting new people.

The leave-taking from her father had been painful. They

had always been close, and he had supported his daughter's dreams. She was sure she had seen tears in his eyes when he told her good-bye on the platform.

In contrast, her stepmother, whom her father had married when Katherine was very young, had merely waved good-bye and declared that she wouldn't be surprised to see Katherine back at home within a matter of weeks.

Susie, her half-sister, thought Katherine had lost her mind even to want to go out to such a backwater place as California when there was so much to do right there in New York City. All she could expect to find out there were farmers and orange trees. Kate knew, though, that Susie was glad to get her out of the way so she would have a better chance with Edwin, the handsome nephew of her father's business partner, William Jacobs. Susie needn't have worried; although Edwin was a handsome man, Kate had never had any interest in him as a beau.

The woman's voice broke into her thoughts. "My nephew done fell down a well and drowneded. Wasn't too bright, that boy."

Katherine's thoughts traveled back over the past year. Her stepmother, Lila, had become more distant from the family. She was so involved in all her social activities that she was seldom at home. And when she was, she belittled Katherine for her devotion to nursing and her lack of interest in finding a suitable husband, a man who could support her in style.

Susie was like her mother. She loved the social life. The only things that seemed to matter to her were the latest fashions, dinner parties, and who was seeing whom. Katherine, on the other hand, was her father's daughter. Both of them enjoyed reading, talking business, and even an occasional game of bridge. Since her early childhood, they had been devoted to each other. While he also cared for Susie, Katherine knew that she was his favorite.

She leaned her head against the window and looked out into the lightening morning. The sun had begun to poke up over the hilltops. Telegraph poles whizzed by, and occasionally the train passed a cluster of houses.

Katherine had hoped that the woman would take her silence as a hint, but she kept right on talking. She talked so incessantly about her dog, her assorted aches and pains, and her lazy husband who was angry that she was making the trip that Katherine wanted to jump up and move; but there were no empty seats. To top it all off, someone behind her had lit a cheap cigar, filling the cramped car with smoke. At least it helped mask the stink of the woman!

The conductor came through. "We will be stopping in a few minutes to take on water. Everyone please stay on the train."

Katherine thought it would be wonderful to get a few breaths of fresh air. She hated the cramped feeling of the railway cars. When the train finally came to a stop, she excused herself and, with her handbag over her arm, managed to squeeze out in front of the fat lady and into the aisle.

As she moved toward the front of the car, Katherine noticed that the button salesman had slouched down in his seat, his derby hat pulled over his face. Light snores came from his open mouth. Katherine moved on past him. *I hope he sleeps all the way to San Francisco.*

The conductor had opened the door and was standing out on the platform. After checking the watch that hung from a chain on his vest, he moved into the next car. As soon as he walked away, Katherine quickly stepped down and moved to the side of the steps, out of the light that came from the car.

Oh, it was great to breathe the fresh air.

She looked off into the darkness and saw a long trough swing down toward the train. Then she heard the rush of water pouring into the engine's tank.

Suddenly something hard was jammed into her back and a hand grabbed hold of her shoulder. The sound of a revolver cocking startled her.

"Hello, Kate."

Chapter 2

KATHERINE HAD LITTLE TIME TO REGISTER any shock at what she had just heard. A firm shove between her shoulders sent her flying forward.

"Get movin', Miss High-and-Mighty! Keep your eyes from wanderin' and your mouth shut if you like breathin'."

Numb with fear, Katherine felt herself being dragged away from the train.

She tried to scream, but only a squeak came out before a heavy hand clamped down over her mouth. Without thinking, her gut instinct took over, and she bit down on a finger with all her strength. The man grunted with pain.

"Bitch!" he hissed. He jerked his hand from her mouth and slapped her sharply alongside her ear. Shooting pain and dizziness filled her head as she lost her balance and fell to her knees. However, the man brooked no delays and violently jerked her back to her feet and pulled her farther from the train.

As Katherine stumbled along, she desperately tried to think. No one had ever struck her in all her life!

In a dazed state, she allowed the man to drag her into the dark woods that ran alongside the tracks; the soles of her shoes were not much protection against the rough stones that were scattered about. Her fear kept her from being aware of the pain in her head, hands, knees, and feet.

Finally the man flung her to the ground behind a clump of bushes. Katherine landed hard on her back.

"Not a peep," he ordered.

Katherine felt as if her eyes were swimming in her head. She couldn't focus on anything. She heard the whistle of the train as it prepared to leave the water station. Her fear escalated.

"Why are you doing this?" she demanded. The sound of the train starting to move reached her ears. "Why are—"

"I said shut up!" the man barked, and peered through the bushes toward the departing train. A thin smile spread across his face.

Slowly Katherine's vision focused. Past the gun barrel she could now see him. A striped suit. A bowler hat. "Wait! Wait a second! You're that button and thread salesman, aren't you?"

"I ain't no button salesman, sweetie," the man said.

The sounds of the train grew fainter until there was nothing left but the sound of her racing heart.

"You've been following me," Katherine said accusingly.

"I knew it! You were paying attention to me. You like me, huh?"

"About as much as I like a toothache." She slowly reached up, gingerly felt her ear. It stung when she touched it.

"Ah, come on . . . you were givin' me the eye on that platform. I saw you."

"If you think that, you've got scrambled eggs for brains."

"You think so? Way I see it, I handled this pretty darn smart. I didn't even have to force you from the car. I just sat back and watched you get off the train. I didn't have to do a damn thing. You come along gentle as a lamb and ain't no one the wiser. Bet you feel pretty dumb now, don't ya? Who's the smart one?"

"If you touch me, my father will hunt you down and kill you." The fear that she felt when she'd first been taken was slowly receding. Now anger began to take its place.

"Big deal. I ain't afraid."

"Why are you doing this? I don't know you."

"But I know you," the salesman said as he sat on his haunches, waving the gun around. "I've seen you go in and out of John Tyler's office a buncha times. You even smiled at me once, and I followed you for a whole block."

"You're lying. I wouldn't smile at someone as sleazy as you."

"Well, lying or not, I've got you now, don't I?" He grinned proudly.

Katherine decided it was useless to try to talk with this disgusting creature. She thought about the tall cowboy and wished that he would suddenly appear. But that was not to be; minutes later she found herself sitting on the ground, her back to a small tree, with her hands tied around its trunk.

"If you'll be quiet, I won't gag you. Let out one squeak, and I'll stuff a dirty rag in your mouth."

It was getting lighter now. She figured an hour or two had passed since she left the train. She leaned her head back against the tree to try to relieve some of the pressure on her bound arms, but was instantly alert when the salesman came near and tickled her cheek.

"Get away from me, you slimy toad!"

He only laughed and tickled the other cheek.

To her relief, he went back to a small fire and fed it more sticks. She could hear the crackle of the flames, and a thin stream of smoke rose toward the blue sky. She hoped he knew what he was doing, or he could set the woods on fire.

Staring intently at the salesman, Katherine tried to think if she had ever seen him near her father's office, but she could not remember him. Why had he taken her? What was happening?

Her ears picked up the sound of a motorcar approaching, and she wondered if she dared to scream if it came near. The sleazy little worm still had the gun and could shoot her. Was it worth the risk?

Finally the motorcar came into view. The big black sedan stopped not twenty feet from where she was tied. She called out, "Help! Help me!" and saw the salesman double over with laughter.

Katherine couldn't believe her eyes when a familiar figure got out of the car. "Eddy, help me!" she called, pulling desperately at her restraints.

The handsome blond man was dressed in jeans, boots, and a western-type shirt. With a look of concern, he walked toward her, went behind the tree, and cut the rope binding her hands.

"Oh thank God! This little weasel tied me to the tree and hit me, Eddy! He hit me in the face!"

Eddy reached down and helped Katherine to her feet. She stood within his protecting arm and glared at the man tending the fire.

"I thought I told you not to hurt her," Eddy said.

"Ah shit, I didn't hurt her much. I was just tryin' to keep her big mouth shut. Besides, she started it. Look where she bit me," he said, and held out his hand.

"He put it over my mouth, Eddy. What did he expect?" Suddenly the strangeness of the situation struck her. "Wait. Wait just a minute. What's this all about? What are you doing here, Eddy?"

"Just relax, Kate."

"I can't relax! Why did he take me from the train? He's been on the same train with me since New Orleans. Was he following me?"

Squirrelly got up and threw a handful of sticks into the fire. "Would you believe how dumb she is? She got off the train all on her own when we stopped at the midway watering tank. I didn't have to do a thing. Now she's standin' here thinkin' that you come to rescue her. You got rocks for brains, sweetheart."

"Keep quiet, Squirrelly," Eddy said with a hard look.

"Do you know this slimy little worm, Eddy?" Katherine asked.

Eddy was embarrassed and looked away from her. "Come on, Kate, get in the car."

It was then that she noticed the man sitting behind the wheel of the motorcar. He didn't look at her. All she could see of him was a scar that ran down the side of his face. Eddy opened the back door of the car and stood waiting for Katherine to get in.

"I don't understand this! Please, Eddy, tell me what's going on." The fear that she felt when Squirrelly had taken her from the train began to return. She had so many questions that she couldn't begin to count them, but two kept coming back. *Why is this happening, and why is Eddy here?*

"You'll not be hurt, Kate, I promise."

"But I've missed my train."

"You'll just be a couple of weeks late getting to San Francisco, that's all. We'll stay out here in the country for a little while. Maybe we can even do some hunting. They tell me there's plenty of deer out here."

"You know I don't like to hunt."

"Then why did you make all of those trips to John's lodge if you didn't like to hunt?"

"I just went to keep him company and cook for him."

"Didn't you ever use that expensive rifle he bought you?"

"I shot some bottles and tin cans."

Eddy laughed. "The way John was bragging about you, I thought you had shot a moose!"

"Well, I didn't," Katherine said with a frown.

She didn't like this. Not one bit. Edwin Jacobs had been courting her sister, Susan. She had never been attracted to him, although he was charming. Why was he here? How did he know this Squirrelly character?

"Eddy, what is going on?"

"Kate, please. Just trust me," he answered, holding out his hand.

In the end, she realized that she didn't have a choice; she had to trust him or, at the very least, go along with him. She couldn't get away. The only thing to do was bide her time and wait for her chance. She took Eddy's hand and got into the backseat. He slid in beside her.

After putting out the fire, Squirrelly got into the front seat, turned, and leered at her. He held up his hand and there, hanging from his fingertips, was one of her lace bras.

"Look at what I got."

"Give that to me, you pervert!"

"Pervert? What's that mean? She talks pretty fancy, don't she?"

"Give it to her," Eddy said sternly.

Squirrelly grinned, showing a large gap between his front teeth. "And if I don't?"

"Give it to her now, Squirrelly."

"I got my orders from the top guy; I ain't takin' no orders from you."

"I'm in charge out here. You'll take orders from me." Eddy reached over and grabbed the bra from his hand. "How did you get this anyway?"

"Oh, she gave it to me. She's sweet on me, ain't you, darlin'?"

"I am not! My valise came open on the train, and everything spilled out. I stuffed this one in my pocket, and he grabbed it when we were struggling." Katherine took the bra from Eddy and tucked it back into her coat pocket. "I really want to know what is going on! Why are you with these men, Eddy?"

"I'll tell you all about it later, Kate."

The car was traveling at a fast clip down a rutted road that snaked between the trees. The sun had risen in the sky, and the day was already getting hot. "Cover her eyes." The voice came from the man behind the wheel.

"Right." Eddy whipped out a scarf and tied it over her eyes. "Sorry, love, but this is necessary."

"But—"

"Don't be scared, nothing's going to happen to you."

Katherine was quiet as the car bounced along the rough road. Silence filled the vehicle. Periodically Eddy gave her hand a squeeze, but it did little to make her feel any less uneasy. After what seemed like an hour, but was probably only half that, the car came to a stop. She heard two doors open as the men in front got out, and then the door opened on her side of the car. A hand reached in and yanked her out. "Don't touch me!"

"Well, la-di-da, ain't she a fine lady." She recognized Squirrelly's voice.

She heard Eddy get out of the car, and then one of his hands was on her waist. "Come on, honey."

"Where are we, Eddy? Why do I have to have my eyes covered?"

"I don't see any reason for them to be covered now." Eddy jerked the scarf off.

She blinked in the bright morning sunlight. When she was able to focus her eyes, she saw that they were in front of a rough log cabin, with one door and one window on the front. It stood alone, surrounded only by rocks and trees. She was in the middle of nowhere.

"What is this place?"

"It's the Waldorf-Astoria!" Squirrelly said, and giggled.

"You'll be all right here. I'm staying with you," Eddy said reassuringly.

"Me too." Squirrely giggled again, this time licking his lips.

Katherine shot him an angry glance, which set him tittering even more.

How could Eddy expect her to stay in the same place as that fool? Why was she here? What were they going to do with her?

Eddy turned and pointed back toward the car. "Let's get our things—"

Seeing her chance, Katherine jerked away from him and ran up a small incline of rock at the side of the house. This might be her only chance. She had to make it count!

Running and stumbling on the loose rock, Katherine tried to break away. It was hard going, but slowly she made her way up the small hill. Halfway to the top, her foot slipped and she fell. The sharp rock cut her knees, but she jumped back up and kept moving.

As she neared the top of the rise, she felt a hand grab hold of her ankle.

"Now, where do you think you're goin'?" Squirrelly's voice came from behind her.

Quickly, and with all the strength she had, she kicked her foot back, feeling the heel of her shoe connect with something solid. Squirrelly let out a shout and a string of curses as he fell and then slid down the rock.

With her legs churning, the pain from the small cuts forgotten, she reached the top of the hill. Before her lay a vast area of small trees and shrubs. She had hoped that she would be near a road, another house, or that she could catch a glimpse of someone. Instead, there was nothing. Tears of disappointment filled her eyes.

"Where you gonna go?" a gravelly voice said from behind her.

Katherine spun around to see standing on the hillside the scar-faced man who had driven the car. She'd not heard him on the rocks! Hard eyes stared at her. They reminded her of the eyes of a wolverine she'd seen at the zoo.

"People that live in these parts respect what's out there," he said, low and menacingly. His hand reached to his belt and grabbed the hilt of a knife, slowly pulling it free. The sound of the blade sliding from the scabbard chilled her. He held the large knife out to his side so that she could see it clearly. "You ain't got no respect."

A bead of sweat slowly ran down her cheek. She didn't know if it was from the heat or the fear that sliced through her.

"But this here's something you better respect," the scarred man continued. " 'Cause if you don't . . . ," he said, and made a slashing motion with his arm.

"Hayden!" Eddy yelled, scrambling up the hill. "There's no need for that. Kate was just coming back down to the house. Weren't you, Kate?"

"Yes. Yes, I was," she answered, making her way back

down the rocky hill. Hayden was dangerous! Even now he still had the knife out, his eyes boring holes into her.

"Put the knife away, Hayden," Eddy ordered.

Silently, his eyes never leaving Katherine, Hayden slid the knife back into its scabbard. Without a word, he turned on his heel and headed back toward the car.

She stifled an impulse to thank Eddy for his help. Why should she thank him? He appeared to be in on this bizarre plot, whatever it was.

"Bitch! I'm not forgettin' this!" Squirrelly had stumbled to his feet, his handkerchief held to his nose, a crimson stain of blood on the white fabric. His clothes were covered in dust and dirt from his tumble down the hillside.

"Shut up, Squirrelly," Eddy said sternly.

"To hell with that! She's gonna pay!"

"I said shut up!"

Squirrelly stared at them for a moment, the hatred evident in his eyes. He kept dabbing the handkerchief against his nose before he, too, stalked off toward the car.

"Eddy, I . . . ," Kate started, but no further words came.

"Don't mess with those two, Katherine. They'd just as soon hurt you as look at you. Just do what we say, and everything will be fine."

His tone was comforting. Katherine didn't know if she'd ever been more confused in her entire life.

Edwin grabbed her by the elbow and led her into the cabin.

Chapter 3

"Next stop, Muddy Creek!"

At the sound of the conductor's voice, Tate sat up and looked out the window. The first scattering of small houses came into view. The train would soon be pulling into the station. He stood and pulled his satchel and a large paper sack down from the rack above the seat, slung the bags over his shoulder, and started to move toward the back of the train.

He made his way through the other passengers who were gathering their belongings. When he reached the end of the car, he looked for the woman whose bag he'd dumped. She wasn't in her seat.

He stood on the small platform that separated the cars and waited for the train to come to a stop. He peered through the door into the car behind him but saw no sign of her.

Tate hoped Jorge would be waiting for him. He'd sent a message ahead from Fort Davis to the Muddy Creek station agent asking him to notify Jorge Gomez to meet him today.

If the message hadn't gone through, he would be stranded here for the rest of the day.

As soon as the train came to a halt, he swung down onto the platform. The sun was high overhead. The temperature in June often got above one hundred degrees, and this day didn't appear to be an exception. Tate pulled a handkerchief from his back pocket and wiped his brow.

Suddenly he heard a shout. "Señor Castle! Señor Castle!"

A short Mexican man with a large-brimmed hat and a wide grin came hurrying from the back of the depot. The foreman's clothes were dust-covered.

"Jorge! Am I glad to see you. I was afraid you hadn't received my message." Tate picked up his satchel and the sack and went toward him, holding out his hand. The two men shook vigorously.

"Señor, is good that you're back. Little one, she miss you."

"I missed her too. It's been almost three weeks."

As they talked, the two men moved through the station. Up ahead of them, a man knelt to embrace two small children who were peppering his cheeks with kisses. Their mother stood nearby smiling. The reunion made Tate even more eager to get home.

"You make the sale, señor?" Jorge asked.

"I made the sale. We couldn't have asked for a much better deal. The problem was that the commander of the fort was away, and I had to wait a week for him to return. That's why it took me so long."

"Still . . . it is all very good." The foreman's grin grew even wider. "When they want them?"

"We've got to have them ready by the first of the month. The commander's sending a detail down to drive them back to the fort. We've got a lot of work ahead of us."

"That we can do, señor."

They walked outside the station and stopped in front of a battered old pickup truck. Tate set the large sack and his satchel in the back and climbed into the cab. Jorge slid behind the wheel. When he started the motor, it backfired, sounding like a pistol shot. The engine sputtered once, twice, and then came to life. Jorge put the truck into gear, and they started to move.

"We're going to have to work on this old thing," Tate said.

"She noisy, but she run once she started. She get us where we go."

"We've got to make her last for a while yet. After we get the money from the fort for the horses, we'll trade her in on something better."

The truck bumped down the road that led out of town. The houses they passed were set farther and farther apart, and soon nothing lay ahead of them but the Texas prairie land. Tate tilted his head toward the open window and breathed in the fresh scent of prairie grass.

The two men were silent, comfortable with each other. They had been friends for many years. Jorge and his wife, Yelena, were with Tate before Emily's birth. Looking back on all that had happened, he didn't know how he would have managed without them.

"Did the fetlock on that old Hammerhead heal up?" Tate asked.

"It heal, but he run into a fence and got a big scratch down his side. I cover it with pine tar. He look a mess, but he always rarin' to go."

"Maybe we shouldn't have called him Hammerhead; he's living up to his name." After a few moments, Tate continued. "Have you seen that spotted stallion lately?"

Catching the spotted stallion had been a desire of Tate's since the moment he first saw him five years ago. What a beautiful, proud animal! He wanted to catch him to breed his mares, but, more important, he didn't want any harm to befall him.

"Sí, I have seen him," Jorge said. But I'm not the only one. Señor Wilbur from over east came by the other day."

"What did he want?"

"He want to know if I seen the wild herd that is led by the stallion. I say no." Jorge laughed. "I see him, but I don't tell."

"I'm glad you didn't," Tate said with a tight face. "Wilbur wants the stallion. But I don't like the way he plans to go about getting him. I don't believe in creasing a horse to stun him. Not many men are that accurate, and most of 'em either kill the animal or miss, scattering the *manadas*."

"Señor Wilbur is stubborn man. He not going to worry about killing or scattering the mares."

"He's a dang fool if he thinks he's a good enough shot," Tate said through gritted teeth. His fist was curled into a tight ball. "Another thing, where do you aim? A place close to the withers? A foot behind the ears? A vertebra a little forward of the hips? No, I won't have Wilbur trying to catch that horse by creasing him. He has a herd of nice mares and produces good foals. I wonder why he doesn't go after the loose stallions. There are ten or twelve of them following his mares. They're the ones the spotted stallion has run off."

"Yelena and little one baked a cake for your return," Jorge said, turning the talk from the stallion.

"I bet Emily liked that."

Jorge smiled. "She sat on table and stir."

Tate knew Jorge and his wife were very fond of his little six-year-old. They didn't have any children of their own and had taken to Emily from the day she was born.

As Jorge turned the truck down the road toward the ranch, Tate feasted his eyes on his home; the sturdy frame house looked as if it had been there forever. A stone chimney rose up from each end, and a long porch spanned the front. The homestead was set amid a grove of mesquite trees, with the occasional yucca scattered amongst them. In the network of corrals behind the house, horses grazed. He and Jorge had worked most of the winter with the horses, breaking them to halter. Home. He loved it and never wanted to live any place else. However, as much as he loved this place, he'd move to a city quicker than scat for Emily to receive the care she needed. He'd do it without a backward glance.

As soon as Tate stepped out of the truck, Old Bob, his eight-year-old dog, came to meet him, his tongue hanging out the side of his mouth. Tate reached down and scratched the mutt's shaggy head. "Hey there, Bob. Have you been looking after things while I was away?"

Yelena stood on the porch holding Emily. Dressed in a blue, light cotton dress, the child was all smiles and waved both hands. Her curly dark head bobbed with excitement. Tate hurried onto the porch, dropped his bag and paper sack, and reached for her.

"Hello, little sweetheart."

"Daddy, Daddy!" Emily fell into her father's grasp and wrapped her arms around his neck, then patted his right cheek with one small hand and bestowed wet kisses on the other. "Daddy, I'm glad you're back! Did you bring me a present?"

Tate kissed her forehead. *Has it been only three weeks?* It seemed like forever since he last held his little girl. "I've missed you, Emily. Have you been good for Yelena?"

Emily hesitated before answering, "Sometimes."

"Now, what does that mean?" Tate chuckled.

"I hit Yelena."

Tate pulled his daughter away from him and looked down into her blue eyes. "Why did you do a naughty thing like that?"

"She said that I couldn't wear my pretty dress with the pink ribbon."

"Your Sunday dress? Were you going somewhere?"

"No. I wanted to play outside in the sand, and she wouldn't let me."

"Yelena was right to say no."

"I don't like her."

"Now, I don't want to hear you saying things like that. Yelena cares a great deal for you. If she tells you not to wear your nice dress, you do what she says."

"Are you mad at me, Daddy?"

"Of course not, sweetheart, but I want you to be a nice girl. I think you should tell her you're sorry."

Emily turned in her father's arms. A look of rebellion came over the child's face and then her eyes went down to the paper sack lying on the porch. "Sorry, Yelena," she murmured. "Now can I have my present?"

Tate sighed. "You can have it, but I don't want to learn that you hit Yelena again. Promise me." Emily quickly nodded her head, her eyes never leaving the paper sack. Tate leaned down and picked up the bag.

"What is it?" Emily asked excitedly.

"Let's go in the house and find out."

Tate carried his daughter into the kitchen and set her on the edge of the table. Her thin legs hung down limply. She walked, but her uneven gait made her hips so tired she could only go short distances. Damn Hazel, the girl's mother, for going off and leaving her!

The shoe had slipped off the foot of Emily's shorter leg. Tate reached for the shoe and lifted his daughter's short leg up onto his knee. He cradled her tiny foot in his hand.

"I got on my new shoes, Daddy."

He had bought the shoes the last time he went to Alpine. Emily had loved the bright red color at first sight. "I see you have, little sugar bun."

"I can walk in them when Jorge holds me."

"You can?" He slipped the shoe gently back on Emily's foot and buttoned the strap. "You'll have to show me after you open your present."

Emily reached her hand into the sack. "What is it?" she said again.

"Pull it out and see."

Emily pulled out a doll that he had bought in Alpine. It had a baby face, blue eyes, a pink mouth, and long brown hair. Its dress was pink with a matching pink satin sash. "Oh, Daddy, Daddy! She's got a dress just like mine!"

"Do you like her, sweetheart?" Emily's smile was all the answer he needed.

Emily hugged the doll close to her. "Does she cry?"

"Bend her over and you'll find out."

Emily bent the doll back and forth. Her smile widened when she heard the doll coo, "Ma . . . ma."

"Lay her down," Tate said. "Her eyes will close."

Emily laughed with delight. "What's her name?"

"The lady at the store said that she didn't have one," Tate said. "You'll have to give her a name."

Emily thought about it for a while, her little nose crinkling up from the effort. Finally she said, "I think I'll call her Sarsaparilla."

"That's a pretty long name for a baby."

"I like it," the girl said defiantly.

"Maybe you should shorten it up a little."

"Well . . . then I'll call her 'Sassy.' "

"That sounds great, honey."

"Are you hungry, señor?" Yelena asked as she set plates on the table.

"My belly's so empty it thinks I've forgotten about it." Tate laughed as he lifted Emily up and sat down with her in a chair. Emily snatched her doll from the table and started bouncing it on her knee.

"Jorge coming," Yelena said.

"Great. I've not had a good meal since the day I left."

By the time Tate finished eating, Emily had nodded off to sleep. One arm hung down toward the floor, but the other held her new doll tightly to her chest. The excitement of her father coming home, and the doll, had been too much for the child.

Tate carried her to the small room off the kitchen and laid her down on her bed. She woke and smiled up at him. He pulled the curtains shut on the purple-and-yellow-streaked evening sky, sending the room into near darkness. He kissed her forehead.

"Can you tell me a story, Daddy?" Emily asked sleepily as Tate changed her clothes and tucked the doll into the crook of her arm.

"Not tonight, honey."

"Please?"

"Daddy's got to talk to Jorge. Yelena will."

"I've heard her stories," Emily complained.

Tate pulled a thin blanket up to his daughter's waist, then leaned down to give her one more kiss good night. She put her arms around his neck and squeezed him tightly.

"Daddy, you smell funny," the little girl said.

"I do?"

"You smell like flowers."

Tate grinned.

*   *   *

Tate went out onto the porch, where Jorge sat in an old bentwood chair. The vivid colors of the sky had darkened as the sun started its disappearing act over the western horizon. Stars had begun to spring to life above them, twinkling in the early evening sky. It had been a hot day, but the air had already started to cool down. A light breeze carried the scent of sage.

Tate lit a cigarette and sat down on the edge of the porch. Old Bob trotted from the yard in back of the house and sat at his master's feet. The dog gave a contented sigh before settling down.

"I got a good price for the horses, Jorge. I'll be able to pay you now."

"You owe me nothing, señor."

"I said I'd pay you for helping me break those horses, and I will."

"You give me and my *esposa* a home. We feel you family, you and the little *niña*. That's all the payment we need."

"You're our family, both of you. I couldn't have managed all these years without your help. My sale to the fort should put us in pretty good shape."

"What put you in pretty good shape would be if you get the spotted stallion."

"You know how hard I've been tryin', Jorge. But he's man-shy. I've had him boxed up a couple times, and he always manages to get out. One time he almost ran me down. He was mad as hell. It'll be hard to get near him again."

They sat in near silence for a couple of minutes, the only sound that reached their ears coming from a lone coyote calling his mate. Tate took a couple of drags on his cigarette before saying, "There's only one thing we haven't tried."

"What's that?"

"We could drive his mares in. If we did that, he'd follow them. But he might kick down the fences."

"We can try, señor. That one smart mustang. Maybe he smarter than us," Jorge said with a chuckle.

"After we deliver the horses to the fort, we'll have some time to try an' catch him. We'll just have to be careful and not lead Wilbur to him."

Yelena came out and sat down beside Tate on the porch. "The little one happy with the doll," she said as she pulled a shawl around her shoulders. The night air had become cooler with each passing minute.

"She asleep?"

"Sí, señor. She only hear start of story." Yelena smiled.

"I'm afraid we're going to have to use a firmer hand with her. She's startin' to act up. I don't want her to be a spoiled brat."

"She have good days, and she have bad days. She not run and play like other children, and she get tired being in house."

"Is she still crawlin' on the floor?"

"Sometimes she crawl. She don't like to walk. I help her. Jorge help her."

"I don't want you running to her every time she calls. She's got to learn to do a few things for herself."

"Sí, señor."

"It not as bad as that, señor," Jorge said. "She try to do the best she can. She want to walk. Oh, how she laugh when I held her up and she walk next to me. But she cry sometimes when she fall down."

Tate could hear the pride in both of their voices when they talked about Emily. It was hard for all of them to deal with the little girl's handicap.

"I wish I could find someone to make her some shoes so she would have an easier time walking." Tate put out his cigarette and threw it out into the yard. "I'm sorry she hit you, Yelena. I want you to tell me if she does it again."

"It just a little hit, señor."

"A little hit's still a hit, and she shouldn't have done it."

"It not her fault her little leg so short, señor."

Tate sighed. "I know. It's nobody's fault. It's just hard to know what to do. If I had the money, I'd take her north to a clinic. Maybe they'd have an idea of how to help her."

"If we get the spotted stallion, we have the money," Jorge said.

"Even if we did manage to get him, it'd take time to get enough foals from him to sell."

"We get the foals if the mares follow him in. If he mount half of them, we have ten, twenty foals. We get the stallion, we have money."

"Maybe," Tate answered. He stood. "I'm turning in. I need a good night's sleep."

He lay in his bed wide awake. He was still bothered that Emily had hit Yelena. He remembered the times that Hazel had been peeved at him for something or other, and the first thing she'd try to do was slap him. She'd tried it often but had only succeeded the first time. He'd been ready after that. Emily wasn't going to grow up and get into the habit of hitting when she wasn't pleased about something. She wasn't going to grow up to be like her mother. He'd never spanked Emily, but if he heard of her doing it again, he would be tempted.

Finally, after much tossing and turning, Tate fell asleep.

Chapter 4

JOHN TYLER SAT BEHIND THE DESK IN HIS OFFICE on the sixth floor of the Tyler building in a state of near panic. His shoulders slumped; he buried his face in his hands.

"Oh God, oh God, Kate, what have they done to you?" he muttered.

He stared down at the sheet of paper lying on his desk and read again the printed words.

> We have your daughter Katherine. If you want to see her again, get $100,000 ready in small bills. We will be in touch again. Tell anyone and she dies.

The note had been in the morning's mail and had been postmarked from one of the central post offices right there in New York City. There were no distinguishing marks on the envelope or the note itself; it was written on a tablet that could be bought at any five-and-dime.

His eyes focused on the words "Tell anyone and she dies."

John's right hand reached out and lifted the silver picture frame sitting on his desk. His wet eyes looked upon the smiling portrait of Kate he had made shortly after she'd graduated from nursing school. *Lord, she looks so much like her mother it's eerie.*

What to do? What to do? The thoughts careened around inside his head. He was used to making decisions over large financial matters, but never in a million years could he have imagined that he would have to make a decision like this.

Before she left on her cross-country trip, he made Kate promise to wire him at certain points along the way. She'd thought that he was being overprotective, but he insisted on it. She sent a message to him when her ship docked in New Orleans and wired him from scheduled stops on the train route. She was to telegraph him from Marathon, but no message had come. At first, he thought that she'd simply forgotten. Nevertheless, he had worried, and now the ransom note had arrived.

Kate was the brightest light in his whole life. He'd been deeply disappointed to discover after he had married Lila that she was so enamored with society life and fancy clubs. Socializing meant more to her than the family. As sorry as he was to admit it, Susie, his other daughter, was a carbon copy of her mother. The two of them talked about nothing but shopping and dances! Kate was different; she was more like him. She had ambition. She had dreams, and she worked hard to fulfill them. She'd been at the top of her class in nursing school and had worked at the municipal clinic helping the poor. Lila had never approved of Kate's becoming a nurse. She didn't think it a suitable profession for a respectable young lady of the upper class. John couldn't have been prouder of his elder daughter, and now this!

Whom can I turn to? I have to do something!

The more that he thought about it, the more John realized that there was only one person that he could rely upon—his partner, William Jacobs. If he couldn't trust him, he couldn't trust anyone. He got to his feet, snatched the note off his desk, and walked down the short hallway to William's office. Pausing for a moment outside the door to calm himself, he knocked and entered.

There were no papers strewn about; no clothing hung from the coatrack, and no cigar burned in the ashtray. Then he remembered that William had mentioned that he was taking his nephew, Edwin, out to Pittsburgh to review one of the company's smelting plants. He wouldn't be back until the next day.

John trudged back to his office and sank into his chair. He spread the note back out on the table and stared at the message. He put his face in his hands.

What can I do?

After all of the employees had left the office for the day, John turned the lights off and headed for the door. He put on his hat and walked out of the building. The June air was warm after a light summer drizzle had washed away the harsher smells of the city. John drew in a deep breath. His walk was brisk; he'd spent all day deciding on his plan of action, and he wanted to do it before he changed his mind.

Passing a bakery, he caught sight of his reflection in the storefront window. His thick gray hair, bushy mustache, and stomach paunch all showed him to be a man who had left his younger days behind.

He passed a newsstand. The owner shouted out to him to buy the evening edition, but he pressed on. It was hard to believe that the city could still be normal when his world had been turned upside down. He wove his way past an elderly man hailing a cab as he engaged in a shouting match with the driver of a brand-new Ford car that blocked the curb.

Three blocks farther down the street, John entered a doorway and stepped into the dim light of his favorite restaurant. A squat, balding man wearing a vested suit stood just inside the foyer. He smiled as John entered.

"Mr. Tyler, you're early tonight. Would you like your usual table?"

"I'm not here for dinner, Tony," John said. "I need to ask a favor."

"Anything, Mr. Tyler. You know that."

"I need to make a long-distance telephone call, and I want to be sure that absolutely no one knows about it."

"Certainly, sir. Come back to my office. I'll make sure you're not interrupted." Tony led the way down the hallway to a door at the rear of the restaurant. "Come, come."

John entered the tiny office, removed his hat, and sat down behind the desk. "Thank you, Tony. I appreciate this." The restaurant owner shut the door behind him.

John took out the ransom note and spread it on the desk. He took the telephone receiver from its cradle, held it to his ear, and dialed the operator. "Operator, I would like you to ring the Texas Rangers headquarters in Waco, Texas."

John waited nervously for an answer. Sweat began to bead on his brow. Finally, after giving the name of the officer he needed, John took a deep breath and waited.

"Holmgaard," a man said in a thick Texas drawl.

"Hello, Lyle. This is John Tyler in New York."

"John! What a surprise. I haven't heard from you for a good long while."

"Too long. I think the last time was back in '31 when one of our shipments got derailed down near Houston."

The two men talked for a couple of minutes about times past before the Texas Ranger said, "Now, John, I like chattin' about the good ole days as much as the next fellow, but something tells me that isn't the reason for your call."

"Ever the Ranger."

"It's been too long for me to be anything else."

John took a deep breath and looked down at the ransom note. "Lyle, I desperately need your help. My daughter has been kidnapped, and the bastards say they'll kill her if it gets out that I've gone to the authorities."

"I don't know if I can do you much good down here if your daughter was kidnapped up there in New York."

"She was taken in Texas, Lyle. I think she was kidnapped from the train."

For the next twenty minutes, John told the lawman about Kate taking the boat to New Orleans and the train across southern Texas on her way to California. He told Lyle that she had sent him a message when she arrived in

New Orleans and another from Marietta, Texas. She was to send another from Marathon, but it didn't come.

"And when did you get the note?" Lyle asked.

"The ransom note came this morning, mailed from right here in New York City. It demanded one hundred thousand dollars, or Kate would be killed. It also warned that she'd meet the same fate if I contacted anyone."

"Damn kidnappin'. It's a shame what some folks'll do for money. Give me a description of her, John."

"Kate is twenty-five years old, a tall girl, with long blond hair and blue eyes. I know most fathers would say this, but I think she's a beautiful girl." The emotion of the day had begun to wear John down. "I don't know what else to tell you, Lyle."

"That's enough for now, John. I'll check into this and get back to you."

"No, no . . . don't call me. I'll call you about this time tomorrow. I can't take the chance of someone knowing that we've been in touch. I don't know who'd want to do this to Kate, but I'm not going to take any chances."

The two men said their good-byes and hung up.

John sat in the silence of the restaurant office and collected his thoughts. What he had done tonight was risky. If the kidnappers knew he'd contacted a law officer, it was possible that they would follow through with their threat to kill Kate. Regardless, he'd finally decided that he had to give Kate a chance.

Feeling the first stirrings of hope since he'd received the note, John took out his wallet and laid a one-hundred-dollar bill on the desk. He grabbed up his hat and left the office.

Tony was waiting just outside the door.

"No one can know about this, Tony. It's a matter of life and death."

"You can trust me, Mr. Tyler. No one will know."

"I knew I could count on you," John said, putting a hand on the other man's shoulder. Without another word, he left the restaurant.

John decided to walk the rest of the way to his home. At this late hour, it would have been more sensible to hail a cab, but he needed the time alone to organize his thoughts. For the first several blocks, he walked with his head down, the weight of Kate's circumstances bearing down on him. He'd done all that he could to give her a fighting chance. But if need be, he would give his whole fortune to get her back.

He turned through the gate and walked up the curving drive to the house he had bought when he married Lila. The three-story brownstone stood in one of the exclusive streets of the city. It had more rooms than they would ever need. Betsy, Kate's mother, would have scorned such opulence. When they were first married, they'd had only enough money to afford a one-room apartment in Pittsburgh. But, by God, they had been happy!

Malcolm, the butler that Lila had insisted they hire, had the door open by the time he reached it. John had always wondered if the man could see through the heavy oak door.

"Good evening, Mr. Tyler. Mrs. Tyler is in the library."

"Thank you, Malcolm." John handed him his hat and walked into the large foyer, his heels clicking on the marble floor. He pushed open the double doors of the library and went in. Lila and Susie stood in the center of the room. Susie giggled. Both of the women were dressed in evening gowns, and each held a glass of red wine.

"You're early," Lila said with a smile. Even though she was nearly ten years younger than her husband, age lines had begun to show around the corners of her mouth. Alabaster skin, high cheekbones, long dark hair worn in a bun at the back of her neck, and green eyes, all combined to make her a very beautiful woman.

"I left the office early . . . long day," he murmured.

"You remembered that we're going to the Kleins' tonight. They are having a reception for Senator Forrest. Everyone's going to be there."

"I'm not going, Lila," John said as he plopped down onto the sofa.

"But, Daddy! You have to go," Susie said, planting a kiss on her father's forehead. It was easy to see that Susie was her mother's daughter. They could pass easily for sisters. They had the same elegant bearing and charming mannerisms. He often wondered if there was anything of himself inside his younger daughter.

"I'm sorry, sweetheart, but I think I'll pass."

"I, for one, wouldn't miss it for the world!" Susie said. "Margaret told me that Kenneth Caldwell III is back from a semester studying in Oxford and is full of all kinds of interesting stories. If I don't hurry, someone else will catch his eye!" and with that, she gathered up a beaded purse and a fox stole.

"What about Edwin?" John asked. "Won't he be upset to hear that you were flirting with another man?"

"He's in Pittsburgh. It's not my fault he left me all alone!" she flung over her shoulder. The doors swung shut behind her with a bang.

"Are you sure you won't come to the party?" Lila asked gently.

"I told you I wasn't going when you asked me the first time. Forrest is a self-serving egotist and a poor excuse for a senator, to my way of thinking. He'll not get another dollar from me."

"I've already promised a hundred dollars, John."

"Then pay it out of your allowance. I didn't promise it."

"Why are you so irritable tonight? Did something happen at the office today?"

John stood up from the sofa and walked across the library to a small cabinet against the far wall. He pulled out a glass and filled half of it with Scotch. He wasn't much of a drinker—his wife and daughter drank more—but he needed something tonight.

"I've got a lot on my mind, Lila."

"What is it, dear?"

"Kate has been kidnapped. I got a ransom note today."

"What?" Lila gasped, setting her glass down on the table. "Oh my God! This is terrible! What did the note say?"

"It said that I was to give them money or they'd kill her."

"How much do they want?"

"One hundred thousand dollars," John said, taking a stiff belt of his drink.

"Are you going to pay it?"

"Of course, I'm going to pay it. I don't have any choice."

"I knew it. I knew that something like this could happen," Lila said, pacing across the library floor. "When she told me she was going to California, I knew it was a bad idea. No respectable young woman would make such a wild trip across the country alone."

John looked at her with eyes as cold as a frosty morning. "You mean my daughter isn't respectable?"

"Oh John. No. No, I didn't mean that, and you know it," Lila said, rushing over to her husband's side and placing a reassuring hand on his shoulder. "What are you going to do? Did you contact the authorities?"

For the briefest of moments, John thought about telling his wife of his conversation with Lyle, but in the end thought better of it. There was no point in dragging her more deeply into the whole mess. No, he would carry that burden alone.

"I don't think that we should," he answered. "And I don't want you to say a word about this to anyone. I mean it, Lila, no one. Not even Susie."

"But Kate's her sister," Lila protested.

"I don't want her to know."

"I won't say anything to her if you don't want me to, but she loves Kate. We both do." She went to the bureau, inserted a cigarette into a long holder, and lit it with a silver lighter.

"I wish you wouldn't do that," John said.

"I'm sorry, dear. I need something to steady my nerves. This has been quite a shock."

"I just can't get used to seeing women puffing on cigarettes."

"This is 1933, John. Half of the women in this city smoke cigarettes."

"I don't give a damn what half the women in the city do. I don't want my wife smoking."

"I'm sorry." Lila pulled the cigarette from the holder and snuffed it out in the ashtray. "I know that this is tearing you apart, but you've done all you can do. If you go to the authorities, the kidnappers will hurt poor Kate. We'll just give them the money and get our daughter back."

John stared blankly ahead. Lila was right; they'd just have to pay and get Kate home.

"About this party?" he mumbled.

"Don't you give it a moment's thought. You stay home, and Susie and I will go. We have to put up a brave front."

"Thank you, my dear."

Lila gave her husband a light kiss on the cheek. "Get some rest."

John was relieved to be alone. He sank wearily down into a reading chair and stretched his legs out in front of him. Before sleep began, he wondered what Kate was doing.

He hoped and prayed that the time would go fast and his little girl would be home soon.

Chapter 5

KATE STOOD IN FRONT OF THE DIRTY WINDOW. Outside, the midday sun beat down on the empty landscape. The only thing she could see was a scattering of scrubby trees and bushes that dotted the rocky hillside.

"Stay away from the window."

Kate looked over her shoulder to see Squirrelly leaning against the door frame with a mischievous smile plastered across his face. "Why?" she asked. "There's nothing out there."

"Because I said so, little Miss High-and-Mighty, and I don't want to hear no sass."

"Get out of here," Kate said, turning to face the man. "Eddy said this was my room and for you to stay out."

"Well, la-di-da. There's only two rooms in this cabin, and there's four of us. I figure that I'll be stayin' in here with you before too long."

"Shut up and get out." *Oh, how I hate this man!*

"Sister, you better wise up to the fact that you can't depend on sissy little Eddy. I'm the only thing standing between you and ole Scarface out there. He's one mean son of a bitch. If he decides he wants you, he ain't gonna let Eddy stand in his way."

"So who's going to protect me from you?"

Squirrelly leered as he took a step away from the door and into the room. "I thought maybe you and I could make it out of here together. That is, if you're nice to me."

"You can forget that," Kate said sharply. She pressed her arms across her chest and planted her feet squarely on the floor. *Where is Eddy?!* "I'm not going anywhere with a skunk like you."

"We'll see. Either that scar-faced wild man or me is gonna be sharin' your bed tonight. If I was you, I'd be hopin' 'twas me."

The mere thought of touching such a disgusting man turned her stomach. "You make me want to throw up."

"Oh, you talk big. You keep that up, an' I'll be all excited!"

She was bitterly disappointed in Eddy. She hadn't yet discovered how he happened to be associated with these men. Eddy had to be in on her kidnapping. He had to know that her father would pay any amount to get her back.

"Come on, rich girl," Squirrelly said, a mad gleam in his eye. "Say somethin' tough."

"I'm a lot tougher than you think. I was a nurse in a clinic in the roughest section of New York City. You're nothing compared to some of the guys I've worked on. I've sewn up knife wounds, dug out bullets, and stuffed guts back into a man's belly. I think I can handle a little weasel like you."

Before Squirrelly could utter another insult, the door to the front of the cabin shot open.

"Squirrelly!" Eddy shouted. "I told you to stay away from her."

Squirrelly shrugged his shoulders, stuck his hands into the pockets of his pants, and backed out of the room. "We was just talkin'. She's got some pretty tall tales to tell." He threw a smile over his shoulder and sauntered out of the doorway and into the other room.

"Eddy," Kate called. "Will you come in here for a minute?"

Eddy came as far as the doorway. "Are you all right?"

"Yes, I'm all right," she said. "I need to know why you brought me here and how long I have to stay. I want to know what's going on."

"Why don't you tell her?" Squirrelly hollered. "Tell her how we're waitin' for old John Tyler to cough up a chunk of money."

"Is he telling the truth, Eddy?" Kate asked.

Eddy was silent, his gaze leaving her to drift along the floor.

"Are you in on this?"

"I'll explain it all later, Kate."

Awkward silence filled the room. Kate knew that it was useless to keep asking Eddy the same questions, so she instead said, "Squirrelly said that either he or that other man would share my bed tonight. I'd kill myself first, and then how would you collect the money?"

"Don't pay any attention to him. He's just trying to upset you. You don't need to worry about Hayden either. He's had his orders. I gave you my word that you wouldn't be hurt, and I meant it."

"Just the same, I want a bar on this door."

"That's impossible, Kate, but a promise is a promise. They won't bother you. I'll sleep here in front of your door tonight."

"Hey, little Miss High-and-Mighty," Squirrelly yelled. "Can you cook?"

"I don't cook for hogs!"

Squirrelly laughed loud and long. "She's got a mouth on her, ain't she?"

"Ignore him, Kate," Eddy said, backing out of the door. "I'll bring your supper." He pulled the door shut, and she was alone.

Kate sat down on the side of a bunk that had been built into the wall; her meager surroundings were of little comfort. She looked with disgust at the dirty straw-stuffed pad. The floors in the cabin were made of wide plank. The walls were of the same. She wished that she had something that she could put against the door, but the only items in the room were the bunk and an old cast-iron stove that had been used for heating. There wasn't even a chair to sit on.

She stood up and made her way back to the window. She'd already tried to open it, but it wouldn't budge; they'd probably nailed it down from the outside. If she tried to break the glass, they'd certainly hear her. She only had one choice.

Wait.

*   *   *

Hayden entered the cabin carrying a bucket of twigs and a few small pieces of wood. He opened the door of the firebox in the cookstove and shoved some of the dry sticks inside. He grabbed an old newspaper from the table, wadded it up, and shoved it into the box, then struck a stick match and lit it. After adjusting the damper, he kicked shut the firebox door.

"I ain't never seen no fire done like that," Squirrelly said. "That thing gonna get hot enough to melt butter?"

Hayden shot him a look of disgust and went back outside. He returned with an armload of cut wood, opened the firebox, and shoved it onto the burning sticks.

"Say, that there's pretty slick. You act like you know what you're doing."

Hayden grunted and turned away. He pulled a can of beans off the shelf above the stove.

"How ya gonna open that?"

"Shut up," Hayden snarled. "I'm about sick a your mouth."

"I want to see it if you open it with your teeth." Squirrelly almost choked on his laughter. It was fun to irritate the ugly bastard.

Hayden turned his back on him.

A rap on the window glass caught Squirrelly's attention. Eddy stood in front of the cabin, an unhappy look on his face. He jerked his head, signaling the other man to join him.

"What's got you in such a snit?" Squirrelly asked after he'd stepped out of the cabin.

"Don't rile him," Eddy said. "You might find yourself on the business end of that knife of his."

"Well, who told him to come along anyway?" Squirrelly spat, kicked a loose rock and sent a cloud of dust into the warm evening air.

"That's none of your business."

"That's where you're wrong, Eddy old boy. Mr. Jacobs said I was a partner in this deal. I think I got the right to know why it ain't just the two of us."

"Hayden knows the territory out here, and we don't. In case you haven't noticed, this isn't New York City. Things work a little differently out here. We might be glad we have him later on."

"I'd love to have seen old man Tyler's face when he got that ransom note. Wooey, I bet that was somethin'! How are we gonna know when he's forked over the money?"

"We'll know." The plan was simple. Edwin was to wire his uncle after Kate had been kidnapped; then he'd check for an answering wire, in code, every three days. The station that the message would be wired to was Muddy Creek.

"So what are we gonna do with her after we get the money?"

"What do you mean?"

"What do you think I mean? She knows who you are. She ain't gonna go waltzin' back to Daddy with her trap shut. We're gonna have to kill her."

"Don't even think about it," Eddy said, turning a vicious look toward the thug. "How we handle that isn't your affair."

"She can identify me. That makes it my affair."

"When she's safe at home and we have our money, she'll keep quiet. She isn't going to want anything to happen to her daddy."

"What's to keep him from goin' to the law?"

"He won't. Uncle will see to it."

"Damn, I hope so." Squirrelly pulled a handkerchief from his back pocket and wiped his brow. "They can give you the chair for kidnappin'. Look what they did to that dumb bastard that took Lindbergh's kid."

Eddy looked back toward the cabin. How he hated dealing with Squirrelly! From the very beginning, he'd had to remind himself why he needed to go along with this whole mess. This was his big chance at freedom from his uncle. Eddy knew that the mighty William Jacobs would have no qualms about letting his nephew take all the blame for the embezzlement, but maybe this time he'd outsmarted the old fox. Let the smug bastard get hung with that indictment!

I'm going to make sure that no harm comes to Kate.

Suddenly he remembered that she was in the cabin alone with Hayden, and started back. When he reached the door, he was relieved to see Hayden still at the cookstove. The door to Kate's room was closed.

"Who's going to take her to the woods when she's got to pee?" Squirrelly called after him.

"It won't be you." Eddy went inside the cabin. "Hayden, is there anything around here that would serve as a chamber pot for the lady?"

Hayden laughed for the first time. It was more of a dry cackle than a laugh. "There's a bucket in the shed." He turned back to the stove and stirred the beans.

Eddy went back out the door, and Squirrelly fell in step with him.

"So Miss High-and-Mighty is gonna do her business in a bucket?" There was a pleased grin on Squirrelly's face.

"You're the most repulsive man I've ever met."

"That's what my mama done told me . . . but I have a hell of a lot of fun!"

Eddy rummaged around in the shed until he found a gray granite bucket. It was dirty, and the inside looked as if a pack rat had made a nest there. He dumped the contents on the ground and headed for the nearby stream. Hurrying because he didn't want to leave Kate in the house with Hayden, he washed out the bucket and headed back to the cabin.

Night fell fast in the hills. By the time Hayden slammed three granite plates on the table, it was nearly dark. Eddy dished a couple of spoonfuls of beans onto another plate, carried the food to Kate's door, and knocked.

"Kate. It's Eddy. I have something here for you to eat."

Cautiously Kate opened the door and looked for any sign of Squirrelly. Eddy held out the plate of beans and said, "I'm sorry this is all we have. Hayden says he'll hunt tomorrow."

"Thank you," she said, snatching the plate from his hands and shutting the door in his face. The sounds of Squirrelly's cackle of laughter carried from the other side of the cabin.

Kate awoke with a start as the door to her room suddenly opened.

"It's me, Kate," Eddy said. "Don't be afraid."

"Where are the other varmints?"

"I've no idea where Hayden is, but Squirrelly went out into the woods. I tried to find you a chamber pot, but all I could find is this bucket." He set it inside the door.

"I need a light."

"I'll give you a candle and some matches. Use it only when you need to and make sure to keep the light away from the window; otherwise Hayden will come in and take it."

After Eddy had left, Kate looked around for something to hang over the window to provide a little privacy. There was nothing but the skirt she was wearing. Without any hesitation, she unhooked it, let it fall to the floor, picked it up, and hung it on the two nails above the window. She had been wondering how she was going to relieve herself, and, as mad as she was at Eddy, she was grateful for his thoughtfulness.

She lit the candle, letting some of the wax drip onto the table, and pressed it down, securing it. She relieved herself in the bucket and wondered what her stepmother would think of this miserable indignity.

Susie or their mother would have gone into hysterics, and Hayden might have cut their throats. *I intend to survive and see that these men, including Eddy, pay for their crime.*

She couldn't understand what would cause Eddy to team up with these two unsavory characters! She knew that he had wanted to court her but had respected her lack of interest. She'd assumed that he would eventually marry Susie. Did her father's partner, William Jacobs, know what his nephew was up to? She was certain that he couldn't possibly know. Mr. Jacobs was such a refined man. Her father trusted him, or he would not have let him buy into his firm. Surely he would be mortified!

She sat on the bunk and took off her shoes. They'd been ruined when she scrambled up the hill. Even if she could get out of the room, how would she get away? She couldn't walk in these shoes. If she could reach the car, she could drive it away, but she doubted that Hayden would ever leave it alone long enough.

Seeing that the candle was burning down, she blew it out. Carefully laying aside the stick matches Eddy had given her, she thought briefly of trying to set the cabin on fire but dismissed that idea as a bad one. The only thing she could do was wait for the right opportunity to get away. She had to be patient and wait until the scar-faced man was away from the cabin. She sure didn't want any more encounters with him and his knife.

She heard the sound of a door opening, followed by Eddy's loud voice.

"You sleep over there, Squirrelly. I don't want you going anywhere near that door. Do you hear me?"

At least Eddy hadn't lost all his ethics. Her ears picked up the sound of Squirrelly's voice.

"I told ya! He just wants her for himself!"

The scar-faced man's rough voice answered, "Leave her alone."

"I ain't gonna do nothin'," Squirrelly whined. Kate wondered if he was as afraid of the other man as she was.

"See that you don't," Hayden growled. "If you want her

after this is over, that's between you and Jacobs. But as long as I'm here, and the money ain't, you'll not bother her."

Kate sat in the dark, her ears alert, the last of Squirrelly's mutterings fading into the night.

She must have slept. She awakened to the sound of someone lighting the cookstove. She lifted her skirt from the window and saw that it was daylight. It frightened her that she had slept all night. Hurriedly she got up and used the bucket to relieve herself, put on her skirt, and sat down to wait for what would happen next.

Chapter 6

Tate woke from a good night's sleep. He stretched and yawned. God, he was glad to be home. Waiting at the fort had been dull, but the trip home had been anything but. Dealing with that woman on the train had been a real eye-opener. He didn't even know why he'd jumped to help her with her valise; it seemed the gentlemanly thing to do at the time. How was he supposed to know that it'd pop open, leaving him with a handful of female undergarments that weighed no more than a heap of feathers? She hadn't appreciated the gesture. But then, what could he have expected from a fancy-dressed woman who had never done a full day's work in her life? She'd be as helpless as a babe in arms when it came to taking care of herself in this part of the country. He had to admit to himself that she was pretty, though, despite being helpless and more than likely brainless.

Hearing Yelena moving around in the kitchen, he dismissed the woman from his mind, flung his feet over the side of the bed, and hurriedly dressed. He had more important things to do than think about someone who'd embarrassed the hell out of him.

Yelena had fired up the cookstove, and the familiar smell of breakfast cooking caused his stomach to growl.

"Morning, Yelena."

"Morning, señor," she replied, turning from the stove where she was frying strips of meat. A pan of golden biscuits sat on the back of the stove. Yelena's biscuits were exceptional. He dipped water from the reservoir into the wash pan. It was a luxury to wash in warm water. He'd washed in cold for nearly three weeks in the barracks at Fort Davis. The commander didn't believe in coddling his troops.

"Jorge out with the mare. He thinks she foal sometime today." Yelena set a platter of meat on the table.

"Why didn't he wake me?"

"He say you tired, you need sleep. She not foal for a few hours yet." Yelena set a pan of biscuits on the table and went back to the counter for a crock of butter.

Tate didn't hesitate. He filled his plate with split biscuits and reached for the meat and the bowl of gravy.

Yes, it was wonderful to be home.

The day was hot and windy. Tate spent most of the morning in the barn with Jorge. The mare, Lucy, didn't foal until shortly before noon. The birth was a hard one; they were beginning to wonder if they might lose her. Jorge had to pull the foal. The filly was strong, and Jorge laughed with pleasure.

"Looky there, señor! Looky there! She strong and standing, looking for her dinner!" Jorge straddled the filly and guided her head toward her mother's teat. The filly sucked lustily.

Tate went to get a large helping of oats for Lucy. The mare gobbled up the treat as Tate stroked her head. She had earned it.

When Tate came out of the barn, Emily was sitting on the edge of the porch. Old Bob lay on the ground at her feet.

"Hello, sweetheart. Are you ready for dinner?"

"Yelena says we don't have any Post Toasties."

"You didn't get your Post Toasties this morning? I'm going to town today. Do you want to go with me and we'll get some?"

Holding tightly on to the porch post, Emily pulled herself up so she could stand. Tate hurried over and scooped her up in his arms.

"Can I go? Can I really go?" she asked excitedly.

"We'll go right after we eat." He carried her into the kitchen and set her down on a chair.

"We're going to town after a bit, Yelena. Make up a list of what you need. Put Post Toasties at the top."

"Sí."

Tate lathered his hands and washed. A fresh towel hung at the end of the wash bench. He carried his wash water to the porch and threw it out into the yard, barely missing Old Bob. Jorge came out of the barn.

"Better hurry, Jorge, if you want anything to eat. I'm hungry as a wolf."

Jorge laughed. "You not like the mess they feed you at the fort?"

"I liked it all right, but it's been three days since I was at the fort," he growled.

Jorge followed Tate into the house. "How my *bella chica*?"

"Pretty girl?" Emily said with a big smile, pleased that she knew the Spanish words. "Jorge, you're so funny!"

Still laughing, Jorge threw an arm around her little shoulders, gave her a gentle hug, and kissed her forehead.

"You Spanish is good, my *bella chica*."

"We both your pretty girl," Yelena said, putting her hand on her husband's shoulder. All three of them laughed.

They were as affectionate as the day they'd come to the ranch, over six years earlier. Tate felt a twinge of envy and wondered if he would ever find love like they shared.

When they sat down to eat, Emily ate everything Yelena put on her plate. She was excited about going to town. "Hurry, Daddy! Hurry!"

Emily was beside herself with excitement as they approached the town.

Muddy Creek was little more than a cluster of unpainted buildings that lined both sides of a dusty road. The town got its name from a thin ribbon of muddy water a half mile to the south. After a flash flood in 1917 that almost washed away the buildings on its bank, the town moved to higher ground and had enjoyed a bit of prosperity since the rail line had come through.

The stores, their fronts decorated with tin signs advertising everything from Copenhagen chewing tobacco to NeHi soda pop, lined a wide boardwalk. The street was empty except for a few dusty cars and several wagons. Saddled horses were tied to a rail, their tails swatting at biting flies. The high, midafternoon sun beat down. A pair of chickens pecked and scratched their way across the street. As in most small towns, groups of men were gathered about gossiping and talking politics. The United States flag fluttered from a tall flagpole in front of a small neat building at the far end of the street. Tate planned on stopping at the post office before he and Emily headed home, but first they needed to tend to the list that Yelena had given him. After parking the pickup truck, they crossed the street to Fulbright Mercantile.

With Emily on his arm, Tate entered the store through a squeaky door. Neatly stocked shelves full of bottles and tins lined the store walls. Barrels full of crackers, beans, and coffee rested on the floor in front of a long oak counter with a shiny brass cash register on one end. Tate's nose was filled with all of the tempting scents that floated through the air.

They had been in the store for only a moment before Dickson Fulbright, the owner, came out of the storeroom with a warm smile and greeting. A short, middle-aged man with a shiny bald head, bushy mustache, and pince-nez glasses, Mr. Fulbright had been a fixture in Muddy Creek for decades. He'd opened up the store with his wife. She passed away nearly six years earlier after losing a bout with pneumonia. Well respected by the entire town, Mr. Fulbright, a very neat man, obsessively wiped his hands on his apron.

"Did you make the sale?" he asked.

"Yep," Tate said matter-of-factly. It bothered him that everyone in the town knew everyone else's business, but he'd never known it to be any other way.

Tate set Emily on the long counter, where she smiled up at the grocer. She kicked her little legs out in front of her, the heels of her small shoes lightly hitting the counter's paneling.

"How are you, young miss?" Mr. Fulbright asked, wiping his hands against his snow-white apron. Tate couldn't remember seeing him without the apron. He wondered if the man even wore it to bed.

"Daddy brought me a doll that says 'Ma-ma.' Her eyes close, and she's got a pink dress just like mine!"

"Now, I've seen a lot of things, but I don't know if I've ever seen a doll that closes its eyes." Mr. Fulbright winked at Tate.

"I'll bring her next time," Emily said.

"You do that." Mr. Fulbright reached into a jar on the counter and handed Emily a stick of peppermint candy. Emily looked at her daddy, accepted the candy, and said, "Thank you."

"Don't open it until we are on the way home," Tate cautioned. "You'll be sticky clear up to your elbows."

After Tate had handed the grocer the list Yelena had given him, he scanned the headlines on the stack of newspapers lying on the counter. Mr. Fulbright began to fill the order.

Alpine "Lonestar" Gazette

August 1, 1933

Nazis Pass Law to Purify German Race

Adolf Hitler announced a new program to weed out Germans who are less than perfect. Doctors will sterilize them for the glory of the Reich.

Amelia Earhart Breaks Record

Amelia Earhart flies from Los Angeles, California, to Newark, New Jersey, in 17 hours 17 minutes.

Tate shook his head. *What is the world coming to? This guy Hitler is going to mess around and cause a world war.*

Seeing that Mr. Fulbright had not filled his order, he picked up Emily. "I'll be back in half an hour."

The grocer nodded, reached up to the shelf behind him, and brought down a can of baking powder.

Tate walked back to the truck, perspiring in the hot sun. He noticed that the chickens had given up their pecking and headed for cooler surroundings. Smart chickens. He got into the vehicle, rounded the corner, and drove into the alley behind the mercantile. At the end of the block, he came to a stop in front of the weathered building that housed the feedstore.

"I'll be right back, and we'll go to the post office," he said to Emily as he leaned in the open passenger's window. She nodded her head absentmindedly as she twirled the candy stick and watched the stripes go around it.

Tate returned to the truck with a bag of oats on each shoulder, dropped the bags into the back of the pickup, and slid behind the wheel. Emily glanced up at her father with one end of the candy stick stuck into her mouth.

"Hey, now. If you're all sticky, you can't go into the post office."

"I won't get sticky," she mumbled past the candy.

"Put the paper back on the candy. And wait until we're headed home."

Emily silently obeyed but held the candy stick tightly in her hand. She ran her tongue over her lips, savoring every bit of peppermint goodness.

Tate pulled the truck to a stop in front of the post office, got out, and reached for Emily. At the door, he paused and held it open for a young woman and a small boy. The woman smiled, but the boy never even glanced up; his head was bent down as he worked on a candy stick. Emily stared at him. Tate tipped his hat and went inside.

"Glad you're back, Tate," Leroy Gaines, the town postmaster, called out from behind a barred cage. He wore a visor cap and bow tie. The sleeves of his shirt were held in place with garters. Wide suspenders extended from his pants over his ample belly to his broad shoulders. The air in the post office was hot, and rivers of sweat poured down the man's jocular cheeks. Leroy didn't seem to mind as he grinned from ear to ear. He bounced up out of his seat, pulled three envelopes out of a cubbyhole, and slapped them down on the counter.

"Thanks, Leroy." Tate scooped the letters up and glanced at them. There was one from the government and two from relatives who had moved to the West Coast. None to Emily from her mother. He put the letters in his pocket.

"Sell your horses?" Leroy asked.

"Sure did." *Does everyone in the county know I've been to the fort to sell my horses?* With Emily on his arm, he said his good-byes and left the post office.

They were nearly to the truck when a voice from behind them called out, "Hey there, Tate."

Tate turned at the sound and saw a familiar face. The man coming toward him was short, with bowed legs and long arms. Light blond hair, a smooth baby face, and an easy smile made him look more like a preacher than what he really was. Nothing about him suggested that he was a well-known and feared Texas Ranger.

"Hello, Lyle. What brings you all the way out here?"

"Well," Lyle started, flashing the easy smile, "I could say we're meeting accidentally, but the truth of the matter is that I came to see you."

"Uh-oh. I don't like the sound of that."

"Now, is that any way to talk to an old friend?" Lyle said, his smile getting wider and more preacherlike.

"Depends on why you came to see me."

The Texas Ranger's smile vanished, and his brow creased in a serious look.

"I need your help, Tate."

"No, Lyle. The last time you came here for my help I was almost killed. I don't know what kind of case you've got, but I can't get involved. I may not be a very good parent, but I'm the only one Emily's got."

Lyle turned to look at the little girl, his preacher's smile back on his face. "And a fine hello to you, Miss Emily."

Glad to have been brought into the conversation, Emily blurted out her important news. "Daddy brought me a doll that closes its eyes. Come out to my house, and I'll show her to you."

"You know, I just might do that."

"You'll not talk me into anything, Lyle."

"I wouldn't think of trying, Tate," Lyle said. As he turned back toward him, Tate noticed that he'd kept the smile. "Thing is, I've got a problem that I think you can help me solve. You know this country better than just about anybody. Just give me a couple of minutes, and I'll be out of your hair. If Yelena's planning on making some of her biscuits and milk gravy, I could come out tonight. She does make the best durn biscuits in Texas."

Tate thought for a moment before he said, "I agree to that." The least he could do was feed the man.

"You'll eat with us?" Emily was all smiles. "Yelena will make a cake."

"She needn't go to all that trouble." Lyle laughed heartily. "Well, all right. She can go to a *little* trouble."

"We'll see you tonight," Tate said.

"Tonight, then."

Lyle turned and walked away, his bowlegs rocking him down the dusty street. Fifteen feet away, he stopped, turned, and fixed an earnest look on his face. "By the way, I heard Hayden's back in these parts."

"I thought he was long gone from here," Tate answered.

"So did I, but something brought him back."

"Nothing good, I reckon."

"I'd reckon the same. We'll talk tonight."

Tate watched as Lyle walked on, rounded a corner, and was out of sight. He opened the pickup door and set Emily down on the seat. He slid behind the wheel and started the truck but didn't put it into gear. Lyle had put too many thoughts into his head.

A tug on his arm pulled him back to the present. He looked down to see Emily clutching the peppermint stick. "Can I eat my candy now?" she asked.

"Let's wait till we get the groceries," he said. "Then it's all yours."

"Yay!" Emily shouted.

The entire way back to the ranch, Tate rolled Lyle's request around in his head. He thought back to the day, not long before, when Lyle had saved his life. The debt that he owed could never truly be repaid. But his allegiance to Lyle was far more than a debt. The Texas Ranger was a good man; the kind of man that he was proud to call a friend. It would be hard to refuse Lyle, but for Emily's sake, he would. As the ranch came into sight, one final thought stabbed into Tate's mind.

Hayden is back.

Chapter 7

Yelena, EXPECTING THE TEXAS RANGER AT THE TABLE, had outdone herself. There was venison from the smokehouse, biscuits and gravy, and a delicious cake for dessert. Emily's happy voice and laughter filled the ranch house kitchen.

After Yelena had washed the dishes and put Emily to bed, Lyle and Tate went to the front porch. The moon hung low and amber on the horizon. The only sounds came from the horses and a lone coyote howling.

Lyle sank down in the bentwood chair with a groan. He stretched out his legs and patted his bulging stomach. "If I ate like that every night, there wouldn't be a horse in Texas that could carry me. That woman makes the best damn biscuits I ever ate. If I thought I could, I'd steal her away from you."

"Well, get that idea out of your head, because you'd have to take Jorge too. He can be a bit of a handful when he gets his back up." Tate chuckled.

"It might be worth it for those biscuits."

As if on cue, Jorge ambled out onto the porch and sat down on the steps.

Tate lit a cigarette, took a drag, and blew his smoke into the night air. "You don't need to worry about holding your tongue, Lyle. You can talk freely in front of Jorge. What I know, Jorge knows. I trust him with my daughter's life."

The three men sat in silence for a moment. Lyle shifted his weight in the chair and cleared his throat. "Your word's good with me, Tate, but what I've got to say needs to be kept among the three of us for a while."

"Done," Tate answered, and Jorge nodded his head.

"I need your help to find a missing woman," Lyle continued. "Her father thinks she was taken from the New Orleans–Texas train after it passed through Simon."

"Anyone I know?" Tate asked.

"No. The woman's name is Katherine Tyler. Her father's an old friend of mine who lives in New York City. The last he knew, Katherine was on the train that left Marietta. He knows that she got that far because she sent him a wire. The next wire was to come from Marathon. It didn't come. Yesterday he got a note asking for money and warning him not to call in the authorities or his daughter would be killed."

Lyle paused, stretched his legs, and continued. "I did some checking around but didn't get much information. After talking to the depot agent at Simon, where she got off to check her baggage, she boarded the train from Marietta. I kept heading up the line to see if anyone had seen her, but she hasn't been seen. I've never met her, but she's the type that most folks around here wouldn't forget. From what I hear, she's a beautiful girl. Tall and blond."

"Did you say she got off the train at Simon?"

"That's what the depot agent told me. 'Bout the only other thing I got out of the man was that there were a couple of strangers hanging around the Simon station with Katherine. The baggage handler got the best look at them. Said one was a cowboy, but that the other one really stood out. Some dandy in a striped suit who looked like a salesman, but he never tried to sell anything in Simon, never even opened up his case. Something doesn't quite sit right with me about those two. Could be just a coincidence, but I've got a missing woman's father asking for help, and I'm gonna check out every possibility."

"Wait a minute," Tate said. "What day was this?"

"Last Thursday."

The last piece of the puzzle was filled in, and the realization hit Tate square in the chest. "It was me. I was the cowboy at the station."

"What?" Lyle practically jumped out of the chair.

"I'd been up at Fort Davis cutting a deal for our horses. I came south to Simon and was waiting to catch the train from Marietta," Tate explained, his mind searching back to that night. "The depot agent was right. There were two other people on the platform with me. A young woman and a man with a wooden case. I guess he could have been a salesman, but I didn't get much of a look at him. It was dark, and he stayed to the other side of the platform. The woman wasn't traveling with him. It didn't look like they knew each other."

"What luck!" Lyle said. Even in the near darkness, Tate could see his bright preacher's smile. "Did she say anything to you?"

"She asked me if the train was on time," Tate answered, the calamity of the woman's bag left unspoken. "That's all."

"Still, you've seen her. Did you see where she got off?"

"No. When we got on the train, I went ahead to the next car. When I arrived at Muddy Creek, I looked into her car, but I didn't see her. Didn't see the salesman either."

"Between Simon and Muddy Creek," Lyle mumbled.

"You think this is the same woman?" Tate asked.

"It sure looks like it. The big question is where she got off the train. There's only one stop between Simon and Muddy Creek."

"No. There's two," Tate corrected the Texas Ranger. "The Texas and New Orleans' scheduled stop is in Los Rios, but it also stops at the midway watering tank. Whoever kidnapped her wouldn't have tried to take her off at Los Rios; too many people would be on the platform. That leaves the midway watering tank."

"You're right." Lyle lit the cigar he pulled out of his breast pocket and smoked in silence for a few moments. Finally he said, "I guess it's time for me to ask you that favor, old friend. What I'd like is for you to go down to that watering tank and see if you can pick up anything. If that salesman was involved, I doubt if he'd be the kind of man that was much used to horses. That means they'd have had to take her out by car. Cars leave tracks."

Mulling over the request, Tate was silent for quite a while. Finally he gave his answer. "Well, I guess I can do that much for you, Lyle. I just don't want to find myself tangled up with any more rustlers or outlaws. I have to think about Emily."

"Wouldn't have it any other way," Lyle said with his reassuring smile. Some folks might think that the smile wasn't real, but Tate knew better. "You're not that much different than John Tyler. He's a fine man who's worried sick about his own daughter."

"Sounds like Hayden," Jorge said from the steps. He'd been silent up until now, but Tate knew that his foreman had a keen mind and had been listening to every word. "If he around, may be a part of it."

"You're right, Jorge," Lyle said gravely. "This is just the type of thing that would draw Hayden. Just like a fly to shit. If that salesman fella is the type of man I think he is, he'd need help finding his way out of a cardboard box, let alone Big Bend country. If he took Miss Tyler, he'd need help from someone who knows the land."

Tate nodded in agreement. "If there's any easy money to be made, Hayden would know about it. Speaking of money, is your friend going to pay the ransom?"

"He'll pay. He'd do anything to get his daughter back." Lyle stared at Tate for a moment to let the weight of his words sink in. "There was one strange thing about the ransom note, though."

"What?"

"According to John, it was mailed from right there in New York City. That means that somebody back there is the ramrod. Probably the brains of it all, more than likely. How would Hayden get involved with someone in New York?"

"Possibly through that lawyer over in Alpine, the one that represented him when I filed the charges against him last time for rustling."

"That's a thought."

"Either way, if Hayden's involved, that woman's life is in danger." Tate flicked his cigarette out into the yard. "Jorge and I need to get the horses ready that I sold to the army. The commander of the fort is sending a detail for them. But I can take a couple of days and see what I can find out."

"Thanks, Tate. If anyone can trace that girl, it's you. You're the best tracker in the area."

"I'll send you a wire if I find anything."

"No need. As soon as I hear back from John, I plan on coming back this way. You can tell me then."

"If there's anything there, it won't take me long to find it."

"Fair enough." Lyle puffed on his cigar and patted his stomach. "Well, I guess I'd better head on back to Alpine. I've got some business there before I can go back to Waco. If it isn't one thing, it's another. Hard times bring out the worst in some folks."

"You're welcome to spend the night, Lyle," Tate offered.

"Thanks, but I better head on out. Good to see you, Jorge." Lyle extended his hand as Jorge stood and took it.

Tate walked with Lyle toward the man's automobile. The night had become cooler and was made even more so by a light breeze from the northeast. Old Bob lay in the yard gnawing on a deer bone.

"If this Tyler woman is the same woman I saw on the train, I'm not sure how safe she'll be out in this country. She didn't look the type that could blow her own nose, much less defend herself with someone like Hayden." In his mind, Tate could still see her standing on the platform in her city clothes. Pretty and helpless.

"Then I think we'd better find her as quick as we can," Lyle said as he got into his automobile. "John Tyler's a friend, and even if he wasn't, I'd still want to find the woman. I hate to think of her out there in the wilds with Hayden."

"I'll do what I can."

"I know you will, Tate," Lyle said as he put the vehicle into gear. "I know you will."

Tate watched the car go down the road until he could no longer see the taillights. He went back and sat on the porch beside Jorge. His foreman passed him a cigarette, and the two men smoked in silence for a couple of moments. Tate looked off into the Texas night.

"What do you think of all this, Jorge?" he finally asked.

"You do what you must do, señor."

"What about the horses?"

"A couple of days not matter. The horses ready for delivery. Patrol not get here until next week."

"I want to be here when they come for them. This sale's important. But before I go we'll talk about it, just in case I don't get back in time."

The two men parted for the evening. Tate went into the house, stopped in his daughter's room, and placed a kiss on her forehead, then went into his own bedroom. He undressed quickly and slid between the cool fresh sheets.

There's nothing like sleeping in your own bed in your own house on your own land. The older I get, the more I appreciate it.

Tate lay on his back with his hands under his head. Thoughts of the woman filled his mind. She had embarrassed the hell out of him. He hadn't thought that he could possibly feel sorry for her, but he did. A woman like her in the hands of a man like Hayden was something he didn't want to think about. Unless they got to her in time, Hayden would either kill her or ruin her for life.

He couldn't very well refuse to help. It would only take a few days out of his life, and it might mean hers.

Tate drifted off to sleep still thinking about the woman's clothes, her clear blue eyes, and the contents of her spilled bag. He could almost smell the fragrance that drifted up from the soft underwear.

Chapter 8

WILLIAM JACOBS TURNED IN HIS SWIVEL CHAIR and looked out the window. Rain streaked the glass as a peal of thunder rolled across the city. But the rotten weather did nothing to dampen his mood. He could hardly keep the smile off his face.

Pulling a sheet of paper from his breast pocket, William felt a thrill at its words, even though he had already read it a dozen times. The telegram he had received from Edwin was the news he had been waiting for. They'd been able to take Kate without any trouble. What a stroke of luck!

Thoughts that he had been suppressing for years now swam around in his head, intoxicating him with their promise.

It won't be long now until I'm in complete control of Tyler-Jacobs Steelworks. People in the highest social circles in the city will accept me! John Tyler will be back at the steel mill in Pittsburgh where he belongs! He doesn't know how to play the game. He doesn't know which politicians to butter up, which bankers to flatter. He's in for the shock of his life; he's going to lose everything to William Jacobs, his business partner!

William's thoughts began to wander toward how he was going to word the next ransom note when the telephone rang.

He picked up the receiver from the cradle. "Jacobs," he said gruffly.

"Hello to you, my clever man."

"Oh. Hello, dear," he said, pleased when he heard the soft, caressing sound of her voice. It surprised him that she would call at the office, because they had planned to meet later. He listened to her for several minutes, then said, "Now, dear, I promised I'd be there, so I will." He cocked his ear toward the door. He heard footsteps coming toward his office and became instantly alert. Cupping his hand over the mouthpiece, he talked into the receiver in low tones.

"Everything's going just the way I planned. Before you know it, it'll all be over," he said with a snort. "How would you like to have that mink coat we saw in Macy's department store window? We'll figure out how to explain your having it. Couldn't you say that stingy old father of yours gave it to you? No?"

More steps echoed from the hallway, closer than before.

"Well, if that won't work, how would you like a piece of jewelry from Tiffany's instead?" William continued. "I'd really rather you have the mink coat. You'd be so beautiful in it. You'd be the envy of every woman you know. Hell, you'd be the envy of every woman in the city. I can hardly wait to show you off as mine."

The steps came to a halt at the closed office door. A light rapping sounded against the door frame.

"Better go now. Meet you at the same time. Good-bye, dear. I love you." As he hung up the phone, he said, "Yes?"

The door opened slowly, and John Tyler stepped into the office. "Busy, William?"

"No. No, of course not. I was just confirming an order. Come in."

The man who sat in front of William's desk bore little resemblance to the man who had been his business partner for the past five years. John Tyler looked as if he had aged ten years since a few days earlier. His eyes were bloodshot, and heavy dark bags hung beneath them. His hair was disheveled, and his clothing looked just as unkempt. William would have sworn that the man hadn't slept in a week. He looked as if he was at the end of his rope.

After they had chatted for a moment about business, William asked, "Are you all right, John?"

Silently, and with shaking hands, John pulled a scrap of paper from his coat pocket and passed it across the desk to his partner.

"What's this?" William glanced at it and jumped to his feet. His fists clenched and his voice bellowed. "What the hell is this?"

"They've got my Kate," John said hoarsely.

"What do you mean they've got your Kate? Kidnapped her?" William asked with disbelief in his voice.

John Tyler sat immobile in the office chair. It was obvious that he was physically and emotionally exhausted. William had to strain to hear him; his words were little more than whispers. "That's what the note says, William. They want a hundred thousand dollars."

"A hundred thousand dollars?" William echoed as incredulously as he could manage. "Maybe this is a prank. Some sort of a joke."

"I'm afraid it's all too real," John answered, going on to explain how Kate's messages from her trip had stopped.

"Damn it all! What in the hell is the world coming to? It isn't safe for decent people to travel anymore," William said as he pounded his fist down onto the desktop.

"Since the Lindbergh baby was taken, there's been a rash of kidnappings. You read about this sort of thing all the time now."

William stepped from behind the desk and paced the floor in front of the window. The storm seemed to be growing in intensity. "The crooks have found a way to get easy money. Damn it all! I hate to think of our Kate in the hands of scoundrels."

John pinched the space between his eyes with his thumb and forefinger. He sighed. "I've been worried sick about this, William. I can't eat and I haven't slept a wink since I received the letter. I knew I had to do something, but I didn't know what. Kate's always been my special girl. The kidnappers must have known it."

"You know how I feel about Kate, John. I love her as if she were my own daughter." William paused, trying to choose his words carefully. There were things he had to find out, things that only John himself could tell him, but he couldn't rush it. He had to squeeze them out of him. "It's no secret that I had high hopes for her and Edwin making a match of it, but it seems it will be Edwin and Susie instead. Speaking of which, have you told your family?"

"I told Lila, but I decided not to tell Susie until this is all over. I don't want her to worry."

"This is outrageous!" William exclaimed. He exhaled sharply and dropped heavily down into his chair. "If I could get my hands on the sons a bitches who did this, by God, I'd not have any trouble ending their miserable lives!"

The men sat silently, the only noise the steady drum of the rain as it beat on the windowpanes. William looked at his business partner and wondered what he would think if he knew that the mastermind behind his daughter's kidnapping was sitting not three feet away. He asked, "Do you have any idea who would do such a thing?"

"Who knows who it could be?" John exclaimed. "The houses we live in make it obvious that we have money. Someone must have decided that they wanted some of mine."

"You're right."

"I just want my daughter back," John muttered, looking down at his hands.

William knew that it was time to ask the most important question of all. Softly he asked it. "Are you going to pay the ransom?"

"Of course, I'm going to pay. They can have every dime I have or can rake up if it means I can get Kate back." John looked up with eyes that were red and moist, but coolly determined. "I've thought about it, William, and I'm not certain I'll get her back even after I pay the money. Why would they let her go? So I have done the only thing I could think of to do. I contacted a friend in the Texas Rangers."

"What?" William blurted out before he could catch himself.

"If there's anyone who can find her, it would be Lyle Holmgaard. You remember, he helped us when we had that shipment derail in Texas a few years ago. I had a few clues that I could give him to work on. Kate had been sending me wires along the way, and when they stopped, I had some idea where she might have been kidnapped. Amazingly it was right in Lyle's backyard. He said he'd do what he could. All we can do is wait and hope."

William swiveled in his chair again to look out the window. "Do you think that was the wise thing to do?" he asked sharply. "Have you thought this through carefully? You could get her killed, you know."

"I had to do something. She's very dear to me."

William was silent, trying to get a grip on his racing heart and thoughts. This changed things. He hadn't thought that Tyler would straighten his back and actually contact the authorities. He thought he'd hand over the money and that would be that. By God, he'd have to be extra careful from now on.

"I'm just as sorry about this as I can be, John. You know I'll do anything I can to help you get her back," he said as sincerely as he could. "Don't worry about things here. You can depend on me. I can take care of things here in the office, if you would want to go out there."

"No, William. I appreciate the offer, but I've got to wait here for the next ransom note. Besides, I doubt that there's much that I could do in Texas besides get in the way." With that, John managed a weak smile. He went to the door and paused. "I think that I'm going to go home. Lila will be anxious to know if I've heard anything. William, I want you to know how much I appreciate you. I knew I could depend on you."

John left and softly closed the door.

William sat back in his chair and made a steeple with his fingers in front of his face. He was alarmed by the news that Tyler had gone to the Texas Rangers. He despised complications in the business world, and this was no different. Still, if this were a complication that he himself could deal with, that would have been okay. But this would be in Edwin's hands, and that might be cause for worry. He realized that he needed to get word to his nephew.

After making sure John had left the building, William put on his hat and overcoat and walked out the door. A heavy rain continued to fall. Now the weather matched his mood. He stood on the sidewalk and scanned both sides of the street for any sight of Tyler; it wouldn't do for him to run into him now. Seeing no sign of the man, he turned on his heel and walked toward the telegraph office.

He walked with his head down, paying little attention to anyone he passed. Few others were out in the stormy weather; most people were content to stay in, where it was warm and dry. William ignored the wet, his mind busy composing the telegram. Finally, as he entered the telegraph office, he decided.

REMEMBER THE OVERTURNED SHIPMENT? STOP.
SAME HAS BEEN NOTIFIED. STOP.

After he had sent the message and stepped back out into the deluge, William Jacobs felt pleased with himself. He had sent a message that only Edwin would understand.

As William continued to walk up the street, he paused to look in a jewelry store window, glancing at the display of rings, necklaces, and bracelets. Unsatisfied with the selection, he moved on. Jewelry from just any store would not be good enough for his lady love. It would have to come from Tiffany's.

With every step, he became more confident that he would succeed. It had been a risky move to kidnap Katherine Tyler, but as a successful businessman in his own right, he knew that there was no reward without risk. He was going to buy out John Tyler with John's own money. He would control the business and take his place among the social elite.

The most important decision had already been made. It was how to deal with Edwin after he'd received the ransom money. William already had plans in the making to get rid of him. He had given strict orders to the man who had found Hayden, and was assured that Hayden would know what to do when the time came.

William Jacobs walked on in the rain with a smile on his face.

Chapter 9

Tate saddled his horse at daybreak. As he tucked the last of his gear into his saddlebags, he looked up at the shimmering sun as it rose above a low rise of hills to the east. Today would be like most days. Hot and windy.

While eating breakfast, he asked Yelena to tell Emily that he would be gone for a couple of days but that he might even be back tomorrow.

"She is 'fraid, señor, you not come back."

"I'll be back."

"I tell her."

Jorge got up to pour coffee from the blackened pot on the cookstove. When he set it back down, Tate said, "Jorge, I don't want to leave, but I do owe Lyle a couple of days of my time. Be on the lookout for anyone you don't know coming near the house. Lyle said Hayden is back, and he hates me worse than poison. I'd not put it past him to come here if he thought I was gone."

"I keep my eye out, señor."

"Hayden's got scars on one side of his face now. I don't

think you've seen him since he was in that knife fight. He's the meanest son of a gun that I've ever met. He has no more feeling for man or beast than a rattlesnake."

"You see a snake, you shoot it, señor."

"I will if the time is right. I should have shot him several years ago when he tried to knife me in the back. He blames me for his scars, but hell, I was just trying to protect myself when that Mexican renegade stepped in and sliced his face. He had been waiting for a chance to get at him. Hayden has enemies all over the Southwest. If it hadn't been the Mexican, it would have been someone else. Thing is, Hayden doesn't see it that way. He blames me and may decide to come here."

"We be waiting for him," Jorge said confidently.

Tate took another bite of his biscuit. "This shouldn't take more than a day or two. Lyle's a good man, the kind who doesn't ask favors unless he really needs help. You and Yelena, keep your eyes open."

"If you see a strange car coming up the lane, Yelena, get Emily and go to the cellar and bar the door."

"Sí, Jorge, I know to do that."

"By the way, Jorge, there's one more thing," Tate said, turning to his foreman. "I don't trust Wilbur. He had dealings with Hayden several years ago, although he denied it to Lyle and it couldn't be proven. Wilbur doesn't know this, but Lyle found out he and Hayden are shirttail relations, and to Wilbur's thinking, blood is thicker than water. Besides, he doesn't like me very much anyway, because we've been able to capture some of the wild mares.

I don't think Wilbur is in on this kidnapping, but he's got his eye out for easy money."

"Wilbur girl like you, señor." Yelena had a sly, mischievous smile on her face. "She come and make over our *niña* when you gone."

"Sophie has too much of Wilbur in her to my liking. She seems like a nice enough girl, but I pity the man who gets her."

"She not for you, señor?" Yelena teased.

"Definitely not. If I ever think about marrying again, and I'm certainly not planning to, you can bet I'll think long and hard about it. I would have to find someone who would accept Emily, because she's the most important thing in my life."

Tate got up from the table and walked over to a bag that he'd yet to unpack from his trip to the fort. He pulled a parcel from it and walked back to the table.

"This is for Emily," Tate said as he placed the package on the table. "I saved a present for her. You can give it to her after she's had her breakfast. It's a Sears catalog. That should keep her busy for a while."

"Oh, sí, señor. She love to look at toys."

"She cut up the last one I brought her."

"She did." Yelena smiled. "But she cut better now. She cut heads off the pictures in that catalog. I help her. We make up paste and put them on that white paper the cheese wrapped in."

Jorge glanced proudly at his wife. "My *bella amante*. She know what baby like."

Yelena smiled and shook her head. "You *dulce*, Jorge."

"I've got to get going, sweet Jorge," Tate teased as he pushed away from the table.

Tate went to Emily's room and placed a kiss on her forehead. It seemed like only yesterday that he held his brand-new baby girl in his arms for the first time. She was growing up so fast. He knew she would be disappointed when she awakened to find him gone.

Why did I agree to do this for a woman who made me feel like a fool on the train?

Tate felt good to be back in the saddle again. The horse he was riding was a coal-black mustang he'd had for several years. Jack liked to run. As soon as he was out in the open, Tate let him stretch his legs and pulled him up when they reached the railroad tracks. The horse's sides were heaving. From this place, it was only about a mile to the water tank.

Tate walked the horse alongside the tracks and approached the tank slowly. He dismounted and tied Jack to a sapling, then picked his way among the rocks, cacti, and bright red ocotillo flowers that bloomed low to the ground.

Scrutinizing the ground carefully for evidence, he tried to visualize where the engine had stopped and where the passenger cars would have been. Stepping over the train tracks, he went to the south side of the rails. The nearby woods would have been a good place to whisk the woman out of sight in a matter of seconds.

Walking carefully, he scanned the earth until he found what he was looking for. Squatting down, he verified the print of a woman's shoe in the sandy soil. It was faint but unmistakable. The imprints led him farther into the woods, away from the train tracks. Beneath a stand of juniper trees, he stood and wiped his forehead with his handkerchief. It was hot and getting hotter as the sun arched overhead. He followed the footprints to where he found the remains of a fire.

Only a greenhorn would have built a fire in this place. As dry as it's been, he could have set the whole woods on fire. Luckily some of the wood used was green.

Circling the remains of the fire, he scanned the ground for further signs of the woman. Finally, on the ground in front of a Mexican piñon tree, he saw signs that someone had moved about in the dirt. Looking closer, he found blond hairs stuck in the bark, and he surmised that the woman had been tied to this tree. The back of her head had rested against the rough trunk. He looked around for evidence that she had been harmed, but could find none. Tate found the tire tracks of a car, a heavy car, on a nearby trail that had been cut through the woods years before. He went back for Jack and returned to follow those tracks.

Miles went by. Tate followed the tire tracks. The sun rose higher in the sky, and the temperature climbed along with it. High above, a lone eagle circled hungrily, searching for some smaller prey that might dart out of its hiding spot. He figured it wouldn't be long before the bird gave up its hunt and waited for evening.

Seeing Katherine Tyler in his mind's eye, he recalled her beauty. Nature had bestowed fine-boned, delicately carved features upon her as well as wide-set sky-blue eyes. Her soft-spun hair was a curious mixture of silver and gold, or maybe it had just looked that way in the evening light.

She was slender to the point of fragility. The set of her mouth and chin, the candor in her eyes, and the way her head rode proudly on her long neck all showed her strength of character. Tate had been wrong in his first impression of her. This was no empty-headed beauty the kidnappers had taken, but a strong-willed, determined, and dignified woman. Her eyes had looked unwaveringly into his. The straightforwardness of her stare had slightly unnerved him. Later he'd felt a strange quiver in his stomach when he lifted her undergarments.

Tate pulled his mind back from the image of the woman. After stopping Jack at the top of a rise, he looked over the landscape, then scanned the countryside with his binoculars. Tall crags of rock and clumps of brittle-looking trees were evidence that this was a wilder, more remote area. The whole place was desolate. Few ways to get in or out. The perfect place to hide.

The only building in sight was the old Billings cabin that had stood there for fifty years or more. A small tendril of smoke rose from the cabin's lone chimney.

A greenhorn wouldn't have brought her here, but someone like Hayden, who knew the area, would have. Tate had no doubt now that Hayden was involved.

Kate wasn't sure exactly how long she had been at the cabin, but she thought that it had been three days. Her nights had been long and fretful. When she hadn't been tossing in a fitful sleep, she'd stared at the door, afraid one of the men would burst through it. She was not sure that Eddy could protect her from the other two men. The man that they called Hayden scared her more than the repulsive salesman. With the scars on his face and the way that he stared at her with his mean eyes, he reminded her more of a wolf than a man. He always wore that wicked-looking knife, and when he spoke, it was usually a snarl. Eddy and the salesman seemed to be careful when they were with him, as if they feared him too. She hadn't been alone with him that she knew of. For that, she was thankful.

It was midmorning of the third day that a knock sounded on Kate's door.

"Who is it?" she called out.

"It's me, Kate," Eddy answered as he pushed the door open and stepped into the room. He had large dark bags under his eyes, and his clothing was rumpled. "I need to talk to you."

"I don't have anything to say to you, Eddy."

"Please, Kate. Don't be difficult. I don't have much time."

"What do you want?" she asked from where she sat on the bunk. With each passing day, her dislike of Eddy had grown. Even hearing his voice caused anger to boil up inside her. "Haven't you done enough to me already?"

"Hayden and I are going to town."

"What?" Kate shouted. "You're going to leave me here with that brainless fool?"

"He'll not bother you. He's got strict orders to leave you alone."

"Strict orders? He isn't capable of following any order, strict or otherwise. He's an idiot and you know it."

"Keep that stout pole I gave you yesterday wedged tightly against the door. He'll not be able to get in."

The idea of being left alone with Squirrelly was almost as frightening as being left alone with Hayden.

Eddy was not happy that he had to leave her. But better she be here with Squirrelly than with Hayden. Neither Squirrelly nor Hayden knew the telegram would be addressed to Grover Electric Company and R. Edwin. (It was the name he and his uncle had agreed upon.) And he had to take Hayden along because the bastard wouldn't give him the keys to the car.

"You'll be all right if you just stay in the room and keep the door braced with that pole. I won't be gone long." Kate could see that there was more that Eddy wanted to say, but he hesitated. He looked at her for a moment longer before blurting out, "I want you to know I'm really sorry about this, Kate."

"How much?" Kate angrily asked.

"What?"

"How much money are you hoping to get out of my father?"

Eddy looked down at the floor. "It's not just me, Kate. I'm taking orders just like the others. Someday you'll know all about it."

"Who are you taking orders from? What have I ever done that would cause someone to do this to me?"

"No one wants to hurt you, Kate. On that, I give you my word. But someone needs money badly, and your father has plenty of it."

Anger washed over Kate like a warm flood. That someone was using her for simple greed was infuriating. Her father had given so much to charity and had supported numerous families with his generosity. Now these blood-suckers wanted to bleed him dry!

"My father will pay, Eddy. Never doubt that. But remember this, Eddy: My father was brought up in the steel mills. He can be as tough as the steel he helped make. He worked hard to buy that plant. Anyone would be a fool to harm something that is his. He'll find you and make you pay, if it takes the rest of his life."

"Get a move on, Jacobs. Hayden's waitin'." Squirrelly leaned against the door frame, a loose-lipped smile on his face.

Eddy turned back to Kate. "I'll hurry back. Keep the pole lodged against the door." Then turning, he spoke sternly to Squirrelly. "I'm warning you. If you bother her, I'll blow your head off."

Squirrelly giggled. "You ain't got the guts!"

"You'll find out. You mess up this deal, and if I don't kill you, I know someone who will."

Squirrelly's giggle turned into a hearty laugh. "Old William Jacobs has the guts. He's got the guts of a government mule."

Eddy pointed his finger in Squirrelly's face. "Shut up, goddamn it."

"Are you talking about Uncle William?" Kate demanded.

"Who else would we be talking about?" Squirrelly said, and then to Eddy, "I'm getting kind of tired of you pointing your finger in my face and giving me orders. You're not the head dog of this."

Is Squirrelly saying that William Jacobs is the head dog? Kate thought. *Eddy didn't deny it.*

The two men stood staring at each other after Eddy had closed the door and waited to hear the pole wedged against it. He then turned and walked out the cabin door. From the window, Kate saw him follow Hayden to the car and then watched them drive away.

She was frightened, really frightened. She looked around for something to use to defend herself. There was no doubt in her mind that Squirrelly would try to molest her. She had seen evidence of his lust when he jerked his hips toward her in an obscene gesture. If he tried anything, she would fight him until her last breath.

Kate looked out the window, for a long while, at the desolate landscape, listening for movement in the other room. She thought of the torment that her father must be feeling. Then she thought of Susie. What would her sister think when she learned Eddy's true nature? Would she still be so madly in love with him? Susie saw only Eddy's handsome face and glib tongue. Who could blame her? Kate had always thought of him as a nice young man, if a little full of himself. Never in her wildest dreams would she have thought he or William Jacobs would be involved in something like this.

After nearly an hour with no sound coming from the other room, Kate began to wonder if Squirrelly had left the cabin. Then, without a warning, *bang.* The door shook from the force of the blow against it, startling her. Kate ran to the door to make sure the pole was lodged tightly against it. She jumped back when another force hit the door. The third blow splintered it, and the pole fell away. Squirrelly stood in the doorway, a bottle in one hand, grinning like the idiot he was.

"Get out of here," she shouted.

"Make me." He continued to grin and walked into the room. He took a big swig from the bottle. Some of the dark liquid ran down his chin, staining his shirt.

"Get away." She grabbed up the pole that had been against the door. "Get away."

Squirrelly jerked the pole from her hand. "Ah, come on, sweetie pie. You've been giving me the eye ever since we got on the train in New Orleans. Admit it . . . you like me."

"I don't. I don't like you at all. I don't want anything to do with you. Get out of this room!"

"And if I don't?" Squirrelly took another step toward her.

"Eddy will kill you when he comes back."

Squirrelly threw his head back and laughed hysterically

Fear made Kate's knees weak. Out here in this wilderness, she was alone with this treacherous man. She stiffened her knees and held up her head. Damned if she would let him know she was afraid of him.

"There's no reason for you to be hoity-toity, little Miss High-and-Mighty. You think you're better than me 'cause your papa's rich? You'd be surprised to know that my papa is rich too."

"What is he? A crook?"

"Yeah, but he's a rich crook. You'd also be surprised to know how many of your society friends I've screwed."

"Shut up! I don't want to hear about your sordid affairs."

"Oh, don't give me that. You know what screwing is, don't you?" Squirrelly gyrated his hips at Kate, simulating his description of sex. He moved so forcefully that a bit of liquor spilled from the bottle onto the floor.

"Shut up and get out of here."

"We could have a good time while your lover boy's gone."

"He's not my lover boy. I don't like him any more than I like you."

"In that case, I'll be your lover boy."

"I'd rather have a warthog than you," Kate said coldly.

"Maybe you'd rather have Hayden. I hear he's plenty rough with his women. Likes to smack 'em around a bit. I'll be nicer to you than he will." He walked closer, until only a couple of feet separated them.

"Get away, you mud-ugly guttersnipe."

With that, Squirrelly's teasing attitude disappeared, and what replaced it frightened Kate. His eyes glinted with anger as he snarled, "Call me that again, you high-toned bitch, and I'll screw your eyeballs out."

"Just try it, you guttersnipe," she said again, goading him recklessly.

Squirrelly took two big steps toward her, pulled back his hand, and slapped her so hard her head bounced back against the wall. Pain shot through her skull. For a moment, she was dazed, her eyes unfocused. When reality returned, he was there, his knees on the bed, grinning at her.

"How do you like that, Miss Prissy-Tail? Maybe you're the kind that likes it rough."

"My father will kill you," she mumbled through the pain and shock. She could taste blood inside her mouth.

"Yeah? He won't be able to swat a fly when we get through with him."

"We? Who do you mean?"

"Who do you think? Your old papa is so smart he don't know what's right under his nose. In the meanwhile, I'm gonna have me some fun with the cream of New York society. You can tell your snooty friends about it when you get back home—*if* you get back home—that you were screwed by a real man."

When he slapped her, the bottle of alcohol had slipped out of his hand and landed on the bed. The dark liquid had soaked the mattress, the strong stench filling her nostrils. The odor mingled with Squirrelly's foul breath and unwashed body.

"Don't touch me! Get away!"

"Not on your life. I'm about to plow you. It's somethin' I've wanted to do from the moment I saw you." He grabbed her and yanked her close to him. "Mmmm, you smell good, sweetie. How do you want it? Rough? Or are you going to lay back and spread your legs for me?"

Kate pushed against him with all her might. Squirrelly smirked at her attempt to push him away and stepped away from the bed. When she looked again, he was taking off his belt. Desperate to stop what was about to happen, she grabbed for the whiskey bottle. Her hand grasped the wrong end to swing, so she threw it at him. He dodged. She swung her fists at him with all the strength that she had left. Still smirking, he shoved her down on the cot. As his weight pressed down on her, she grabbed a handful of his hair and screamed and screamed and screamed.

God help me. He's going to rape me!

Out of the corner of her eye she saw something, and Squirrelly collapsed on top of her.

Chapter 10

Panic-stricken, Kate tried frantically to push Squirrelly off her, but his dead weight pinned her to the bed. Suddenly he was lifted up and tossed to the floor like a sack of grain. A man stood next to the cot, his hand extended toward her. Kate looked up into a face that was strangely familiar, but she wasn't sure. The man's hat was pulled low over his forehead.

"Come on, let's get out of here," his gruff voice ordered.

"I'm not going anywhere with you." Kate was still dazed.

"Do you want to stay here and let this animal rape you?"

She looked down to see Squirrelly lying limp on the floor, his britches almost to his knees. Blood oozed from the side of his head.

The man grabbed her hand. "I said come on."

Finally Kate recognized the unmistakable gentle drawl of the cowboy from the train. *The cowboy from the train!* He looked the same as he had when they boarded the train together: same clothes, same rudeness. Her shock at seeing Squirrelly lying on the floor, however, was greater than her surprise at seeing the cowboy. "Is he dead?" Her mouth was dry, making it difficult for her to talk.

"What do you care? He was going to rape you, and probably kill you."

"How do I know you're not one of them?" she said defiantly, yanking her arm free from his grip.

"You're Miss Tyler, aren't you?"

"Yes. How did you know?"

"Your father contacted the Texas Rangers. They're looking for you."

"Are you a Texas Ranger?"

"No. Now, are you coming or not? Make up your mind. I'm not waiting around here until Hayden gets back. He's one mean son of a bitch."

"I'm coming." A quick thought passed through Kate's mind. Going off with this strange man couldn't possibly be any worse than waiting around for Eddy and Hayden to come back. Besides, the farther she was from here, the better. She reached for her bag, flung it over her arm, and hurriedly followed him out the door.

The sun clung to the very top of the hills, its disk a deep red. The purple color of twilight filled the sky. Shadows on the ground were growing larger by the second. Soon it would be dark.

Out in back of the cabin, the cowboy stopped and looked down at her feet. "Are those the only shoes you have?"

"Here? Yes."

"Well, come on. They'll have to do." He grabbed her arm again and pulled her across the yard and into the dense

bushes at the back of the cabin. Kate stumbled along behind him, her heels digging into the soil.

"Hurry up, I hear the car coming." He stopped and
pushed her down behind some underbrush.

"Stay here and don't make a sound, no matter what you
hear."

"You're leaving me now?" Eddy and Hayden were coming back!

"You'll be all right. I won't be gone long," he said gently.
"Don't move, or I won't be able to find you when I come
back." He was gone without a sound.

Kate stared blindly into the darkness. When she heard a
pair of car doors slam, she had to will herself to keep
breathing. The door to the cabin creaked, and then a string
of obscenities reached her ears. Hayden was in a rage.

Where is the cowboy?

"You goddamn stupid fool! You let her get away!" Hayden
shouted at the unconscious man on the floor. He drew back
his foot and kicked Squirrelly. "I should kill this useless son
of a bitch!"

Eddy stared down at Squirrelly and gritted his teeth. His
pants were unbuttoned and bunched around his knees. No
doubt he had intended to rape Kate, but there was no evidence that he had completed the job. How had Kate managed to fight him off and get away? Blood oozed from the
wound on Squirrelly's head. Eddy hoped that the little shit
had a headache for a month. The important thing now was
to find Kate. Hayden snatched a lantern from the wall, lit it,
and headed for the door.

"What are you going to do?" Eddy asked.

"Find her. What else?"

"Don't hurt her."

"I'd like to wring her damn neck," Hayden muttered. He spat a stream of tobacco at Squirrelly's motionless body. "She got the jump on him while he was thinking with his pecker, or maybe somebody helped her."

"You said nobody knew about this cabin," Eddy accused.

"Don't be stupid, Jacobs! Damn cabin's been here for fifty years or more. Fella named Castle knows about it."

"How would he have found out Kate was here?"

"Probably snooping around, looking for me. He found the cabin, saw her, and figured she must be my woman, so he snatched her."

"Do you know him?"

"He's been doggin' me for years. I owe that bastard plenty, and he'll get it as soon as I catch up with him."

"Would he hurt Kate?"

"What do you think?" Hayden said with a chilling laugh. "Him and me ain't like you city fellas. Soon as he gets her alone in the woods, he'll take his, just like I would've took mine."

"Oh God! Poor Kate."

"To hell with her! All she means to me is money." Hayden flung open the door. "Stay here while I look around. I don't want your tracks messing up hers."

Before Eddy could say anything in reply, Squirrelly groaned and blinked his eyes. Slowly, and with great effort, he managed to lean up on one elbow. His hand rubbed the growing knot on the back of his head.

Eddy bent down beside him and nudged him with his hand. "What the hell happened here?"

"Ohhhh, my head," Squirrelly moaned.

"What happened here?" Eddy repeated.

"The son of a bitch hit me. I'll kill him." Squirrelly drew his fingers away from his head and looked at the red stain of his own blood. "I'll kill him."

"Who?" Hayden uttered the word sharply as he came back inside the cabin.

"How in the hell do I know? He looked like one of the clods that live around here."

"An Indian?" Eddy asked.

"No, he wasn't no Indian. I just got a glance at him before he whopped me."

"I know who he was," Hayden said as he went to the door and stood looking into the dark night. "Castle." Inside, he was seething.

"Can you find them?" Eddy asked nervously.

"Yeah, but there ain't much point in startin' now. I could spend the whole damn night lookin' for tracks with this lantern and not find a thing. I hate givin' Castle a head start, but I'm gonna have to wait till mornin'."

"But they'll get away!"

"They ain't gonna get far," Hayden sneered into the dark night. "This land's hard enough to get around in during the day. Movin' around at night's gonna be slow. 'Specially if he has to drag that woman with him."

"But you said he might rape her," Eddy protested.

"I ain't goin' till mornin'," Hayden said with a tone that signaled the discussion was over.

Eddy stood in the room that had been Kate's with anger burning in his belly. He knew that he shouldn't have left her with Squirrelly. But now Kate was out there in the wilderness with a man cut from the same cloth as Hayden!

"I need a doctor!" Squirrelly moaned.

"This is all your fault!" Eddy shouted at Squirrelly. "I knew I couldn't depend on you. All you've got on your mind is fornicating."

"Fornicating? What's that?"

Eddy looked at him in disgust and turned away.

The seconds went by like minutes, the minutes like hours. Kate burrowed down into the bushes like a creature of the wilds. She had never known such utter darkness. Something had bitten her arm, and she itched. She breathed steadily to let the terrific pounding of her heart subside a little.

What if they kill this man who came to help me?

She heard the men enter the cabin, and the night was filled with the curses from Hayden's foul mouth. "You goddamn stupid fool! You let her get away! I should kill this useless son of a bitch!"

Kate pushed herself up and waited for the cramped muscles in her legs to relax. *Quiet,* she told herself.

"Shhhh . . ." The hiss came from beside her. "It's me. Give me your hand."

The relief Kate felt almost opened a floodgate of tears, but she held them back. When the man's calloused palm met hers, she squeezed it with all her might and followed him. In the scant light of the rising moon, she could see that he carried a bundle under his arm and saddlebags over his shoulder. They walked on uneven ground. *How does he know where we're going? Can he see in the dark like a cat?* Small bushes scratched against her legs as she struggled to keep up with the stranger's long strides. The thin moon rose steadily in the night sky, but he never slowed.

As they walked on through the darkness, Kate couldn't help but think about the strangeness of her situation. A week ago she had been thousands of miles away working in a clinic. Now she was deep in the Texas wilderness with a man who had no doubt saved her life, and she didn't even know his name.

She stumbled on an unseen branch and threw her arm out to catch herself. The cowboy steadied her and then kept on walking. A short time later he stopped and listened. She stood with her forehead resting on his back, so exhausted she could hardly move.

"You all right?"

"Just tired."

"Let's go on. I turned my horse loose. Let's hope Hayden will follow him. That will give us a little time. We're headed east. Hayden won't start tracking us until morning."

"How do you know Hayden?" she asked, looking up at the side of his face.

"He's wanted to kill me for a long time," the stranger answered without looking at her. His eyes scanned over the area they had covered. "That doesn't matter now. Come on, let's go."

"I can't even thank you. I don't know your name."

"My name is Tate Castle."

"How did you know where I was?"

"We don't have time for this. Come on."

Kate clutched the cowboy's arm. The events of the last few days had left her dazed, and it seemed he was the only real thing left in the world.

"We're going to have to walk out of here. I'm going to break the heels off those shoes of yours." He knelt down to slip a shoe off. He stepped on the high heel, and it snapped off. He put the shoe back on her foot and lifted her other foot to take off the shoe. With both heels off, he said, "That better?"

"It feels strange, but I'll get used to it."

Without another word, the cowboy started walking. Kate followed blindly along. It was as if her mind had set her legs the task of carrying her and they kept stubbornly moving forward, incapable of deciding to stop. She stumbled, bumped against a tree, pushed herself away from it, and staggered on.

When, sometime later, Tate stopped, she bumped into him. He dropped the bundle and caught her arm, steadying her against a tree trunk. "Careful!"

"Sorry," she mumbled.

"We'll stop here. Hold on to the tree."

He picked up a stick and began to move it around on the ground.

"Why are you doing that?" Kate asked.

He continued raking the stick over the ground, making large circles through the sandy soil. Finally he tossed the stick away and knelt down and loosened the ties of the bedroll and spread it out under a small tree.

Kate, thinking her bladder would burst any minute, moved toward the bushes for some privacy. She was embarrassed to have to seek privacy to relieve herself, but she didn't have any choice. It was all so unreal! Her life was in the hands of this man, and she'd never really seen his face, except for that brief time on the train and at the cabin.

"Where are you going?" he asked harshly.

Kate looked at him over her shoulder and kept going. She parted the bushes and stepped into a clearing that would afford her some privacy.

"Wait," Tate said sharply. "Damn it! I said wait!"

"I'll not go far."

Tate moved past her with the big stick still in his hand. He threw his arm out to hold her back while the hand holding the stick swooped down and flipped a small snake out of her path.

Her screech of fear was cut off suddenly when Tate's hand clamped down over her mouth.

"Quiet. Keep your voice down. Sounds carry here in the hills."

"I'm sorry," she whispered. The revulsion of seeing the snake so close and knowing she had almost stepped on it sent the bile rising in her throat. She swallowed and willed her galloping heart to be still.

"If you had to do your business, why didn't you say so? I can't keep running after you." He scanned the clearing and ran his stick over the sparse grass. "It's clear now. Go ahead and do what you came here to do."

Instead, Kate stared at him. "I can't do it with you here," she said through clenched teeth.

"Hurry up. I'll turn my back," he said impatiently.

Her face flamed with embarrassment; she could not believe that she was about to relieve herself with a strange man standing not ten feet away. Kate turned her back and squatted down.

When she finished, Tate led the way back to where he had left his saddlebags. Still shaking from her encounter with the snake and unable to look at the man, Kate followed. *Will I ever be able to face him again?*

He opened a saddlebag and said, "You better eat something. We've got biscuits, peanut butter, jam, and a couple of strips of jerky."

"I'll have a biscuit and peanut butter." Still unable to look at him, she took the biscuit from his hand. "What about you?"

"I'll pass. We've got a full canteen of water, but we'll have to go easy on it. It's been dry. We can't depend on finding water."

Kate ate the biscuit slowly. The cowboy was silent while she was eating, his eyes continually searching the landscape. When she finished, she asked, "You said we had to walk out of here. Where are we going?"

"Muddy Creek. It's a little town to the west of here. We can send a wire from there."

"Is that where you live?"

"I live on a ranch north of town."

A crackling sound came from the underbrush. Kate froze. The sound came again. Shuffling, swishing. Panic flared through her again. She dived toward Tate and clutched his arm.

"What's that?" The sound jarred her nerves.

Tate threw a stone into the brush, and the sound stopped.

"It's nothing. Probably a pack rat."

Even if it had been nothing, Kate couldn't let go of the cowboy's arm. All at once, the traumatizing events of the last few days caught up with her. "I'm sorry." Her tears began to flow. "I'm sorry," she said again.

"Lie back and try to sleep." His voice was low and reassuring.

Kate relaxed against him. She wished she could see his face again. He felt solid and lean. She liked the sound of his voice and the earthy smell of him.

"Tate, do you think they'll find us?"

"Not for a while." He moved his back and settled against a tree. "I don't want to give you false hope. It's going to be a long way out of here, but we can make it. I might have to leave you for a bit and backtrack to see if Hayden is coming. He won't quit."

A profound silence followed his statement. Kate shivered as much from dread as from the cool night breeze. Now that Tate had found her, she didn't want him to leave her alone.

"What will we do if he catches up?" she asked in a small voice.

"We'll do what we have to do. We'll head into the hills instead of towards town. It'll take longer, but we want to make it as difficult as we can for him to track us."

As she listened to the soft, slurred voice of the cowboy, the tension left Kate's tired body. She was exhausted and her feet hurt. It seemed odd to be sitting here, yet she felt safe and wondered why.

Tate pulled the blanket up over them. "It gets cool up here at night. Try to sleep for a while."

She did.

Kate awoke to the sound of a low murmur. Her eyes flew open and searched for the source of the voices. She was surprised to see Tate squatting alongside an Indian boy whose dark hair reached down to his shoulders. Around his forehead was tied a twisted cloth. His clothes were clean but ragged. He wore moccasins that came up to his knees. In his arms he cradled a rifle.

"Oh-oh," she gasped at the sight of the gun. He turned, and his eyes were as dark as coal and expressionless.

"Quiet," Tate hissed at her. He inched toward her and spoke softly, knowing that their voices would carry in this quiet hillside. "This is Luke Ironhorse. He's a friend of mine. He spotted Hayden about a mile down the draw."

"I tryin' to save your ass again, Tate," the Indian said with a grunt.

"Watch your language, kid."

"I know language. I not dumb," the boy said defiantly.

"Smart britches," Tate growled.

"What that mean?"

Without another word, Tate grabbed up his saddlebag and threw it over his shoulder. When he tugged on the bedroll, Kate got to her feet. He packed the bedding into a tight roll and tied it with a string. In a matter of minutes, he was ready to leave.

"What are we going to do now?" Kate asked, suddenly fearful at the thought that Hayden was nearby. She could still remember the sound made when he pulled the knife from his scabbard.

"Follow," the Indian boy said, and started to move through the underbrush and up a small hillside.

"Go on," Tate ordered. She looked over her shoulder to see Tate behind her. The boy moved swiftly and silently, and it was hard for Kate to keep up with him. But she was determined to be as little trouble as possible.

They crossed a dry creek bed, the mud cracked in the hot Texas sun. The glare from the sun was blinding, but Kate kept going forward. Occasionally, bright orange flowers grew from the reddish soil, the likes of which she had never seen before, but now was not the time to stop and admire the sights. It took nearly all of her concentration to keep up with Luke. She could hardly hear the Indian boy move. His moccasined feet glided over the increasingly rocky terrain. Her own shoes, newly heelless, hurt her feet, but she tried to ignore the pain and trudged on.

"Stop," Tate said softly.

"What stop for?" Luke turned to face them.

Happy for the break, Kate bent to put her hands on her knees and tried to catch her breath. The midafternoon sun continued to beat down as rivulets of sweat ran down her cheeks. The climb didn't seem to bother the other two at all.

"Stay with Luke," Tate said to Kate.

Luke moved past Kate and began to head back down the trail. "I go look. You stay with your woman."

Tate shook his head. "She's not my woman."

"I'm not his woman," Kate said at the same time.

"Then why you sleep with her?"

Kate's face turned a fiery red as she waited for Tate's answer.

Tate shook his head again and put a hand on the boy's shoulder. "Take her and go. I'll catch up. I know where you're headed."

Kate's eyes clung to Tate. She didn't like being left with the Indian boy. Tate nodded at her reassuringly and, after pressing his canteen into her hand, turned away. In seconds, he was out of sight.

Without another word, the Indian boy continued on up the hill. Kate focused her eyes on the boy's back, determined not to let him get too far ahead. As they reached a small tree that was growing out from between two large boulders, the boy stopped and squatted down in the shade. Kate sat down beside him and opened the canteen. The water felt wonderful on her dry throat. She turned to offer the canteen to the boy, but he was squirting water into his mouth from a leather pouch.

"Where did Tate go?"

"He look for Hayden."

"What will he do if he sees him?"

"Kill him," the boy said matter-of-factly. "Or Hayden kill him."

Kate was stunned into silence. She scarcely knew the cowboy, but the possibility of his being killed terrified her. Somehow he had managed to find her. He had taken her away from the cabin, away from Hayden and Squirrelly and Eddy. Now he was risking his life to get her out of here.

The Indian boy stood, shaded his eyes with his hand, and looked back down the hill. Without a word, he turned and started moving away. Kate reluctantly got to her feet and hastened to follow.

Luke moved steadily upward. Kate, not far behind him, was panting from the effort of keeping pace. Her shoes, while better without their heels, were little protection against the sharp stones.

Her sheltered life hadn't prepared her for this kind of exertion.

Kate was exhausted when Luke finally motioned for her to stop. His arm pointed at a dark hole in the hillside.

"Stay. I go look for snakes."

"Snakes? Good heavens."

"What mean 'good heavens'? Ain't no bad heavens."

"It's only an expression," Kate explained.

"What you mean 'expression'?" Luke didn't wait for an answer before heading upward again. Kate watched as he approached the dark hole and then disappeared inside.

Moments later, when Luke came out of the hole, he motioned for Kate to follow him. Without hesitation, she began her trek up the hill. Her back was wet with sweat by the time she reached the cave entrance. She peered into the darkness as Luke tossed away a large stick.

"No snakes."

"Well, thank goodness for that," Kate said with relief.

"Why you thank goodness? What 'goodness'?"

Kate could only shake her head. *How can I explain that?*

Chapter 11

KATE STOOD AT THE ENTRANCE TO THE CAVE and looked back down the hill. The sun continued to rise in the clear blue Texas sky. Heat shimmered off the rocks below. A couple of hours had passed since Tate had headed back down the hill to check on Hayden, and she was anxious for him to return. Luke had sat quietly against the cave walls, watching her as she fretted. She didn't want to go into the cave for fear of bats.

"When will Tate be back?"

"Why? You 'fraid I'll scalp you?"

"No, I don't think that." Kate hugged herself closely, regardless of the hot summer day. Her voice had wavered when she denied it.

"I a savage Indian. City women 'fraid of savage Indians."

"How do you know I'm a city woman?"

Luke gave a short snort of laughter. "Only city woman wear silly clothes and no hat. Why Hayden want you? Can you skin rabbit? Can you set up tepee? Are you good on blanket?"

At first, Kate didn't understand what he meant. When it

dawned on her, her face turned deep red with embarrassment. "You're a fresh-mouthed kid. I don't appreciate such talk."

"What you mean 'fresh-mouthed'?" When Kate refused to answer his question, Luke returned to another earlier one, which he repeated. "Why Hayden want you?"

"He wants money from my father."

"You no want Hayden for your man? You want Tate?"

"Absolutely not!" Kate blurted out. *I can't believe the nerve of this boy! How can he say such things!*

"Tate better man."

"I don't doubt that. I don't want either one of them."

"You got no man. Woman need a man. I take you for my woman."

"You're just a boy." Kate turned to face him. "I'm years older than you."

Luke leaned forward, squared his shoulders, and tossed his head back. "What difference that make? I am a man. I take many girls to my tepee."

"I don't want to hear about your girls, you horny little toad."

"I no toad. I an eagle."

Kate suddenly realized that the Indian boy was having fun with her. He smiled as he stood up and walked to the entrance of the cave. Shielding his eyes with one hand, he looked into the distance.

Turning away from the boy, Kate reached for the canteen, opened it, and took a swallow. The liquid felt wonderful on her throat. She thought about taking another gulp but decided not to. "Tate doesn't have water," she said. "I'll save the rest for him."

"Tate come now," Luke announced.

Kate hurried over to the entrance. All she could see were trees, rocks, and the glare of reflected sunlight. "Where? I don't see him."

"He come."

Kate felt immense relief that Tate was near. From the moment that he left them, she had worried that he would meet up with Hayden. The brutal man might injure or kill him. Still, staring long and hard at the trail that she and the Indian boy had taken to the cave revealed no movement. Was Luke teasing her about Tate coming?

"He is not coming," Kate argued. "I don't see him."

"You think I lie?"

"I didn't say that. I just said I don't see him."

"Tate don't want you see him," Luke said matter-of-factly. "You see him, Hayden see him."

"Why do you always talk in riddles?" Kate frustratedly asked. Dealing with Luke was complicated. "And don't you say what 'riddles' mean!"

"Tate tell me what mean 'riddles.' Tate my good friend."

"How long have you known him?"

"Long time. He bring mission school. I learn to read and write my name. I first in family to go to school. I go to Tate's house and take little girl moccasins made by my mother."

"Tate has a little girl?"

Kate looked back down the hill, still seeing nothing but the heat ripples and the harsh landscape. She squinted her eyes and saw Tate climbing the hill.

"There he is," she said.

"Told you he was coming."

"How did you know?"

Luke looked up at a lone eagle soaring overhead. "My brother, the eagle, tell me."

"I'm not so stupid that I believe that." Kate smiled, her spirits lifted now that the cowboy was in sight.

"You not smart like me."

Kate laughed. She was getting used to the boy, and liked him. He was witty and intelligent.

Her eyes stayed on Tate as he approached. He didn't appear to be hurt.

"Are you thirsty?" she asked, handing him the canteen.

"I had one drink this afternoon, but I could sure use another."

"Did you see Hayden?"

Tate drank deeply before answering. "He followed my horse a ways, then backtracked when he realized that we'd fooled him. Somewhere back he picked up our trail."

"Is he nearby?"

"A few miles." Tate took another drink.

The hours of the day drifted by until the sun began its slow descent behind the hills. Shadows grew into deeper darkness, and the sounds of animals, free to come out now that the sun had set, reached the cave. The cry of a coyote calling for its mate sent a shiver down Kate's back. She had heard somewhere that Indians signaled to each other using the coyote call.

Tate and Luke moved away and talked together in low

tones. Kate sat down on one of the boulders beside the entrance to the cave and took off her shoes and stockings. Her feet throbbed. Being careful to keep her skirt around her legs, she picked up one foot and massaged it.

"Your woman wear silly shoes." Luke's voice reached her, and she glanced up to see Tate and Luke watching her.

"How many times do I have to tell you . . . I'm not Tate's woman," Kate said.

"Then you be my woman."

Tate smiled. "You'd probably have to fight Hayden for her."

"I kill Hayden."

"Don't be silly," Kate admonished them. "Will you two please stop passing me around as if I were a peace pipe."

"Peace pipe? Don't pass peace pipe no more. We civilized Indians. Only scalp city women now." Luke put his hand on the knife in the scabbard that hung from his belt.

Tate laughed, his eyes twinkling as he looked at Kate. "Has this kid been scaring you?"

"No," Kate answered, giving a tiny lie, "but he's been trying his best."

Tate walked over to where Kate sat, then knelt down and picked up one of her feet. "Another day's walk and you'll have blisters. What can we do about some footwear for her, Luke?"

"She no need footwear. She only silly squaw."

Tate actually laughed aloud. Looking at his face, Kate saw the small wrinkles bunch at the corners of his eyes, the dark whiskers that grew on his face, and the way that his smile seemed contagious. She couldn't believe how handsome he was when he smiled, and she hoped that she wasn't blushing.

"If you want your woman to have moccasins, I go back to village, but it take all night."

"How far to your village?" Kate asked.

"Not far."

"Why don't we all go to his village and hire a car to take us out? Hayden can't possibly catch us in a car."

Luke glanced over at Tate and shook his head. "Silly woman."

Tate, still smiling, said, "It isn't that easy. The village is a small one in the hills. There won't be a car there." Turning to Luke, he added, "Keep an eye out for Hayden. Last time I saw him, he was over by that small patch that got burned out by lightning this spring."

Luke gathered up his things and took a long drink out of his waterskin. "I bring back moccasins for your woman and food for you. On way back, I make sure Hayden still there."

Without another word, Luke trotted down the hill and into the growing darkness. Within moments, he was lost from sight.

"Isn't it risky for him to go back?" she asked Tate.

"Luke can take care of himself."

"But he's only a boy."

"In this country, he's considered a man. He'll be all right."

Now alone with Tate, Kate found herself at a loss for words. She wanted to ask him about his daughter and how his wife felt about him going out to find her. But their relationship had not reached the point where she was comfortable asking Tate personal questions.

Tate dug into the saddlebags and brought out the cloth-wrapped biscuits and handed one to her.

"This isn't exactly a fancy meal, but it's all we got."

"You eat it. I'm not very hungry." She tried to give the biscuit back, but he refused to take it.

"Force yourself to eat. We have miles to go, and you need to keep up your strength."

Aware that Tate was right, Kate gnawed at the biscuit. "Did you have anything all day?" she asked.

"No, but I'm used to it. Luke will bring food back in the morning."

"Have you known him long?"

"Since he was knee-high to a grasshopper. His people have been in this area since before any white men, and his father and I were good friends. Luke's a smart kid, even if he is mouthy."

"He told me he has been to your house."

Tate turned to look down the hill and made no reply. He picked up one of her shoes and tossed it farther into the cave. "I'm sure Luke checked it out, but I want to be sure that there are no bats in there." He picked up the other shoe and threw it after the first one.

"Hey, those shoes cost me twenty dollars."

"You're kidding, aren't you?"

"No, I'm not kidding," Kate said, instantly self-aware. "But it's all right. They're no use to me without heels."

Tate looked down at her feet. Her toes were red, and on

the side of one foot was the beginning of a blister. "You just stay here. I'll spread the blanket inside the cave and come back for you."

"Don't go," she said. But he was already gone.

It was so quiet that she could hear the pounding of her own heart. Tate was back almost immediately. He scooped her up in his arms and headed back into the cave.

"Oh," she said, surprised. "Put me down. I'm too heavy."

"Not on those bare feet."

"I've never been carried before."

"Your men friends in New York haven't lifted you?"

"There was never any reason to."

"You're not heavy. I doubt you weigh any more than a newborn calf." Tate set her gently down on the blanket.

Kate was surprised the cave was so small. Where she lay was only a few feet from the entrance. "I thought it was bigger," she said. "Luke made it seem like it was deep and full of snakes, bats, and bears."

Tate chuckled lightly. "Luke likes to scare city folks. He gets a big kick out of pretending to be a full-blooded savage and getting them all worked up. Truth is, he's really one hell of a smart kid."

"Do you think he'll be all right?"

"He'll be fine. He knows this area better than anyone. He'll run most of the way to his village. I only hope he doesn't get it into his head to tackle Hayden."

"Why does Luke hate Hayden?"

"Hayden ruined several girls from the village. One of them was Luke's sister. To the Indian way of thinking, any girl who's been with a man not her husband is ruined and only fit to be second wife. Luke will kill him someday unless someone else gets to him first."

"Why do you hate him?" Kate cautiously asked.

"Because he's bad to the core. Always has been. He's cruel to animals and anyone weaker than he is, especially women. If there's easy money to be had, Hayden will be there. He tried to knife me in the back a couple of years ago. Probably would've succeeded if one of his old enemies hadn't taken advantage of the situation and jumped him. That's how he got those scars on his face. For some reason, he blames me."

"Did you get hurt?"

"Just a knife wound in the shoulder."

Tate sat down on the blanket beside her. He took his hat off and ran his forked fingers through his black hair. Kate wondered if some of his ancestors were the Indians that had roamed these hills for hundreds of years. When she spoke, the words didn't match her thoughts.

"Will Hayden find us here?"

"He probably knows about this place," Tate answered while fixing her with a serious look, as if he wanted her to know that they were far from being free of danger. "I'm hoping he'll think we headed straight for town. We're all right for a while. He won't try to track us over the rocks at night. Lay back and get some sleep if you can."

"I don't know if I can. The last few days have been so difficult. Being taken from the train, hauled off to that cabin, imprisoned by those three men . . . I've been too nervous to sleep."

"I know all about Hayden, but who were the other two?"

"One of them is the nephew of my father's business partner. His name is Edwin Jacobs. The other one, the one you saved me from, is called 'Squirrelly.' His father is a big-time crook in New York City."

"He looked kind of familiar."

"He should. He was the button salesman who was waiting with us at the train depot. He'd been following me all the way from New Orleans—from New York, I guess. But he's too stupid to be any more than a hired man."

"So the nephew was in on the kidnapping?"

"I didn't think so at first, but now I'm sure he was," Kate said softly. It was still hard for her to accept that Eddy, her sister's beau, was involved in her kidnapping. The more she thought about it, the more she believed that it must be William who was behind all this. "Maybe his uncle wants to take over my father's company."

"Doesn't seem like much of a partner."

"No . . . no, he doesn't."

"Will your father pay?"

"He'll pay. I don't know what they are asking, but he'll pay."

Tate was thoughtful for a minute, then said, "Did they tell you that as soon as they had the money, they would let you go?"

"Yes."

"Did it ever occur to you that there was no way they could let you live? Not after you'd seen their faces."

"Yes, it occurred to me, but Eddy kept telling me that he would see to it that I wasn't harmed."

"You believed him?"

"Yes . . . no. I don't know. I was determined to get away from them as soon as I could. When we arrived at the cabin, I tried to run, but they caught me and Hayden threatened me with his knife. I don't know where I would have gone even if I had escaped. That cabin was in the middle of nowhere. Speaking of which, how did you find me?"

"With your father's help. He contacted a friend of mine in Waco. A Texas Ranger. Lyle came to me and asked if I would help find you. I know these parts pretty well, so he figured I'd have a better chance than most. He already knew that you had left the train after Simon. I started at the water tower. It wasn't too hard to follow your tracks. There were only a few places where they could hide you. I nosed around a little, and when I saw the car leave with Hayden and the other man in it, I decided to take a chance to see if you were in the cabin."

"Lucky for me you did. I was terribly afraid of Squirrelly. Eddy kept telling me that he wouldn't bother me . . ." Kate's words trailed off as she thought back on the attack in the cabin. She was truly lucky to be alive.

"Eddy was wrong, wasn't he?"

"I haven't thanked you for getting me out of there. I want to do that now. I don't know how much longer they would have left me alone." Kate placed her hand on his arm and glanced at his profile. "Thank you, Mr. Castle."

"Mr. Castle was my father's name. Don't you think you can call me 'Tate'?"

"Only if you'll call me 'Kate.' So far you haven't called me anything."

A smile crinkled the corners of his eyes. "I called you

plenty of things after your bag fell down and cream spilled on my boot. Even my daughter said I smelled like flowers."

"Your daughter? How old is she? What's her name?"

"She's six years old, and her name is Emily."

"Who stays with her and your wife while you're away?" Kate asked, thankful that he'd begun talking about his life.

"I have a couple who has been with me for many years. Yelena and Jorge are my family now."

It occurred to Kate that she was completely relaxed and comfortable sitting in this dim cave alone with this man, although she wished he would talk about himself without her having to ask questions. She had known almost from the first that he was not a talker and asking seemed the only way to get to know him.

"Have you lived here long?"

"All my life. I was born on the ranch where I live. My father brought my mother there after they were married. He raised horses. Now I do."

"Your parents are not living?"

"No, they are both gone."

"I guess you think I'm asking a lot of questions?"

"Yeah, I guess I do, but I was getting ready to ask a few myself. What was a girl like you doing traveling across the country alone?"

"I was on my way to California to join my uncle. I thought I would be perfectly safe on the train. So did my father. It never entered my mind that I would be kidnapped."

"How did they get you off the train?"

"I got off at the water tower to get a breath of fresh air. Squirrelly got off too and put a gun in my back. He tried to force me to go into the woods, and when I refused, he hit me. Later we were joined by Hayden and Eddy."

"Your luggage is probably still on its way to California."

Kate looked up at him and smiled. "You didn't get all the things that spilled out of my valise. I picked up one thing and put it in my pocket. Later Squirrelly grabbed it. Eddy made him give it back to me."

"That was not my finest moment."

"I'm sorry you were embarrassed. I have a lot to apologize for as far as you are concerned." She removed her hand from his arm.

"Shall we call it square?" he asked.

"Square," she answered as they shook on it.

Chapter 12

KATE WOKE FROM A SOUND SLEEP. For the briefest of moments, she was still in her dream, dining with her father at Tony's restaurant. The two of them were happy, eating good food and laughing at one of her father's silly jokes. As reality returned, she peered through the darkness of the cave to the entrance. There she could make out Tate's silhouette. He sat with his back toward her, his wide-brimmed hat still on his head. For a moment, she wondered if he was asleep, but even as the thought crossed her mind, he removed his hat and placed it on the blanket beside him.

Kate hesitated for a moment before she stood up and slowly went toward him. The stone floor of the cave felt cold and rough against her sore, bare feet. Tate's head turned as she approached, but he remained silent.

Kate sat down close behind him on the blanket.

"Did you get any sleep?" he whispered.

"A little," she said, imitating his quiet voice. "I dreamed I was with my father."

"A bad dream?"

"No. It was a nice one. We were dining in his favorite restaurant."

"Are you hungry? There's one biscuit left."

"Thanks, but I don't think I could eat another biscuit."

"Especially one that's been in a saddlebag for three days?"

"I'm sure they were good when you put them in there, but I think I'll pass."

"My daughter, Emily, likes them right out of the oven, with plenty of butter and jam."

Kate was pleased that he now spoke so openly about his personal life. *But what about his wife?* She wanted to ask but was afraid that he would clam up and stop talking.

"How about you? Do you have children?"

"No. I'm not married." In the silent seconds that followed her answer, Kate decided to ask the question that had floated in and about her mind since they escaped the cabin. "What about your wife? Won't she be worried about you?"

"I don't have a wife."

"Did she die?"

"She up and left. She's dead to me," Tate said coldly.

"She left her little girl?"

"Emily hasn't suffered because of her leaving."

Kate looked out into the dark night and wondered about the strange conversation that she was having with this man whom she had known for such a short time. *What kind of woman would leave her daughter? What had happened between Tate and his wife?*

"Tell me about you," Tate said, obviously wanting to change the subject.

"What do you want to know?"

"Anything you want to tell me."

"Well . . . I've lived in New York all my life. My father and mother came to New York from Pittsburgh, where my father worked in the steel mills. My mother died when I was little, and my father threw himself into his work. Now he owns a steel mill, but I don't think that he's entirely happy with his life in New York. Oh, I also have a half-sister. Her name is Susan."

"So your father remarried, then?"

"Yes, when I was quite young. I think that he was lonely, and he thought I needed a mother. My stepmother is a society woman. Sometimes I think that neither I nor my father quite come up to her expectations."

"How about your sister?"

"She's more like her mother. She likes the society life too. Her days are filled with shopping, her nights with dancing."

"And you? What was your life filled with?" A pause. "A man?"

"No, I went to nursing school, and for the last couple of years, I've worked in a clinic in the city. I loved every minute of it! It was very satisfying because most of the people we helped were poor. When my uncle in San Francisco offered me a job in his hospital, I decided to accept it. I wanted to travel, to see the country and help people who need help."

"What did your father think about that?"

"He has always encouraged me to make my own decisions, and he made it clear that he would stand by me in whatever I decided to do. My stepmother, on the other hand, was against the idea. Being a nurse isn't society enough for her. She is sure that I'll be back home in a few months."

Somewhere off in the distance, a coyote howled. Kate's fear of the unknown was replaced by her desire to talk with this man.

"Didn't you like the life of a pampered rich girl?" Tate asked.

"I never thought of myself as being pampered, but I guess I was. I didn't want the life that my stepmother wished for me."

"What was that?"

"She wanted me to find a husband, preferably a rich one, with a family background that would help her socially." Kate made a small chuckling sound. "She was terribly disappointed in me, but she has Susan, who loves society as much as she does."

Kate leaned a little bit closer to Tate's broad back and, just for an instant, thought about resting her head against him. It would be comforting to touch him while they talked, but she didn't dare. Instead, she leaned toward the cave entrance and gazed at the sea of stars in the sky.

"I didn't know stars could be so bright," Kate said. "In New York City, there are so many lights that you scarcely notice them."

Tate snorted. "I know. I've been there."

"You have?"

"When I was younger, I left the ranch for a bit and spent a couple years roaming around the country. City life didn't impress me too much. After a while, I decided home wasn't such a bad place after all."

"At least you got to see some of the world." Then, pointing at the sky, she added, "And you have all these stars every night."

"My father used to tell me stories about sailors who sailed the ocean guided by the stars," Tate said, "and about the pioneers who got their bearings by reading the stars in the sky. At night, they would place their wagon tongues in the direction they wanted to travel the next day. I guess my wagon tongue was always pointed here."

"Wasn't there a trail to follow?"

"The first to go West didn't have a trail. They had to find their own way."

"I've always heard that a lot of the people who came West were massacred by the Indians. Is that true?" She wanted to keep him talking.

"Don't believe what you see in the movies or read in Wild West magazines. More people died from drowning as they crossed the rivers than were killed by the Indians. At first, the Indians were very helpful to the pioneers. Gave them food and shelter, helped them to live off the land. But then, as more and more people came, they began to feel they were losing their land, and they did lose most of it. That's what happened to Luke's people. They are an offshoot of the Chiricahua Apaches. They left the reservation and settled in these hills. I'm not sure how long they will be able to stay here. It's almost hunted out, and they have no way to make a living."

"Why did they leave the reservation?"

"Luke's father told me that there were too many rules and regulations. Different from the life that they had been living for hundreds of years. They probably felt a lot like I did in the city—out of place. They wanted to be free."

Kate realized that life for the Indians was complicated. What she had seen in magazines or heard on the radio was a far cry from the reality. "Does the government help them?"

"Not if they aren't on the reservation."

"But what about the children? Luke mentioned something about a mission school. Who pays for that?"

"Well . . . we did manage to get the government to send a teacher after we built the schoolhouse."

"Did you have something to do with that?" She heard the pride in his voice when he mentioned the schoolhouse. There was far more to Tate than she would ever have thought that night on the train platform.

He grinned. "A little, maybe."

"I'd like to visit a real Indian village sometime. I'm sure that it's different from what I imagine it to be. People back East think Indians are still savages. There isn't anything savage about Luke."

"Except his sense of humor. Maybe you can come back sometime and visit. But first we've got to get out of here and get you back to your father."

In the midst of their easy conversation, Kate felt a

shiver, remembering that they were being hunted by a man who might kill them if he caught them.

"It all seems like a bad dream. I just want to wake up and have it be over." Kate paused, then added, "My father will want to meet you and thank you for helping me."

"I have to admit, when Lyle first asked me to look for the woman who disappeared, I didn't want to come," Tate said, breathing deeply. "But knowing that Hayden could be involved, and Lyle seemed to think that he was, it was a pretty sure thing that the woman would never come back alive, and if she did, she'd be ruined. Knowing all that, I couldn't have stayed home."

"I'm so glad you did come looking for me." For a brief moment, she laid her cheek against his back. "I'll never be able to thank you enough."

Tate felt the warmth of her against his back and was surprised by the strange feeling that swept over him. "Better hold off on those thanks until we get out of here." He stood up, looked down at her, and said gruffly, "You had better get some sleep."

"Will you sleep?" Kate asked, disappointed that their conversation had come to an end.

"I'll doze at the entrance to the cave. You'll be all right."

"I wasn't worried about myself. We've both had a rough day."

"We won't get any rest if we sit here jawing all night." He reached a hand out to her and helped her to her feet. "Can you find your way back to your bedroll?"

"I can find it." Kate placed her hand on his shoulder. "Good night."

Tate watched as she made her way farther into the darkness of the cave and settled herself down onto the bedroll. He sat quietly looking out into the starlit night.

He now had a slightly different opinion of Miss Katherine Tyler. She wasn't the pampered rich girl he had thought she was. She was the victim of a greedy man and his nephew.

The sound of a sniffle reached his ears, and he turned around to look into the darkness. He heard the sound again, realized Miss Tyler was crying, and went back to where she lay on her blanket. He stood silently for a moment, looking down at her. He knelt down beside her and said, "Why are you crying?"

"I'm not crying. I just got choked up for a minute."

"You were crying. What's wrong?"

"I'm sorry. I didn't think you would hear me. I usually don't bawl like a baby," she said, and swallowed a sob.

"You've been through a lot."

"I'm just tired, that's all. I've been telling myself to buck up. Things could be worse. I could be out here by myself, or even worse, still be back in the cabin with Hayden and Squirrelly."

"You don't need to be scared now. We'll be all right here for the night, and in the morning Luke will be back. He will let us know what Hayden is up to."

"There's more than Hayden to be scared of. What about snakes and bats back here? Can I move up closer to you?"

Kate sat up and leaned against him. He put his arm around her.

"You've held up real good."

"For a city woman?"

"That's what Luke calls you. I've never called you that. Well"—he chuckled—"at least not out loud."

Kate didn't seem to catch his attempt at humor. Wiping the end of her nose, she said, "I don't think Luke likes me much. He's always expecting me to do something stupid."

"Luke's had a couple of bad experiences with women from the city."

"Women? He's just a boy."

"I don't mean that kind of experience. I know of one who was especially hateful to him." Tate did not want to tell her it was his ex-wife who had made Luke uncomfortable when he came to their home.

"You'll feel better after you get a good night's sleep." Tate felt the hot tears on her cheek when he placed his face next to hers. He found himself reluctant to move away from her. His heart was doing strange things while he held her.

"We'll get out of here, won't we?" she asked softly.

"I can't promise that, but I can promise that I'll do my level best to get *you* out." His voice came gently to her ears. She leaned her head against his shoulder.

"I know you will."

Shifting his body, he tried to form a more comfortable cradle for her. He raised his head and looked down at her. Her breath was on his mouth. In the dim light, he could see the outline of her face. It was pale and calm.

She lifted her arm and slipped it around his neck,

pulling him to her. He gave a long, shuddering sigh and wrapped her in both of his arms, hugging her close.

"Are you all right now?" he whispered. He didn't want to like this woman. He didn't want to have feelings for her. To him, she wasn't quite real, a fairy or a shadowy woman out of a dream. On the heels of that thought came a contradictory one: This was a real flesh-and-bone woman he was holding in his arms.

Suddenly Tate's arms dropped from around Kate and he stood. He couldn't do this. He couldn't afford to have feelings for her. "Come on. I'll bed you down closer to the entrance."

Kate was reluctant to let go of him. She reached for his hand and held it in hers as he pulled her to her feet. Tate bent down and scooped up her blanket. She followed him through the darkness to the front of the cave, where he laid out the bedding.

"Here you are. I'll be sitting over here where you can see me. You won't be left alone."

"What about you? Are you going to sleep?"

"I'll sleep, but don't worry, I'm a light sleeper." With that, Tate sat down, leaned against the side of the cave entrance, crossed his arms over his chest, and leaned his head back.

Kate felt a fierce wave of longing, a desire that had begun when Tate put his arms around her. Unlike most rich girls, she had no interest in her father's wealth. She dreamed of finding a man who would love her for herself. Instinctively she knew that this man was a man of integrity. He wasn't interested in what lined her father's pockets. As quickly as she thought it, she pulled her thought back. He was just being kind, and she shouldn't make much of the embrace. But, try as she might to make it trivial, it had been comforting to be held in his arms.

How could a woman leave him?

Chapter 13

Eddy sat up on the edge of his bunk. Hayden's bunk was empty. Squirrelly was snoring like a warthog. Eddy rubbed his eyes and wished for a good stiff drink. Things were not going the way he had planned. Damned idiot in the other bunk had upset everything by letting Kate get away. If Hayden killed her, he swore that Squirrelly would meet the same fate, only slowly and more painfully.

If only I knew that she was all right, I'd take off for Mexico right now. But I can't just go off and leave her with these two. I haven't told them yet that John Tyler called in the Texas Rangers. Hayden will be mad as a hornet when he finds out. Squirrelly thinks his daddy can handle most anything, but he'll find out the Texas Rangers are not the kind to be handled by a petty crook from New York.

Squirrelly awakened, stretched, and let wind.

"You crude son of a bitch. Don't you have any decency?"

Squirrelly laughed. "Just because I farted you think I'm not decent. What are you in such a snit for? Mine don't stink."

"You are so crude I wonder how your mother stands you."

Squirrelly let out a whoop of laughter. "Because I am the son of a bitch."

Eddy went to the wash bench, more to get away from the uncouth idiot who was still laughing than to wash.

"That ornery bastard isn't back yet?"

Eddy didn't answer. It was obvious that Hayden wasn't back.

Squirrelly went to the door, threw it open, stood in the doorway, and urinated. "I always wanted to do that," he said with a slack-lipped grin. "I really wanted to do it at home—pee on the sidewalk as people went by."

"What an ambition," Eddy snarled.

"You don't have to be so nasty about it."

"I'm going to town."

"You take the car, and Hayden'll be mad as a pissed-on snake."

Eddy pulled on his pants and sat back down on the bunk to put on his shoes. "I don't give a damn how mad Hayden gets. He's just hired help like you are."

"If you go, I'm going too. I'm not gonna be here when that madman comes back. I hope he finds that little split tail. Before we get rid of her, I'm going to screw her eyeballs out."

"Touch her, and I'll kill you."

"You're always saying that."

Eddy took a clean shirt from his valise, shook the wrinkles out of it, and put it on. Looking into the cracked mirror over the washbasin, he carefully brushed his hair.

"What are you getting all dolled up for? Ain't none of the women I've seen out here so far would know whether your hair was combed or not. I've got to have me one of them before we leave here. It would be something to tell the boys when I get home."

Eddy ignored him. He checked to be sure he had his wallet and anything of value out of his valise before he went out the door and toward the car. Squirrelly followed.

"Okay, hotshot, you've stolen enough cars to know how to hot-wire this one, so get at it."

"What'll you give me?"

"I'll knock your block off and have my uncle report to your father what an asshole you've been."

The threat didn't seem to bother Squirrelly at all, but he opened the door and began to work with the wires under the dash. In a matter of minutes, the car engine was purring and Eddy had to admit that Squirrelly had some value after all.

"Get in," he said, and slid under the wheel. With a backward glance at the cabin, Eddy drove away.

At the train depot in Muddy Creek, Eddy inquired of the agent if a wire had come for R. Edwin. The agent, who looked at Eddy from beneath his visor cap with piercing eyes, made Eddy uncomfortable.

"You fellas gonna be around here long?"

"What's it to ya?" Squirrelly replied, and winced when Eddy dug his elbow into his ribs.

"We'll be here for a few more days. Our company is

looking for land to lease around here," Eddy explained smoothly.

"What for?" the agent asked.

"We plan to run some electric lines," Eddy said. "Now, did you say you had something for me or not? We've got a lot to do."

The agent reached into a tray and placed the telegram on the counter. "Would save money if you fellas would write letters. Of course, it would take four days to get here from New York."

"That isn't the way big companies work." Eddie picked up the message and walked out.

Out on the station platform, Squirrelly said, "That bastard's too nosy."

Eddy dreaded reading the message, but after settling behind the wheel, he unfolded it and read:

THINGS INCOMPLETE ON THIS END. STOP. STICK WITH PLAN. STOP.

"It means he's not got the money yet," Squirrelly said.

"Keep your voice down. Do you want everyone in town to hear you?"

"We ought to get rid of the split tail and head for home. I'm sick of this place. There's nothing here in this town but hayseeds and horse dung."

"I'll take care of Kate."

"You'll kill her?"

"That's not any of your business."

"Maybe Hayden will do the job and save you the trouble."

Eddy felt a shiver of apprehension at the thought of Kate out in the wilderness with that animal of a man. He regretted not shooting both Hayden and Squirrelly in their sleep and taking off for Mexico with Kate. One thing was sure in his mind: He was not going to let them kill her. Squirrelly interrupted his thoughts by saying, "Is there a greasy spoon in this jerkwater town where we can eat? I'm sick of eating beans and squirrels, cats, or whatever kind of animal Hayden cooks."

"Did you know for the last two nights you've been eating polecat?" Eddy enjoyed the look on Squirrelly's face.

"I didn't smell polecat."

"Course, you didn't. He took out the scent bag when he skinned it."

"Ah God, I think I might puke just thinking about it."

Eddy passed his hand over his face to hide his grin. "At the time, you were sure filling your gut and telling Hayden how good it was."

Squirrelly reached under the seat, pulled out a billed cap, and slammed it down on his head. "Let's go to that place down the street that says 'Mustang Eatery.'"

Eddy opened his car door. "Come on, then, but keep your mouth shut."

"I don't have to," Squirrelly said angrily.

"You'd better. We're too near the end of this thing for you to screw up now."

Squirrelly's shorter legs worked to keep up with Eddy's long stride. When Eddy tipped his hat at a lady they passed,

Squirrelly tried to imitate it, but his big hat tipped to the back of his head. He swore softly under his breath and made a grab for it. He righted it on his head as Eddy turned into the door of the eatery.

The place was small. There were no booths, but a long counter with stools took up one whole side. You could see through a large opening into the kitchen where a heavyset woman worked at the stove.

"Ah God," Squirrelly said under his breath.

"It's not Lindy's, but it's all that's here." Eddy was enjoying Squirrelly's discomfort. He knew the little weasel liked to eat at Lindy's and brag that the maître d' there knew him.

Eddy removed his hat and hung it on the peg on the wall. He dug his elbow in Squirrelly's ribs. "Hang up your hat."

Eddy then straddled a stool halfway down the counter. Squirrelly climbed up onto one beside him and slapped the counter with the palm of his hand.

"Stop it," Eddy hissed. "We don't want to bring attention to ourselves."

The heavyset woman came from the kitchen. "What'll ya have, gents?"

"Whatta ya got?" Squirrelly asked.

The woman pointed to the chalkboard fastened to the wall behind her.

"It's there. Can't ya read?"

"I can read writin', but not that scribblin'."

"They've got beef stew or hamburgers," Eddy said. Then to the lady he said, "I'd like the beef stew, please."

"It'll take only a minute," she said, and walked away.

"Hey, what about me?" Squirrely called.

"I wasn't sure a high-toned gent like you would want anything."

"I want the same as my friend here, but I'll take a cold bottle of beer to drink while you're gettin' it ready."

The woman reached under the counter and pulled out a bottle of beer and placed it on the counter in front of Squirrely. She slapped a metal opener down beside it and went back to the kitchen.

"She thinks she's something on a stick, don't she?"

"This is her establishment. She can think whatever she wants."

"I'll be glad to see the last of this place. When I get back to New York, I'll never leave it again."

"It's a good thing," Eddy growled. "You'd not last a week in this place. Someone would be putting their foot in your mouth. You don't have your daddy backing you here."

"My daddy'd take over this place within an hour of gettin' here. These yokels wouldn't know what hit 'em."

"I'm not so sure about that. Folks out here have put up with more than what your daddy could dish out and have survived."

The lady returned with the steaming bowl of stew and set it in front of Eddy.

"Thank you, ma'am. It smells delicious."

The woman smiled a toothless grin. "If you want more, just let me know." She went back to the kitchen and returned with a bowl for Squirrely. He grunted but said nothing.

"Are you gents passing through?"

"Passing through to where?"

Eddy ignored Squirrelly and smiled at the woman. "We're doing some work for a company in New York who plans to run electric lines through here."

"Why would they do that when there are already electric lines?"

"Yeah," Squirrelly said, "why would they do that when they already have electric lines?"

Eddy nudged him with his elbow. "My friend here is trying to be funny," he said to the woman.

"We need more electric lines for the folks out on the ranches," she considered. "Will you be here long?"

"We're hoping to be out of here by the end of the day." Squirrelly stopped speaking when Eddy's knee nudged his.

"We're not sure," Eddy explained to the woman. "It could be today, tomorrow, or the next day."

"If you're here on Friday, we have all the catfish you can eat for half a dollar."

"You can get a good steak in New York for forty cents," Squirrelly said sarcastically.

"You can get a steak here for a quarter," the woman said. "We have so much beef here it's a treat to have something else."

"I enjoy a good steak, but I really like catfish. I hope we're still here on Friday." Eddy finished eating, stood, and placed a fifty-cent piece on the counter. "Enough for me and my friend?" he asked.

"Your friend owes me two bits for the beer."

"Two bits," Squirrelly said. "Ain't you a little high?"

"You drank the beer. Give me the two bits, or I'll call the sheriff."

"Pay her," Eddy said, and reached for his hat.

Squirrelly tossed a quarter on the counter.

"Come on," Eddy said, and went to the door. He waited to be sure Squirrelly was following before he went out onto the street. When Squirrelly joined him, he said, "You are the most stupid person I've ever known. I told you we shouldn't draw attention to ourselves. After the way you treated that woman, she's going to remember us even a year from now."

"So what?"

"You just don't get it, do you? John Tyler notified the Texas Rangers. They could be looking for us right now."

"How do you know that?"

"I got a telegram yesterday from my uncle."

"Why in the hell didn't you say so?"

"I didn't tell you because you didn't need to know. Had you been alert like I told you to be, instead of having your mind on what's in your pants, you would have known someone was lurking about. As it is, you let him get in the cabin while you were trying to rape Kate. You'd better hope Hayden catches up with her and brings her back."

"What about the other guy?"

"Hayden will take care of him."

"I'm going back to the train station and find out when the train leaves here tomorrow," Squirrelly said.

"We're not leaving from here on the train. We're going in this car. We'll drive to Alpine or somewhere else and take the train from there."

"Hayden won't let you take this car."

"It isn't his. My uncle paid for it."

"I don't think that'll cut any ice with him. I think he's half crazy anyway."

"I hate to say it, but I agree with you on that."

After Squirrelly hot-wired the car again, Eddy drove slowly down the street, being careful not to stir up a dust cloud in his wake. On the edge of town, he turned right instead of left, the way back to the cabin.

"Where you goin'?" Squirrelly asked.

"You think I want someone in town to follow us back to the cabin? I'm going to try to find a roundabout way to get there."

Eddy was quiet all the way back. He dreaded what he would find when he got there. Had Hayden returned with Kate? Had he killed her? What about that Castle fella he talked about? Was he a match for Hayden, or had Hayden killed him?

If only he knew Kate was all right, he could dump Squirrelly and head for Mexico. It couldn't be more than thirty or forty miles to the border. He had planned for so long, stashed his money in a bank in Mexico City, and now the only thing standing in his way was making sure that Kate was all right. He never expected to get any of the ransom money. His uncle could have his share. Old William would need it to pay for his legal expenses after Kate exposed him as being part of the kidnapping plot.

As they approached the cabin, Eddy's eyes searched for a sign of Hayden, but there was none.

Squirrelly was out of the car as soon as it stopped. He

stood in the doorway of the cabin and looked back at Eddy.
"He ain't back yet."

Eddy's eyes searched for a sign

"Maybe he's found the split tail and is holed up with her
somewhere. It's what I'd do."

Eddy gritted his teeth and wondered how much longer
he was going to be able to stand the idiot.

Chapter 14

JOHN TYLER SAT AT HIS DESK, running his forked fingers through his hair. On the desk was the note he had been expecting. It told him to place the money in a paper bag and go to the corner of Tenth and Broadway at ten o'clock that evening. A man would approach him and say the word "Katherine." He was to give the man the sack, turn his back, and leave quickly. Later he would receive a telephone call at home telling him where to find Kate. If there was any sign of the police at the pickup spot, he could forget about ever seeing his daughter again, alive or dead.

John was worried. What assurance did he have that Kate would be returned after he had paid the money? None, really, but it was a chance he had to take. He got to his feet and walked quickly down the hall to William's office. After a gentle knock, he opened the door and went in.

William was at his desk. At the sight of his partner, he folded the newspaper he was reading and said, "Come in, John."

"I received another letter this morning telling me where

to take the ransom money." He laid the letter on William's desk.

After reading it, William said, "You're not planning on taking the money yourself, are you?"

"Of course."

"I don't think that's a good idea," William said thoughtfully, a crease of worry spreading across his forehead. "You should be home where you can take the phone call when it comes. Someone else could deliver the money."

"Whom do you have in mind?"

"Me," William said confidently. "I'll deliver it."

John felt a flutter of affection. The caring and giving way in which William had reacted to Kate's misfortune continued to surprise him. How did he deserve such a fine friend? Shaking his head, he said, "I couldn't ask you to do that. It could be dangerous."

"I don't care. Considering how I feel about Kate, it's the least I can do."

"It would be a double tragedy if something happened to you."

"Better me than you. I have no family except for Edwin. But you . . . you have those two precious girls who need their father. I'll take the ransom."

"There's one catch, William. They will expect me to deliver the money. If it isn't me, they might panic and leave."

"I'll wear your coat and hat and carry the paper sack under my arm. They'll be looking for a man with a sack."

"Are you sure you want to do this?"

"I insist. What about your man with the Texas Rangers? Is he still poking around down there?"

"He hasn't had any luck with his search, although he has a good man working on it. I've spoken with him and told him I was paying the money."

William frowned. "I'd call them off if I were you. We don't want anything to go wrong at this late date."

"I suppose you're right."

William rubbed his hands together nervously. "Have you taken the money from the bank?"

"It's in the office safe," John said wearily. "One hundred thousand dollars. I've done what they've asked me to do. Oh Lord, I hope they keep their end of the bargain and Kate comes home soon."

"Everything will work out. I'll come back tonight about nine-thirty and pick up the money. That will give me thirty minutes to get to Tenth and Broadway. Then the bastards can take their blood money and we'll get Kate back." William gave John a confident smile.

"I'll never be able to thank you enough."

"Don't mention it. You would do the same for me."

"I've never had a better friend."

William rose from his desk, extended his hand. The two men shook hands heartily.

"I'd better get on home," John said. "Lila has been worried sick about Kate. Not eating or sleeping well. She will be glad when this is over."

"What did she think about you paying the money?"

"She insisted on it."

"She's certainly a wonderful woman. You're a lucky man, John."

"I know that." John sighed and turned back to face his partner. "Sometimes I think I'm a disappointment to her."

"What on earth would make you say that?"

"She likes the society life, and I don't."

"If it makes you feel any better, I agree with you, but you should try harder to like her friends. You might enjoy them."

It was daylight when Kate awoke. The early morning sun filtered into the cave, throwing enough light for her to see the dark rock above. She blinked rapidly for a moment before she remembered where she was. She looked around for Tate. He was where she had last seen him, lying on a blanket between her and the entrance to the cave. Her sleep-addled mind remembered how he had held her when she cried. She felt ashamed for having shown such weakness and didn't want him to think she was going to cry every time she turned around.

Kate didn't know what got into her, but everything now piled on her at once, making her realize the gravity of her situation. She was here in the wilds with a man she completely trusted even though she had known him for only a few days. And to top that, a thoroughly disreputable creature was trying to kill them. She had known immediately that Hayden was coldhearted and persistent as a wild animal when he chased her up the hill with his knife in his hand. What would she do if he killed Tate? This man had become very important to her, not only because he was her rescuer but because he had touched something in her heart that had never been touched before.

Tate suddenly rose up off the blanket and got to his feet. Kate saw him glance at her quickly, then move out of the cave. He stood next to the large boulder at the entrance and, shading his eyes against the rising sun, peered down the slope. He gripped his rifle tightly and pulled it up toward his shoulder. Kate threw back the blanket and stood. As quiet as she had been, Tate glanced over his shoulder at her and put his finger to his lips in a motion for her to be silent. She nodded in understanding and moved as quietly as she could down the side of the cave until she was standing behind him. She placed her hand on his shoulder to let him know she was there. Tate never turned his eyes from the slope, but nodded his head to acknowledge her presence.

Kate put her lips near his ear and whispered, "Is someone coming?"

"Someone's out there. It might be Luke, but I don't know yet. I only saw the bushes move. Stay inside until I know for sure."

For a few tense minutes, Kate stood stone-still behind Tate, her mind a tornado of thoughts. *What if it's Hayden? Will Tate be able to stop him, or will Hayden kill us both?* Fear gnawed at her stomach. Her eyes stayed locked on Tate, alert for any sign that trouble was coming.

Finally he lowered the rifle. "It's Luke. He'll be here in a minute, but keep quiet. Hayden may be following him."

Another minute passed, then suddenly Luke appeared at the entrance of the cave. "I come back."

"I never doubted it for a minute," Tate said.

"Your woman did."

Kate's mouth opened to voice her denial, but a realization entered her mind before she could speak: Tate hadn't bothered to deny that she was his woman.

"Did you see Hayden?"

"I see him. He back up draw but headed this way. He lost tracks but find again. Get your woman. We go." Reaching into a bag that hung from his shoulder, he pulled out a pair of moccasins and handed them to Tate.

"For me?" she said to Luke.

"No. I bring moccasins for Tate."

Tate motioned for Kate to sit down. He knelt in front of her and raised one of her bare feet. Her feet didn't hurt as much as they had the night before, but they were still sore. Tate slipped her foot into the moccasin. The sole was cushioned with fur.

"They feel wonderful," she exclaimed. "Thank you, Luke."

"I get for Tate. Thank him."

"Well, then, thank you, Tate."

The cowboy's eyes twinkled, and he smiled one of his rare smiles. "You're very welcome." Just as easily, the smile disappeared, and he was all business as he turned to Luke and asked, "How far back is Hayden? Will he see us when we leave?"

"Not if we go now." Luke started off toward a dense grove of scrub oak.

Tate tucked his bedroll under his arm. With his hand on Kate's back, he urged her along. The warm Texas sun felt good on her skin after the cool air inside the cave. The men moved swiftly, but Kate had no trouble keeping up.

"Won't he find my shoes in the cave?" Kate said softly.

"It doesn't matter if he finds them. He'll know we were there anyway. Now we need to find a place where we can defend ourselves if necessary."

"Where are we going?"

"Luke knows. He's spent his whole life in these hills. He knows them better than any man."

They moved on for hours, the sun rising higher and bearing down with ever more intense heat. The landscape blurred; every rock, tree, or flower looked like the last. Kate was desperate for a drink of water but didn't want to ask them to stop. She set her mind on keeping up with Tate, staying no more than two steps behind him. An hour later Luke finally brought them to a stop. Tate moved up beside him.

"Your woman need water," Luke said, nodding to Kate as she wiped the sweat from her brow.

"We'll rest here for a minute," Tate said.

Luke took a water bag that hung from his belt and handed it to Tate, who put his hand on Kate's shoulder and said, "Open your mouth." When she did, he filled it with water from the bag. "We have to be sparing with the water. You can have more later."

As the liquid filled her mouth, Kate couldn't remember having ever tasted anything so delicious. She wiped her mouth with the back of her hand. Tate gave the bag back to Luke. "Aren't you going to have some?" Kate asked.

"Later. We need to move on."

Tate pointed to a ridge ahead of them. "We're going up there. I'll be able to see in three directions and get a good look at what's below. We'll also be in the shade and not easy to spot."

"You think you'll see Hayden?"

"Not likely. He's too good a tracker to expose himself."

By the time they reached the top of the ridge, Kate's legs were weak and trembling. It hadn't looked so steep when they started up. Tate handed her the canteen. "That was a hard walk. Take a good long drink. There's a place not far from here where I can fill it. We'll spend the day here, and tonight, if the moon is out, we'll head south along the creek. Hole up again tomorrow and maybe make it to Muddy Creek by tomorrow night. I figure it's a good ten miles. Does that scare you?"

"It scares the heck out of my feet."

"Then let's give them a rest," Tate said. He picked up a stick, walked into the brush, and moved the stick over the ground. "All clear. Not a snake in sight. You can have some privacy here."

While Tate and Luke surveyed their back trail, Kate sat down on the ground, took off her moccasins, and rested her head on her knees. It was quiet and peaceful.

She raised her eyes to see Tate rushing toward her. Her pulse quickened. With his hands, he was motioning for her to move farther back from the ridge. She grabbed her handbag and her moccasins, got swiftly to her feet, and stumbled back into the shadows. The stones hurt her feet, but she scarcely noticed.

"Hurry! A rider is coming this way." Tate grabbed the knapsack and went to the far side of the ridge and started climbing behind it. Kate followed and was only halfway up when he threw down the knapsack, came back to take her hand, and hauled her up behind a huge boulder. Pressing her down, he knelt beside her and whispered, "A Mexican is coming out of the dry creek bed on horseback. He's looking for something."

The sound of a horse's hooves striking stones that lined the creek bed and the squeaking of saddle leather were all that Kate heard. Her heart hammered and her brain hummed. She clung to Tate's arm and he squeezed her hand. *Dear God, don't let them hurt Tate or Luke!*

"Where is Luke?" she whispered.

Tate moved away from her and peered over the rim of the boulder. "He isn't far away. He knows where we are."

Then, through the utter terror that possessed her, a thought came to her. She was so panicked it felt as if a tight hand was squeezing the breath out of her body. She had taken a handkerchief and small hairbrush from her handbag back where she had been sitting and left them there. How stupid! She clutched Tate and put her lips to his ear.

"I left my handkerchief and brush back there. He will be sure to see them."

He shot an inquiring look at her, and she felt even more panic. Her skin prickled, and her breath seemed stuck in her throat.

Leaving her side, Tate searched through the loose rocks that lay on the ground around them until he found one the size of his fist. Gripping it in his hand, he looked over the edge of the boulder. He stepped back and, with all his strength, threw the rock in the direction of the creek bed. She heard the sound of the rock as it struck hard against the boulder above the bed. This sound was followed by a rush of loose rock down the side of the hill. The Mexican heard it too and kicked his mount into a run. His cursing in Spanish reached her ears as he rode past.

Tate scrambled out from behind the boulder, dashed across the open, and was back seconds later holding her handkerchief and brush. He sank down beside Kate.

"I'm sorry!" she whispered as she grabbed his arm.

"Shhhhh . . . it's okay. All we needed was a little diversion. Now I've got to make sure he goes on up the stream."

Reacting to his words, she tightened her hand on his arm. The thought of being left alone on the ridge filled her with terror. Then, reaching into the depths of her reserve courage, she loosened her hand on his arm and leaned away from him. She closed her eyes. It seemed to require all her strength to keep from bursting into tears.

When his arm drew her close, she offered no resistance, instead wrapping her arm around his lean body. All thought left her, and she gave herself up to the joy of being held by him. Her cheek was pressed to his shoulder, and she could feel the scrape of whiskers when he laid his cheek against her forehead. Then, as quickly as their embrace had begun, he gently pushed her away from him. His eyes glinted devilishly as they watched her face.

"As pleasant as this is, I need to go see what that fellow is up to. You'll be safe here. Just remember, should we get separated, go along the creek bed until you reach the river. Then head west until you reach Muddy Creek."

"Why are you telling me this?" She took a deep breath, trying to steady her nerves.

"Because I want you to know what to do in case I don't come back right away." He pulled away from her, picked up his hat, and slammed it down on her head. "I don't want you getting sunstroke either."

"What about you?"

"I'm used to this heat and you're not. I'll go upstream and find a tree to climb. I don't think he'll backtrack, but I need to be sure. Don't worry," he said when he saw the concern on her face. "When I get back, Luke should be here and we'll have some food." Without another word, Tate moved away from the boulder and was gone.

Alone, Kate huddled against the stone as the merciless sun stood guard above her. She clutched Tate's hat, her only shade, and watched the hot breeze stir the dry leaves. Each minute Tate was away seemed like an hour. She longed for the watch she had dropped during her struggle with Squirrelly. She had no idea how long Tate had actually been gone, but it seemed as if it had been two hours or more. Kate was beginning to be sick with apprehension.

The sun had moved directly above her. The heat was stifling. She took off the hat and fanned her face, trying to keep her thoughts away from the possibility that something had happened to Tate. Finally she decided that she just wouldn't think about it. She would think about something else. But, try as she might, she couldn't stop herself and stared in the direction he had gone until her eyes watered from the sun's glare.

An eagle spiraled in the sky above her, climbing higher toward the sun until it was only a speck in the vast emptiness. *Oh, to be able to soar high above this parched land like an eagle!*

Kate sat and waited, hardly conscious of the fact that the back of her shirt was soaked with sweat and the rivulets ran between her breasts.

It took several seconds for the sound to break through to her. She took off the hat and turned her ear to the north. The sound that finally reached her was horse's hooves striking stones. *Has the Mexican returned?* She pulled herself to her feet ready to flee should the need arise. A sense of foreboding filled her and would not be willed away. Suddenly the thought came to her that, once again, she might be about to be killed.

Had he already hurt Tate? She wouldn't allow herself to think of the possibility that Tate had been killed!

She thought about running, but even in her near panic, she realized there was nowhere to go. It would be easy for a man on horseback to run her down. As the sounds grew closer, her terror increased. She blinked rapidly, then saw Tate on horseback. He pulled the horse to a stop and dismounted. He came toward her quickly, his long strides covering the distance between them. When he had almost reached her, she launched herself against him, clutched him tightly, and buried her face in his sweat-soaked shirt. His arms pulled her to him.

Kate was soundlessly and helplessly crying.

"Don't cry," he said softly. "Everything's fine. I told you I'd be back."

Kate raised a face wet with tears, her eyes swimming, her lashes spiked with them. "I thought something had happened to you! I thought the Mexican or Hayden had found you!"

"But they didn't." Tate wiped the tears from beneath her eyes with his thumbs.

"But you were gone for so long," Kate said, stifling a sob.

"I know. I had to be sure I wasn't followed."

"Then how did you get the Mexican's horse?"

"Come down by the creek. We'll sit in the shade, and I'll tell you about it while we eat what Luke brought from his village." He looked at her face and grinned. At that, Kate's tears subsided and a smile of her own spread across her wet face. Her heart sang like a bird.

He's back! He's safe!

Chapter 15

HAYDEN WAS ANGRY. He was angry not only at himself but at that damn Indian kid. This wasn't the first time that he'd had to deal with the little son of a bitch. Shortly after he'd had his way with the kid's sister, the boy had come at him with a knife. He should have killed the brat then, but he'd thought that that would be the end of it. He'd thought wrong. How in the hell could he have known that the Indian would team up with Castle?

As he stood in the hot sun, Hayden's anger escalated. He was sure that the Indian boy was the one who had sneaked in and slipped the halter off his horse. It was a favorite Indian trick. Now, with his horse gone, he would be delayed. He might have made a mistake when he let the boy live; but this time, when he got his hands on the little bastard, he'd choke the life out of him.

Hayden continued to stomp around on the rocky ground, cursing the Indian and Castle. He even had a special curse for that damned idiot Squirrelly. If it hadn't been for him trying to rape the girl, she would never have run away from the cabin, and he wouldn't be out in this damned heat!

Shaking his head, Hayden brought his mind back to the matter at hand. There were signs that someone had been in his camp, but they were faint. He followed them past a cluster of small scrub trees and a low rise in the rocky soil. He was standing at the top of the rise, scanning the ground for any trace of the Indian, when, off in the distance, he saw something that grabbed his attention. There, riding directly toward him, was a horseman.

Lowering himself to the ground slowly so as not to attract attention, Hayden fixed his eyes on the rider. The bright sunlight of the early Texas day made it hard to make out any clear details, but Hayden felt certain that from what he'd seen it was a Mexican.

Is he looking for me?

He'd had a couple of dealings with the Mexicans across the border. Most of these dealings had involved stolen goods or whiskey, and he'd always made out pretty well. Lately he'd had an ongoing agreement with a group of *bandoleros* to buy whatever gold Spanish coins they managed to find or, more than likely, steal. In turn, Hayden had his own buyers. It had been a good deal. Maybe, if he was lucky, the rider might have come across signs of the woman and Castle. He had to find out.

He moved down the low hill and toward the rider's path. If he moved quickly, he might be able to intercept the rider and take his horse.

Hayden stood in the thin shadows of a stand of scrub trees and waited. Damn that Indian! He needed a horse. He had never been fond of walking, and besides, with a horse he'd have a much better chance of finding Castle and the girl. The minutes ticked by, and still he waited.

Where was that rider? He should have come by now!

Finally, his patience at an end, Hayden moved away from the stand and picked his way to a higher vantage point. The sun had continued to rise in the cloudless sky, and he could feel the blazing rays beat down on him. Peering out, he saw nothing: no horse, no rider, only heat waves shimmering on the horizon.

Cautiously he worked his way back toward the spot where he had last seen the rider. There was nothing. Moving quickly, he hurried down the creek bed. If he could pick up the rider's trail, he might be able to catch up with him. He needed that horse!

When he reached the Mexican's tracks, he found that the rider had indeed taken a different route. He had turned to the north and moved down into a dry creek bed. The horse's hooves had cracked the dry mud of the bed, making it easy to follow.

It took nearly twenty minutes for Hayden to catch up with the Mexican, and when he did, he was surprised to find him stretched out on the grassy slope, his arms lying limply at his sides. Moving to the man's side, Hayden found that he wasn't dead, just unconscious. This was no accident. Working swiftly, Hayden searched the Mexican's pockets and found nothing worthwhile. If he was bringing coins, whoever waylaid him had taken them. Glancing around, Hayden cursed: The man's horse was nowhere to be seen. Could this be the work of Castle or the Indian? If it had been a robber, the Mexican would be dead. Castle was a weak man who wouldn't kill unless he felt he had to.

Indecision racked Hayden's thoughts. Among his choices was to make his way back to the cabin, get the car, and go to Muddy Creek. If Castle did make it out of here with the woman, the first place he would go was that shitty little town. The problem was that Hayden didn't want to go there. He was too well known in Muddy Creek. But if he could pick up that prissy tenderfoot Jacobs, he could have him look around and find out if Castle had been to the depot to send a wire. On the other hand, if Castle was the one who stole the Mexican's horse, then Castle was nearby.

"Is Luke all right?"

Kate and Tate sat beneath a tree, sharing some of the food that Luke had brought from his village. It wasn't much, but Kate ate ravenously. Tate smiled gently as he answered, "He's fine. Luke's a wily little cuss. He turned Hayden's horse loose. Now Hayden will have to move by foot, and that means we'll have a little breathing space. Especially since we have a horse."

"Where is the Mexican?"

"He's lying back there along the creek bed. Luke knocked him off the horse when I distracted him. When he wakes up, he'll have a hell of a headache."

"So, then, where is Luke?" Kate asked as she took a bite of a biscuit even tougher than the ones that had been in Tate's saddlebag. To her hungry stomach, though, it tasted delicious.

Tate chuckled. "He's around here somewhere. He's keeping an eye on Hayden. We're wondering if the Mexican was looking for Hayden. The Texas Rangers know that Hayden has dealings with an outlaw band across the border. They think it's something to do with gold coins. If they catch him, he'll be put away for a good long time."

"I don't like the idea of Luke keeping an eye on such a dangerous man. He's just a boy. Hayden's mean enough to hurt or kill him if he takes a notion." The image of Hayden pulling out his knife came back to her once more, and she shivered.

"Luke won't let Hayden catch him. He has the advantage of being small and quick. Besides, he's had a lot of practice trailing. He'll stay out of Hayden's way." Tate handed the canteen to Kate. "Have a drink of water."

She took a couple of swallows and held it out for Tate to take.

"You can have more if you want," he told her.

"No. That's enough for now."

As Tate reached to take the canteen, his fingers gently touched Kate's, sending a shiver through her body. She looked away quickly, sure that she was blushing, and hoped that he hadn't noticed.

"We'll wait here for Luke and then go find shelter." Tate looked up at the sky and added, "Dark clouds are rolling in from the southwest. Looks like we might be in for a storm."

Kate ate the rest of her food in silence. With the brief rest and bite to eat, she felt much better. When Luke finally appeared, she said, "Thank you for the food."

"Me and Tate don't need you dead."

"So you'll keep me alive by feeding me, huh?" Kate chuckled. "That's nice to hear."

Luke moved over to where Tate was and sat down on his haunches. He took the water pouch from his belt and took a long swig from it. "Hayden find Mexican. Searched his pockets."

"What then?" Tate asked.

"He move off way he come." Luke hung the pouch back on his belt. "I find tracks of longhorn down the draw."

"There are a dozen or two wild ones in this area. They've been breeding out here for years now. Let's hope we don't run across one of them while we are on foot."

"I climb tree when I see longhorn."

Her curiosity raised, Kate asked, "What are you two talking about? What's a longhorn?" She couldn't imagine anything that would make Luke run and hide.

"A longhorn is a breed of steer with horns a yard wide," Tate said, holding his hands apart to illustrate. "They've got a hump on their backs and long skinny legs. They're fearless. A longhorn will attack a man on foot." Tate looked concerned. "Most of the ranchers around here quit raising them because they're too hard to handle. A bunch of them got loose. Some of them were never rounded up. They're wilder than a scalded cat and twice as mean."

"That's why I run," Luke added.

Tate hung the food bag over the saddle horn and held the stirrup so Kate could mount the horse. "We need to get to shelter before the storm breaks."

"I don't think I can get on the horse in this skirt," Kate said as she tried to throw her leg over the horse.

"I can cut it with my knife. That ought to do it."

"Go ahead," Kate said.

Tate got out his knife and split the front of the skirt up to her knees. He then did the same to the back. "Try that."

Kate put her foot back in the stirrup, and this time easily threw her leg over. Her skirt barely covered her legs, but in the overall scheme of things, it was a minor detail. "This is much better. Thank goodness this isn't a wild mustang."

"The horse is well broken."

Kate didn't tell him that she was an experienced rider and had ridden some spirited horses, for fear that he would think she was bragging. As it turned out, she didn't have to handle the horse. Tate walked ahead holding the reins, and she felt rather useless sitting atop the horse.

The dark, rolling clouds were nearer. The sun drifted in and out of them, and a spirited breeze began to pick up, making the hot summer day much cooler. Luke and Tate kept looking at the sky. She worried they would not find shelter before the storm hit.

"Couldn't we both ride?" she asked Tate. When he didn't answer, she was sorry for even voicing the question. He was walking faster now that they were on fairly level ground.

Kate watched Tate. He was the most confident man she had ever met. There wasn't a man she knew, besides her father, who compared with him. John Tyler was single-minded, fearless, and completely honorable. She was sure that her father would like a man so much like himself.

She was jarred from her thoughts when the horse picked up speed. Tate, leading the horse, was running through a clearing of grassland. She looked beyond him to see Luke

waving. When they reached the boy, he was standing beneath a shallow overhang. Tate stopped the horse, reached
up, and lifted Kate down. Her legs were rubbery, and she
leaned against him.

"This is a good place, Luke," Tate said. "I thought this
was where you were taking us. We can stay dry in here unless the wind changes to the north. Thankfully its coming
from the south now. Even if it swings around to the north-
west, we'll still be able to stay fairly dry. We'll also have a
good view of the surroundings from here."

Luke grinned. "I no dumb Indian."

"Your father taught you well, Little Eagle."

Luke looked pleased and cast a satisfied grin at Kate.
"My father scalped plenty white women."

"Your father never scalped anybody. Stop trying to scare
Kate."

"I scare silly white woman plenty." Luke took the reins
from Tate and led the horse out from under the overhang
and into the dense brush.

"Don't pay him any mind," Tate said as he spread out the
bedroll for Kate to sit on. "He's all talk."

"He doesn't scare me." Kate was surprised at how comfortable she was with the cowboy and the Indian boy. It
seemed as if she had known them forever, and she had complete confidence in them. They had both risked their lives for
her.

Her father would want to do something for them, she
mused silently, but he would have to be careful to avoid
stepping on their pride. It was obvious that they weren't
helping her because they thought they would be paid.

Yeeeow! The primitive cry of a cat came from afar. Kate jerked herself erect and tightly gripped Tate's arm. It felt like time was standing still as she clung to him. The cry came again.

"What . . . what . . . is it?" The silence pressed down on her, and then Tate's voice, low and calm, came close to her ear.

"It's a wildcat." Tate's eyes were searching the rocky ledges. He pulled his rifle free slowly and cocked the trigger. "Don't move. I don't want to shoot it if I don't have to."

Kate was stiff with fear. Apprehension squeezed her lungs until she couldn't breathe. Suddenly she felt Tate's body tense. Looking up at his face, she saw that his eyes had locked onto something, but when she tried to follow his gaze, she saw nothing but bushes and rocks.

"Where is it?" she whispered shakily when she could find the breath.

"To the left and about ten feet up. On that rocky shoulder."

"Where's Luke?"

"He'll have heard the cat and will be looking out for it."

"Oh! I see it." Kate could hardly hold back the low cry when she finally saw the cat facing them. It was larger than she'd thought it would be. She could see its yellow eyes gleaming. Then, with its gaze never leaving them, it let out another piercing scream.

"I've got it in my sights." Tate stepped in front of her, the rifle raised to his shoulder. "He'll either spring when he's directly opposite of us or he'll go on."

The large, slick cat moved with effortless grace along the

rocky ledge, then froze in immobility with its head jutting forward. Its long sweeping tail hung close to its powerful hind quarters. Another piercing howl exploded from his huge mouth the instant before the wildcat's body arched and stretched, its front paws reaching out for another ledge. To Kate, it was like a dream played out in slow motion. The only move she made was to wrap her arm around Tate's waist and cringe against his back. She was only vaguely aware when he turned and put his arms around her. He still held his rifle cocked and ready.

"Oh blessed God." The words came from her stiff, dry throat. "I've never seen anything like that. He was so close."

"He's gone now. I'm glad I didn't have to shoot him." Tate's arms dropped from around her, and he moved to the other end of the overhang.

Kate's limbs returned to life, and she stumbled after him.

He turned as she approached, and she immediately fell into his arms. He could feel her heartbeat as they stared at each other. He held her with his eyes as firmly as he held her with his arms. A blush tinged her cheeks, but her wide blue eyes never wavered.

"I'm sorry," she said miserably, trying to hold the frayed ends of her nerves together so she wouldn't cry. She didn't know what else to say, and for the space of a dozen heartbeats, they regarded each other in utter silence.

"I think we've both learned something the last few days," he said with less than his customary reserve.

Kate dropped her eyes. "I know I have. I've realized that life is fragile and that there aren't many men in the world like you, Tate."

"Why do you say that?" he said.

"Because you don't even know me. I'm not even sure you like me, yet you're risking your life for me. I don't know any other man who would do that." She dropped her eyes to her scratched and bleeding hands.

He reached out and took them in his own, turning her hands palms-up and rubbing his finger over a long, bloody scratch. His hands, used to the rough work on a Texas ranch, felt coarse against her tender skin. "This has been hard on you. I've got a pair of leather gloves in my saddlebag. They'll be too big, but they'll be better than nothing."

"What I need is a bath," she said, watching his finger slide over her palm. Her eyes flew to his, and a surge of hot blood flooded her face.

"That's beyond my power to give you," he said with a laughing glint in his eyes. His smile broadened when a new wave of color tinged her cheeks. "Not that I would look away if I saw you bathing in a stream."

"Tate Castle!" Kate expected to feel mortified but was surprised that she was only mildly embarrassed.

His amusement at her self-consciousness was something that he didn't try to hide. His easy smile disarmed any anger she felt.

"I should be mad at you for saying that!" A faint, tingling thrill passed through her and made a fleeting path across her face. Her laugh was free and warm. "But how can I be, when you've saved my life?"

"In some parts of the world, when you save a life, that person belongs to you, body and soul." The serious words caught her off guard.

"Is that so?" She was almost incapable of coherent speech or thought, conscious only that her hands were still clasped in his and that he was looking down at her with half-closed eyes.

"Do you know what that means?" he asked.

"That you own me?"

"I wouldn't go as far as to say that."

"But you saved my life," she protested huskily.

"Not yet," he said.

She pulled her hands from his and turned away, only to turn back with a glowing smile on her face.

"You did. Twice. Once from Squirrelly and then when you got me out of the cabin and away from Hayden."

His smile answered the radiance on her face. As he feasted his eyes on her, he realized that this was no coy miss who used flirtatious guile on men. She was a woman with all the feminine instincts, but open and natural with her feelings. He had seen many beautiful women, but none who had the inner glow of this one. After his experience with his wife, he didn't want to like this woman from the city, but he did.

"Katherine, Katherine." He laughed. It wasn't a chuckle, but a real laugh. "That suits you much better than 'Kate.'"

She laughed with him, scarcely aware of anything but the tall, slim man smiling down at her. Her eyes slid over his relaxed features, his smiling eyes, and his tall, loose frame. Her heart began to pound with a new rhythm as they hungrily eyed each other.

"A bath is a luxury we can't afford right now." He rubbed his fingers over the stubble on his chin. "I'd like to shave, but that's got to wait too." His slow smile drew little wrinkles at the corners of his eyes. The look on her face altered, leaving it creased with a worried frown.

"Oh, Tate! I don't want you or Luke to be hurt because of me."

His eyes searched her distressed face. She was full of pain. A sense of helplessness threatened to destroy his determination to keep a distance between them. He stared gravely at her for a long moment and let his hard-held breath out like a sigh. He looked beyond her and said, "Here's the kid."

Luke carried the food sack and the water bag. "We eat. Rain is near." Even as he spoke, huge drops of rain began pelting down. Tate nudged Kate farther back under the overhang where he had laid out the bedroll. He motioned for her to sit down on it and then went to the front of the overhang to look at the pouring rain.

"Hayden will be holed up somewhere," he said to Luke. "I don't think we need to worry about him for a while."

Kate watched Tate bend and listen attentively to what Luke was saying, then glance over his shoulder to where she was sitting. Never in a million years would she have believed that she could be attracted to a cowboy. Tate Castle was a most unusual man and one who was beginning to have a firm grip on her heart.

Chapter 16

THE STORM GREW IN ITS INTENSITY; the rain fell in sheets, lightning flashed down from dark clouds, and thunder rolled. At one loud thunderclap followed by forked lightning, Kate jumped to her feet. Tate stepped back to shield her from the splatters of raindrops. Kate had never seen such a display. It was both thrilling and scary. Without being aware of it, she clutched Tate's arm.

"Don't be scared. This is a pretty ordinary storm for this part of the country."

Another dazzling bolt of lightning flared, followed by a clap of thunder that sounded as if the very sky above was being ripped from end to end. The air was filled with a sulfurous stench. Their horse whinnied. Tate and Luke moved as far back as they could go under the overhang and sank down onto the ground, their backs to the storm. Tate pulled Kate down between his outstretched legs and then pulled a blanket up and around them, until only their heads could be seen. Luke produced a blanket of his own and rolled up in it. A flash of lightning revealed low, massive thunderheads above the mesa's black rim.

"Are you afraid, Katherine?" Tate's lips were close to her ear.

A quiver of pure pleasure went through her as he spoke her name. She had never felt so wildly happy in her life. It wasn't for fear of the storm that she trembled.

"No. I'm not afraid." She turned her head and whispered against his cheek. "Tate?" She could feel his breath on her face and smelled the faint scent of tobacco. "Would you think I was crazy if I said I think the storm is exciting?"

"Is that why you're trembling?" His voice was a soft purr in her ear, and she felt the vibrations when he chuckled. Being so close to him set her heart thundering, and little shivers ran down her back.

"You know it isn't." She laughed softly and brought her hand out from under the blanket to push the hair back from her eyes.

The arm around her tightened, and she snuggled contentedly against him.

"Then what is it?" The voice in her ear was lazily teasing, but beneath it was a hint of gentle possessiveness. She couldn't stop the happy laughter that brimmed up in her throat. It was all so new, this wonderful intimacy: being free to tease him and touch him. She caught his hands with hers and held them. She was alive, soaring, her entire existence focused on him and exulting at being held close in his arms. She filled her lungs with the scent of him.

Oh blessed storm! Please go on forever!

Wrapped in her own special enchantment, Kate was scarcely aware of anything except the man who turned his back to the storm and put his arms around her, sheltering her. Rain was sliding off the overhang in a solid sheet. She reached around Tate to make sure his back was covered.

"Are you getting wet?"

"Not much." Tate was silent after the whispered words. He wanted to tell her that she was nothing like he first thought she was. It was hard for him to believe that he was here with her like this and that she was worried that his back was wet. This woman was certainly not like his ex-wife. She did not belong here in his arms, pressed closely to his chest. She should be living the life that she had been pursuing up until the time she'd gotten on the train from Marietta. This realization brought a sudden feeling of discontent to his heart.

"Are you cold?" he asked.

Kate shook her head. She wasn't conscious of the cold or the hard ground or her cramped position. She was aware only of the man with the quiet face, seeking eyes, and tight arms. She didn't feel the cool of the rain, but instead the pull of his whiskers on her hair and his breath on her face. Was that his heart or hers thumping so determinedly between them? She closed her eyes, suffused with joy and wonderment, experiencing a strange peace. He held her gently but securely, holding the storm at bay with his wiry body. She wanted to record, in her memory, this wonderful feeling so she could bring it out and relive it again and again during the bleak days ahead without him. She thought longingly of spending every day of her life with him, making a home for him, having him with her during the long, lonely nighttime hours.

Kate was jarred from her trance when she felt Tate's hand slide down her arm, his fingers tightening around her hand. He held it gently but firmly, and his rough fingers began to move up and down her arm, in a light caress. Kate thought her heart would stop beating. A lump rose in her throat, too large for her to swallow. She turned her face to his shoulder.

"Shhh . . ." She hardly heard the sound that was murmured in her ear, but she definitely felt the lips that lingered there. It was a moment she would remember forever.

Almost as suddenly as it had come, the rain ceased. The dark clouds rolled on as if chased by their enemy, the sun. It was as though nature was showing off for the group beneath the overhang. Even as they stood and stretched, blue sky appeared, and then a rainbow, vivid and magnificent, arched the sky.

Kate stood on weakened legs, keeping her eyes averted from Tate, but knowing that now there was something between them that hadn't been there before. She felt almost giddy with happiness. He had touched her, held her, but then, she cautioned herself, he was only protecting her from the storm. A little of the joy left her when she remembered that he was doing his duty and keeping his promise to his friend to get her back safely.

"Nice, soft woman. Too bad storm has passed." Luke was grinning as he folded his blanket.

"Why do you say that?" Tate asked, and wished that he had not voiced the question because Luke would not let an opening like that pass.

"Why I say that? You a man, she a woman."

Kate looked from one to the other, her cheeks red with

embarrassment. Wasn't there anything this boy didn't talk about openly?

Tate stepped outside the overhang to look around. He wasn't absolutely sure that the storm was over. He studied the terrain on either side of them for as far as he could see. There was a chance that Hayden might be down the trail, waiting for them. But there was an even greater chance that he would soon trap them if they stayed under the overhang. The very silence worried him; there wasn't even a birdsong to be heard. All of which meant to Tate that something or someone was near.

"Get the horse, Luke. Be careful. It's too quiet."

Kate took hold of Tate's arm and looked inquiringly into his face.

"As soon as a storm is over, the birds come out. I don't hear them. Stay here while I look around."

Without argument, Kate stepped as far back under the overhang as she could go, leaned against the wall, and watched Tate move into the surrounding brush. Soon Luke returned, leading the horse. He brought him in under the overhang and wiped him off with a blanket. Then he put the Mexican's saddle back on him. Luke looked at Kate slyly. She wondered if there was something else that he wanted to say to her, but she was reluctant to question him. Finally, after finishing his work with the horse, he came to stand a few feet from her.

"Tate been long without a woman."

"Why are you telling me this?" He had surprised her with his bluntness.

"He need Indian girl to help him. He not need another useless woman."

"Does he have an Indian girl?"

"My sister would marry him. Even be second wife."

"Second wife?"

"Tate man enough for two wives."

"Is it customary out here for a man to have two wives?"

"If first wife can't skin rabbit."

"But it's against the law," Kate protested.

"What law?"

"God's law."

"God have no law here. He up there." Luke jerked his thumb toward the sky. Kate failed to see the sly grin on his face.

"What're you up to, Luke?" Tate's voice came from behind her.

"Silly woman think you no need two wives."

"I don't need one wife"—Tate frowned—"much less two."

Kate kept her face carefully composed. She didn't look at Tate but tilted her chin and spoke slowly. "He's the one that said you needed two wives. I hadn't given it a thought."

"He's good at arranging people's lives. I suppose he told you that he wants his sister to be my second wife? Did he mention that he has another sister that he wants to be my first wife?" As he looked at her, his left eyelid drooped in a wink and his lips lifted slightly at the corners.

"No, he didn't mention that. He didn't have time. Besides, I didn't want to hear it anyway. I'm not interested in how many wives you have or want." Kate lifted her shoulders indifferently and looked away, pretending to be interested in the saddle on the horse.

Tate spoke rapidly to Luke in his native language. From the tone of his voice, he was scolding him. Luke didn't seem to mind. He held up his hand, palm out. To Kate, it looked like a gesture of surrender. Without comment, Luke continued to gather up his belongings. He hung his food and water bag over the saddle horn.

"I can walk for a while," Kate said.

"You ride," Luke said, and picked up the horse's reins while Tate held the stirrup for her to mount. As she settled into the saddle, she was conscious that her skirt barely covered the upper part of her thighs.

With Luke leading the way, Tate, with the reins looped over his hand, followed. He looked over his shoulder at Kate and said softly, "Be quiet."

Not another word passed between the three of them until the shadows had lengthened and the sun had begun to disappear behind the hills. Kate was so tired that she clung to the saddle horn. *How can they walk so far?* But Luke gave no sign of letting up, and Tate stayed behind him. Finally, after what seemed to Kate to be hours, they stopped, and Luke came back to speak to Tate in low tones. Then Luke took off in a trot back in the direction that they had come.

"What's he going back for?" Kate dared to ask.

Tate stepped back and stood beside her. He pointed to a rock formation off to the right. "He wants to climb those rocks and see if he can catch sight of Hayden." Just the mention of Hayden's name made Kate's skin crawl.

"Do you think he's still following?"

"I have no doubt of it."

"Will he catch up?"

"He will. But we've got to choose the spot where it happens. By now, he knows we're headed for Muddy Creek. He'll make his move soon. He won't attempt anything in the dark. He knows Luke's with us and that he can see in the dark like an owl. It's a myth that Indians don't fight at night. Hayden may think that some of Luke's people have joined us."

"Couldn't we try to get behind him?"

"With all this rain, we'll be leaving tracks like a mule walking down a muddy road. Anyone could follow them. As soon as Luke gets back, we'll go on. I know of one place where he won't be able to slip up on us, and, just maybe, we'll be lucky enough to see him before he sees us."

"What'll you do?"

"It depends on what he does." Tate took his hat off and wiped his brow. It had become hot and sultry after the rain. "I'd like him to think that you're no longer with us. I wiped out your tracks back at the overhang in the hope that he might think I've hidden you away somewhere. If he buys it, he might stay still and watch to see if I go back for you. Hopefully he'll stay holed up for a while. It might give Luke time to make it to Muddy Creek and send a wire to Lyle."

"How far is it to town?"

"About five miles."

"Five miles?"

"That's not very far for Luke. He likes to run, doesn't matter the distance. I've never known of anyone who can catch him when he's in full stride. By going now, he'll be there first thing in the morning when the agent comes to open the depot."

"It doesn't seem very safe to run at night," Kate remarked.

"Actually it's the best time. For one thing, it's a lot cooler. For another, Hayden will either be holed up or trying to find us. Even if he's between us and Muddy Creek, Luke will find a way to slip past him."

"But if he sees Luke, won't he go after him?"

"I doubt it. Hayden's like a bull—single-minded. He'll be too focused on finding us to spend much time on an Indian. If anything, it'll make him want to find us even more because he'll think that he only has me to contend with."

"If he catches us . . ." Kate couldn't even bring herself to finish the thought. Deep in her mind, she felt that she already knew the answer. If Hayden caught up with them, someone would get hurt.

"If he does catch us," Tate said, his eyes searching hers, "and I tell you to go, I want you to run towards the east Find a place to hide and stay perfectly still. Luke will find you when he comes back from town."

For the next couple of minutes, both were silent. In her mind, Kate imagined what would happen if Hayden did find them. The thought of Tate being hurt, or even killed, froze the blood in her veins. If he told her to run, could she actually bring herself to abandon this man who had done so much to make sure that she was safe?

"You think Hayden will come tonight?" she asked softly.

"If he comes, he'll come when the sun is low. He'll wait until the sun is setting and then come from the west so that we'll be blinded by it." Suddenly Tate turned his head and acted as if he was listening, even though Kate could hear no sound. "That was Luke's signal. He's leaving now."

"I didn't hear anything."

"It was the whistle of a scissortail. Luke's father and I have used that signal for years. I'm surprised Hayden hasn't caught on to it."

"Luke is leaving now?"

"He must have found a way to slip past Hayden. Come on." Tate tugged on the reins of the horse and moved up the hillside toward the heavy boulders. "We've got to get to a place where we'll have cover."

Kate was frightened. The shadows grew longer with each passing moment, and she felt that the showdown between them and Hayden was growing ever closer. From the moment that Tate had saved her from Squirrelly's clutches, she wanted to avoid this fight, but now that seemed impossible. Even though the day was still hot, she couldn't help shivering.

Tate led the horse around a large boulder and then stood for a minute looking back the way they had come. "This is as good a place as any," he said as he came to help Kate down from the horse. She swung her leg over the saddle and, while tightly gripping Tate's hand, slid to the ground. Once on the ground, Kate had to hold on to the saddle horn because her legs were wobbly.

"What can I do?" she asked.

"Stay here behind this boulder and keep out of sight. Your blond hair shines like a lantern in this sun. Do you have anything you could tie over your head?"

"You want me to cover my hair?"

"As bad as he wants me, I think he wants you more, and it probably doesn't matter to him if he takes you dead or alive. If the ransom money has already been paid, he can't afford to let you live. If you were to make it to the law, you could testify against him. He's already been to prison. He'll do whatever it takes to keep from going back. With all of that, he may shoot you if he sees your blond head poking above a boulder." Tate removed his handkerchief from around his neck and handed it to her. "Here, tie this over your head and stay down. I'll be over behind the rocks on the other side of the trail. If you look up, you'll see me. I'll take off my hat if I see him."

"I'm scared, Tate." The words poured out of her quickly, her fear at what was happening bubbling over. Tears filled the corners of her eyes, and she felt her hands begin to shake.

"It's not a bad thing to be scared," Tate said softly.

"I'm scared for you." She wanted to grab hold of him and not let him go. Her feelings for this man who had risked his life for her had grown into something that she couldn't explain. If he went off and Hayden found him, he could be killed. If that happened, she didn't know if she could go on.

Tate put his hand gently on her shoulder and then slid it up behind her neck. Shivers raced down her spine. "You'll be all right."

"Damn it," she hissed through her teeth. "I'm worried about you."

"Don't be."

The hand behind her neck drew her closer. Her eyes met

his for the briefest of moments before he bent his head and placed his lips against hers, holding them there for a long minute. His kiss was like nothing she had ever experienced before. Her heart swam, and for what seemed like forever, she forgot that this might be the last of their lives. When he raised his head, her eyes were misty. She wanted to say something—to tell him how important he was to her, how he was more than just a rescuer—but the words refused to come. So she said nothing. He looked at her silently, then turned and walked away.

For the next hour, Kate quietly crouched behind the boulder, peeking over the rock only occasionally. Most of the time, her eyes were locked on Tate. This man had become the most important thing in her life. She'd only known him for a few days! She tried to tell herself that it was because they were alone and she depended on him, but her heart told her that wasn't true. Even when they stood on the train platform in Simon, she had felt something. At that moment, she hadn't known what it was, but it must have been attraction. Now she had no more illusions. She had fallen for the cowboy.

Lost in her daydream, she was startled when a hand clamped down over her mouth. She hadn't had the time to let out a sound! Trying with all her might, she tried to move but was held firmly in place.

"Keep quiet, bitch!" The words were huskily whispered in her ear.

Kate knew immediately who it was. For a brief moment, she was frozen, her heart beating wildly. She looked at Tate, but he was still crouched behind the boulder and looking down the trail. He didn't know that Hayden had crept up behind them. Her fear momentarily released its grip, and she instinctively dug her elbow into the man's midsection. A blast of air hit her ear, but the grip that held her never weakened.

"Try that again, bitch, and I'll slit your throat," Hayden growled.

Kate, in desperation, looked toward the boulder where Tate was crouching, hoping to at least see him one last time.

Tate was gone.

Chapter 17

"LET GO OF HER!"

Tate lunged across the gap between himself and Hayden with a ferocious look on his face and his gun in his hand. In turn, Hayden shoved Kate toward him. Seeing Kate come flying across the space, Tate flung out an arm to keep her from falling. Hayden took advantage of the move. His foot lashed out, knocking the gun from Tate's hand. The move had brought Hayden close enough for Tate to strike. He doubled up his fist and swung a jarring blow that flattened Hayden's lips against his big, square teeth. The blow would have felled most men, but it merely rocked Hayden back on his heels. Roaring with anger, Hayden pulled the large knife free of its scabbard and charged. Tate's own anger rose. He dodged the knife and threw another punch. He moved so quickly that Hayden was forced to back up in order to protect himself from Tate's windmill attack.

"Go!" Tate shouted as he shot a glance at Kate. "Get the hell out of here!"

Kate stood paralyzed, the sight of the two men fighting holding her to the ground. Her legs felt as if they were weighted down with iron chains, and her unblinking eyes stayed locked on the men. Even as she heard his shout, fear for Tate kept her from acting.

With a quick feint, Hayden flicked the knife out and cut Tate on the chin. Pain shot through him like fire, forcing him to back away. Hayden lowered his head for a charge, and Tate let him come. Before Hayden could slash him again, Tate's fist struck him with such force that his head snapped up and his body arched back. Hayden staggered for a moment, looking as if he might topple, then planted his feet wide apart and became as rooted to the ground as an oak tree. Tate tried to press his advantage, moving in to fell the man, but Hayden was ready. His big fist thudded against Tate's cheekbone, opening a gash.

Already, Tate could taste the copper blood filling his mouth. As Hayden flashed a bloody mouth of his own, the knife still moving menacingly in front of him, Tate moved to his side and then darted in low, hitting the man hard in the stomach with his head. Hayden lost his balance and fell heavily to the ground, dragging Tate with him. The sound of Hayden's knife clattering amongst the rocks reached Tate's ears. Gnashing teeth tried to grab some part of his face or neck as they rolled. Now on the ground, both men snarled at each other, their faces only inches apart. Hayden brought his head forward in short raps, striking Tate in the face. Blood spurted from his nose. Tate brought his knee up between Hayden's legs, causing Hayden just enough pain to force him to drop his arms. Agile as a cat, Tate sprang to his feet.

A rock-hard fist caught the slow-moving Hayden in the

mouth as he rose to his feet. He staggered back and then began to circle, looking for an opening. Each man appraised the other. Hayden was a rough-and-tumble fighter. While not a brawler, Tate had steel and rawhide in his rangy frame. He moved in, hit, and retreated, dancing away from Hayden's grappling arms.

Suddenly Hayden closed the space between them and grabbed Tate by the arm. With an animal yell, he slammed him down against a nearby boulder. Tate's head bounced off the rock. Dazed, he crashed into the ground. Stars danced in front of his eyes. Hayden lifted one boot to stomp down on the fallen man's face, but Tate avoided the blow, rolled, and then staggered to his feet. He blinked and shook his head, desperately trying to clear it. He would not let this hunk of lowlife beat him down! His life and Kate's depended on it. Ducking under another punch, he lashed out with a fist of his own. The blow struck Hayden in the mouth, shearing off a tooth. His enemy backed away in surprise and spit it out of his bloody mouth. He glared at Tate.

"I'm gonna kill you," Hayden bellowed.

"Is this the best you can do, you stupid jailbird?" Tate taunted. Blood flowed from the deep cut above his eye, from his gashed cheekbone, and from his nose, where Hayden had battered him with his head.

They circled each other again, the hot sun beating down on them. Sweat dripped down into Tate's eyes as he picked his way through the stones that were strewn on the ground.

Suddenly Hayden's eyes left his foe, and he bent down and snatched something up out of the dirt. Sunlight gleamed off the knife blade. Tate's guts knotted. Now he was back where he'd started.

"I'm not through yet, you son of a bitch," Hayden roared with rage.

Hayden charged, his knife in his hand, the blade darting and thrusting like the tongue of a snake. The point of the blade ripped a small gash in Tate's forearm, and the cut felt hot. Trying not to give any ground, he sprang forward and threw a punch, but Hayden jumped back and escaped the blow. Then, holding his knife low, the cutting edge up, he jabbed at Tate. But Tate moved away.

Both men continued to circle, Tate ever watching the knife blade. Finally, after Hayden had missed with another slashing pass, Tate crouched and put all of his strength into his fist, which he sent into Hayden's stomach. As Hayden's head came downward, Tate drove his knee up into the other man's chin. He groaned, but as he fell down, he swung the knife wildly and cut a shallow slit across the center of Tate's chest.

Hot and searing pain filled Tate's body. He wanted to fall down and clutch his hands over the wet wound, but he knew that he couldn't: Hayden would be on him with the killing blow. He had to get the knife away! With Hayden still dazed, Tate moved to step on the arm holding the knife, but he was too slow. His foot found nothing but earth as Hayden rolled and came up slashing.

Hayden's first slash missed. As he turned to slash back in the way that he had come, Tate jumped into the opening and threw a punch at the man's knife arm. His blow landed, but a moment too late: The blade entered into his side. This time the pain wasn't immediate, which he knew to be a sign of a bad wound. Regardless, he didn't have time for pain. Instead, he clamped his hands down on to Hayden's arm, his fingers seeking to find a way to pry the blade from his grasp. For a minute, it was strength against strength, every muscle in both men straining with the effort. Then Hayden yielded, throwing Tate off balance. The shift sent both men falling to the ground. Hayden sprang back to his feet. Tate also got to his feet, although not as quickly as before. He felt sluggish and weak.

Knowing that he had a wounded enemy, Hayden leaped at him, swinging his knife. Tate sidestepped, his left forearm taking the tip of the blade, and smashed his right fist hard into Hayden's face. The second that Hayden hit the ground, Tate was on him, his arm straining to hold the knife away from his body. Tate hammered away with his fist while Hayden clawed at the bloody wounds that he had inflicted. Wildly, bitterly, and desperately they fought, their battered bodies slick with blood. They rolled around in the dirt, their faces close. Tate got his hand into Hayden's hair and jerked his head back. Hate-filled eyes stared back into his own.

"Shit-eatin' buzzard," Tate hissed. Blood ran down his chest and seemed to pour from the wound in his side. The dull feeling that he had first felt was being replaced with a throbbing ache.

"I should have killed you when I had the chance," Hayden spat.

"It'll take a better man than you to kill me."

Suddenly Hayden struck a vicious blow behind Tate's

ear that sent him falling over on his side. He was dazed, unsure of what was up and what was down. Hayden didn't have the same confusion and jumped back to his feet. Still reeling, Tate caught a boot in the jaw that knocked his head to one side. For a moment, Tate lay on his back defenseless.

Almost babbling in pain and insane rage, Hayden straddled Tate's body and lifted the knife to plunge it into his chest. With the last bit of strength that he had, Tate shot his hands up and caught enough of Hayden's thrust to keep it from being a killing blow. Instead, the knife bit into his shoulder. As pain filled him, his life seemed to flash before his eyes. He had failed to save Kate. He had made Emily an orphan. He had allowed this dirty rotten son of a bitch to best him. His frantic eyes saw Hayden prepare to stab him again. This time he knew that he wouldn't have the strength to stop him. This time he knew that he was going to die.

Like a thunderclap, the sound of a gun erupted on the hillside. Through blood and sweat, Tate saw a surprised look come over Hayden's face as he grabbed at his neck. He doubled up and fell heavily to his side as blood poured from between his fingers.

Slowly and with much effort, Tate staggered to his feet, bent over Hayden, and grabbed a handful of his shirt. As he held him there, he saw blood flow from a hole in his neck and his eyes roll back in his head. He knew immediately that Hayden either was dead or soon would be. After he lowered the man to the ground, he turned to see Kate holding his gun in both hands, the barrel still pointed at Hayden.

"Put the gun down, Kate," he gasped. "He's dead."

When Kate didn't respond, he repeated himself, more force-fully this time. "Put the gun down." When Kate still gave no response, Tate stepped over the prone body of his enemy and took the gun from her hand. "It's over," he said.

Kate looked at him with dazed eyes, not seeing or hear-ing him. Suddenly her knees buckled and she tottered, but Tate slipped an arm around her and held her upright.

"It's all right," he said calmly. "It's all right . . . he's dead." There was a minute of taut silence as she leaned heavily against him.

"You're hurt," she gasped as her hand touched the crim-son stain that was growing across Tate's shirt.

"I think I need to sit down."

Kate sprang into action. She grabbed the blanket, spread it on the ground, and eased Tate down onto it. Without hes-itation, she undid the buckle on his trousers and loosened his belt. Pulling his shirt up, she first examined the wound in his side. She couldn't tell how deeply the knife had pen-etrated. Tate winced as she touched him. The slash was bleeding profusely.

She searched among the rocks in the area where Hayden had first grabbed her until she found her bag. She opened it and brought out several white handkerchiefs. Folding two of them together, she made a pad and pressed it into Tate's side. Then she removed Tate's belt from his pants.

"Can you sit up long enough for me to slip this around your waist to hold the bandage in place?"

"Whatever it takes." He clenched his teeth tightly in pain when he moved. Kate hurriedly placed the belt around his waist.

"How bad is it?" Tate asked. Now that his fight with Hayden had ended, the pain from his wounds was worse. The long cut in his chest throbbed with every beat of his heart, but it was the one in his side that caused him the most discomfort.

"I don't know. But for right now I've got to stop the bleeding, or you'll go into shock," Kate answered honestly. She'd seen worse wounds at the clinic, but there she had modern utensils and supplies. Here she had to improvise.

She pulled Tate's shirt apart and saw that she didn't have to deal with the cut across his chest. The wound was not as bad as the one in his side. With Hayden's knife, she cut the sleeves off the shirt and used them to stanch the flow of blood oozing from the cut.

"You won't have a shirt left when I get through with it," she said as she tended to his arm and tried to keep the worry out of her voice.

"I'm glad you're a nurse and not a schoolteacher." His eyelids seemed heavy, but his gaze never left her face.

"So am I," she said, and pushed the hair back from his forehead. "I was so scared when I saw him go at you with the knife."

"Why didn't you run when I told you to?"

"And leave you here with that madman?"

Tate's eyes closed for a long moment before snapping back open. His mouth opened and shut a couple of times without making a sound before he managed to ask, "When . . . when did you pick . . . up the gun?"

"I don't know. I just knew that I had to help you." Tears

began to well in the corner of Kate's eyes. *Stay strong!* she told herself.

"Good thing you did," was all that he managed to say before he felt the sky go dark and the dizziness overtake him. The last thing that he saw before falling unconscious was the first tear streak down Kate's cheek.

Chapter 18

WHEN TATE OPENED HIS EYES, the sky was streaked with the reddish purple colors of dusk. High above, early stars shone brightly, signaling the coming of night. He felt weak as a newborn colt, but the pain that had filled him wasn't as sharp as it had been. A blanket covered him, and he tried to push it off, but his efforts were resisted.

"Don't," Kate's voice ordered. "I've got to keep you warm."

"I feel hotter than hell."

"It doesn't matter. Do you want a drink of water?"

"No, you better save it. We don't know how long we'll be here."

"Take a drink anyway." Kate lifted his head and brought the canteen to his lips. He was glad that she'd insisted, and he drank thirstily. "How is the pain?"

"I've felt worse." He wasn't sure if it was true, but he didn't want to panic Kate. She'd already been through so much.

"I still don't want to move you. I've done what I can to

stop the bleeding. If you were to try to walk or ride, you could bleed to death."

"Luke will be back by morning."

"Will he bring help with him?"

"Probably not. He'll be alone. The sheriff in town isn't the smartest man in the world. He won't pay much attention to Luke. The only thing that'd stir him would be a wire from the Texas Rangers."

"Then we'll just have to wait for Luke," Kate said. Tate was weak. She knew that he could easily black out again. "If we're going to have to camp here for the night, what do I need to do?"

"The sun will be down soon. Do you know how to start a fire?"

"I do. Do we have matches?"

"There are a few in a tin box in my pocket. Find a bare spot over by that other boulder and rake some leaves into it. Pick up some dry sticks, but be careful of snakes."

"Snakes?" Fear knifed through Kate at the thought of another encounter like the one that she had the night they escaped from the cabin.

"Don't worry," Tate said reassuringly. "Take a big stick and stir it around. Snakes are as afraid of you as you are of them."

Using a large stick, Kate scattered a pile of leaves, then stood back and waited to see if there were any snakes. When she saw no movement, she raked the leaves into the bare spot by the boulder, picked up some sticks, and placed them on top of the leaves. She went to her bag and took out the letter from her uncle in California. With the pile ready, she struck a match from the tin, lit one corner of the letter, and held it to the leaves. She fed more sticks into the fire slowly, and before long a steady fire burned. Kate sat back on her heels and watched the fire. She was grateful that they didn't have to worry about Hayden seeing the smoke. Furthermore, she doubted that she'd have to worry about either Eddy or Squirrelly. The mangy vermin were probably back in the cozy cabin with plenty of food and water.

"Where's Hayden's body?" Tate asked.

"It's where he fell."

"We'll need to move it away from here. It could be dangerous to have it close. The smell of blood can draw animals."

"I can do it if you tell me what to do."

Tate tried to sit up. "I . . . I think I can do it."

Kate gently but firmly pushed him back down. "No. No, you can't. Tell me."

With a sigh of resignation, Tate said, "You'll have to go get the horse. Then tie a rope around Hayden's feet and drag him off a ways."

"I can do it," she said confidently. "I'm not squeamish around the dead." She tucked the blanket around Tate's shoulders, stood, and looked down at him. "I'll get the horse."

"There's a length of rope in the Mexican's saddlebags. Hand me my rifle and take the pistol with you." With a faint smile, he added, "I guess I don't need to worry that you don't know how to use it."

Returning the smile, she picked up the pistol from where she had dropped it. She turned the barrel of the gun away and checked to see if there were bullets in the chamber. Seeing that there were, she then placed the rifle by Tate's side.

"I'll be right back," she said as she turned away.

Tate had never felt so helpless. He had almost gotten himself killed because he hadn't shot Hayden when he had the chance. Now he had to depend on this woman, the same woman he'd silently ridiculed as a spoiled city woman while standing on that train platform. How wrong he'd been! She had a lot more starch in her backbone than some men he knew. If he could hold on for a day or two, Lyle would be able to find them and then get her to town and safety. Then she could get on with her life. With that thought came another: He would miss her. If only they could have met under different circumstances.

There was no way she could be compared with Hazel, Emily's mother. Hazel was a selfish bitch who had cared more for herself than for her own child. He had seen no signs of selfishness or arrogance in Kate. She never complained, even when she was dead tired or frightened, or when her feet were so sore that she could hardly walk.

Kate returned, leading the horse. She tied the reins to a scrub tree, lifted the saddlebags, and brought them over to the blanket where Tate lay.

"Did you have any trouble with the horse?" he asked.

"No. I've been around them all my life. We have eight or ten horses on the farm where my father and I used to spend our summers."

Tate lay silently on the blanket, Kate's words rolling about in his head. A summer farm with horses? There was such a difference between her lifestyle and his. It was foolish to think that she could share his life.

Ignorant of Tate's thoughts, Kate pulled a rope out of the saddlebag and held it up for him to see. "It isn't very long," she said.

"You can tie his feet with his belt and then loop one end of the rope around the belt, then the other one around the saddle horn."

Kate shuddered. "I really don't want to do this, but I will."

She went to where Hayden's body lay faceup in the dirt. His eyes stared skyward blankly, and he still looked as confused as he had when he realized that he'd been shot. Disturbed, Kate shook her head. Keeping her eyes away from Hayden's face, she unbuckled his belt and pulled it out of his britches. Quickly, while she still had the nerve, she looped it around his ankles and fastened it. Tate's voice came faintly from where he lay.

"Go through his pockets. You might find something that could tie him to the kidnapping."

Kate quickly searched Hayden's pockets. She found a gold coin, the address of a man in Alpine, and a billfold that contained several hundred dollars. Also in the wallet was a picture of a nude woman lying on a couch. She placed all the items on the blanket beside Tate. Then she wound the other end of the rope around the saddle horn and picked up the reins.

"You don't have to go far." Tate pointed to a small stand of trees.

Kate led the horse, and it moved with little resistance.

Tate lifted his head to see Hayden's body slowly moving away. He hated that Kate had to do this, but it was necessary. She returned a few minutes later and again tied the horse to the scrub tree.

"He needs water," she said, pointing toward the horse.

"Pour a little from the canteen into my hat. It'll be enough to get him by until morning."

Kate did as Tate instructed, and the horse drank lustily. She rubbed the spot between his eyes until he was finished. As she turned around, she glanced over to see that Tate's eyes were shut. Dropping the hat to the ground, she hurried over to him and lifted his hand to take his pulse. It was steady, but not as strong as she would have hoped. She pulled the blanket aside and checked his wounds. Crimson spots had soaked through the makeshift bandages. She still had no idea how they were going to move him.

Gently she pulled the blanket up to cover him. She felt his forehead and found him cool to the touch. She knew that he hadn't had time to get a fever from his wounds, but he was still in great danger. Her greatest fear was that he would go into shock. She took the blanket from Luke's bedroll and spread it over Tate. Nightfall would be coming soon, and with it would come cooler temperatures. He needed to stay warm.

I wish the Mexican had carried a bottle of whiskey in his saddlebag.

For the next couple of hours, Kate sat in front of the fire and looked up at the thousands of stars in the sky. She had never seen them so bright! Once, a noise, like the snapping of a twig, startled her, and she grabbed the rifle and held it in front of her. But when nothing else happened, she went back to looking at the stars.

Finally she decided that it was time to check on Tate. She went to the blanket where he lay, and knelt down. It was dark, but the light from the fire was helpful. Carefully she turned his head toward her. The gash on his cheekbone had stopped bleeding, but his face seemed pale in the firelight. If only she had some antiseptic to wash his cuts, especially the cut across his chest and the one in his side. She placed her hand inside his shirt to search for signs of shock. She had seen many gunshot victims go into shock from loss of blood. The first sign of that shock was that they trembled as if they were freezing. His body was cool, and she didn't feel a tremble.

She looked down to see that Tate's eyes were open and that he was staring into her face. She felt a few seconds of embarrassment.

"I'm touching you to see if you're cold."

"I am cold."

"I'll get another blanket. We have one more."

"No, don't move," he said, but Kate had already risen.

She laid the other blanket on top of him and tucked all of the blankets more tightly around his body. "Now go back to sleep. I won't be afraid as long as I've got the gun."

"If I doze off, wake me if you hear anything. I'm not worried about any four-legged animals. They usually stay away from a fire. Also, if a wind comes up, be careful the fire doesn't spread."

"Go to sleep. Don't worry. I've camped out with my father many times. I know all about campfires."

"When Luke comes back, he'll whistle. It will be the call of a scissortail. Do you know what that sounds like?"

"No, but I won't shoot him. Will he know where to find us?"

"He'll have a pretty good idea. Wake me as soon as it's daylight, and I'll listen for his signal. He's no longer trying to scare you, so you can trust him. The agent at the depot will have told him whether Lyle's in town. If Lyle is there, he'll come back with Luke."

"Will Lyle believe him?"

"He knows Luke. He'll believe him."

Kate felt his forehead with the palm of her hand. His skin was still cool to the touch.

"Now that you're awake, I want to look at your side," she explained.

Gently she pulled the blanket down his body and then parted what was left of his shirt. The pad was as red as before; the bleeding hadn't completely stopped. Loosening the belt, she lifted the pad. Even in the faint light, she could see that the wound wasn't seeping blood, but it was still wet. She'd need to find something else to use as a bandage. She searched through Luke's bedroll and found a ragged shirt. She didn't know how clean it was, but it would have to do. She tore out a sleeve, rolled it into a pad, pressed it to Tate's side, and readjusted the belt to hold it in place. The cut across his chest was in similar condition. She made another pad from the rest of Luke's shirt and moved it into place. Now that his wounds had been cleanly dressed, she lifted his head to her lap and covered him with the blankets.

"Do you want a drink of water?"

"No," he answered faintly. She could see that he was exhausted.

"You're going to get one anyway." She lifted his head and held the canteen to his mouth. He took one small sip. "That's not enough." She held the canteen to his mouth again. "You've got to have water. You've lost a lot of blood."

"When did you drink last?"

"I'm not thirsty now."

After Tate had drunk, Kate lowered his head. She reached across him and picked up the rifle.

"Are you gonna shoot me?"

"Not yet," she said with a smile.

"I wouldn't blame you. I let you down."

"Let me down?"

"Hayden almost got me. He would have, if not for you."

"Didn't you tell me that if you save a person's life, you own that person?"

"I believe I did."

"Does that mean I own you and you own me?"

"That's not such a bad idea . . ." His voice trailed off. She looked down and saw that his eyes were closed. Gently she slid her hand down inside his shirt to feel his heartbeat.

It was strong.

Chapter 19

"SIT DOWN, DEAR. You're wearing yourself out pacing."

John ignored his wife's suggestion, went to the window, pulled back the heavy drapery, and looked out into the darkness. What he could see of the street was empty; the lamp at the end of the drive shed a soft glow. Unlike the empty street, his mind was full of thoughts.

I should have taken the money myself! What was the matter with me that I let William take it? Not only could they kill him because he's not me, but they could hesitate about taking the paper sack.

"Would you like something to drink to calm your nerves?" Lila asked. John turned to look at her, sitting calmly in her favorite chair, a look of concern on her face.

"Not now, dear." Drink would do nothing to ease his anxiety. He had waited impatiently for Lyle to contact him with news of the Texas Ranger's search. With every passing day, his fear that something had happened to Kate escalated. He would gladly have paid double the amount of the ransom to have his daughter returned.

"John?" Lila prodded. "It's too soon for us to hear any

news. These things take time. We should wait another hour or two before we start losing hope."

"I'll never lose hope," John said angrily.

"Dear," Lila replied softly, "you must realize that there are some things that are out of your hands. William is complying with their wishes. We're fortunate to have such a true friend. He loves Kate, you know."

"I'm grateful for all he's done," John said, his voice trailing off as his thoughts returned to the telephone call he was expecting. He'd been told that he would receive word about Kate's whereabouts when the kidnappers received the money. He hoped that they would also tell him that Kate had been released. His nerves were strung as tight as a wire. *Why doesn't the damn phone ring?* If all went as planned, the extortionists should have had the money almost an hour ago! *Something must be wrong!* He abruptly turned on his heel and went to ring for Malcolm.

The door to the library was opened almost immediately by the manservant. "Yes, sir."

"Check the telephone lines to be sure that there's nothing wrong with them. I'm expecting an important call."

"Right away, sir."

Malcolm left the room. When he returned a few minutes later, he said, "The telephone is working, sir."

John simply nodded dejectedly. Sweat formed on his brow, and he wrung his hands together roughly. He returned to pacing the floor.

Suddenly the door to the library opened, and, much to John's relief, William stepped into the room.

"William!" John exclaimed.

Lila jumped up from her chair and ran across the room to where William stood. "I'm so glad you're back! We've been worried about you."

"Have you received the phone call yet?" William asked.

"No. Nothing." John nervously ran his fingers through his already tousled hair. "How did it go?"

"Just as we expected. I went to the place where they told us to go and waited. Damn near broke my neck looking around at all the people, wondering which of them was looking for me," William complained "Then a man came up behind me, took hold of the sack, and said, 'Katherine. Is this for me?' I told him that it was, and before I knew it, he'd snatched it out from under my arm and disappeared into the crowd."

"Did you see his face?" John asked anxiously.

"No. After he snatched it, I spun around, but he was headed into a crowd of people. From the one glance that I got of him, all that I can say for certain is that he wore a billed cap."

"Did he say anything about Kate?"

"Nothing. He only said what I told you." William sighed heavily and looked long and hard at his business partner. "I know that you want easy answers, old friend, but the man who took the money probably didn't know much anyway. He was probably just a courier. Someone who was hired to pick up the money. That way, if he'd been caught, he wouldn't know anything."

Now that William had returned, and still no call had come from the kidnappers, John's apprehension returned tenfold. "First thing in the morning, I'm going to call Lyle. Or maybe the local police."

"We need to be patient now," William said, placing a strong hand on John's shoulder. "We've done all that we can do for the present. They have the money. There's no reason for them to keep Kate now. They'll let her go soon enough. If we do something rash, like calling the police, they may panic and hurt her."

"You're right, William," John said, his voice unsteady. "But I won't be able to rest until I hear her voice. Until I know that she's all right."

"None of us will." Turning to Lila, William said, "Take him up to his room. He has a phone up there he can answer if they call."

"Good idea," Lila answered.

"I'll be in the office first thing in the morning, John. Why don't you come in around noon? If anything comes up, I'll call you. Or if you hear from them, call me."

"Thank you for everything that you've done," Lila said, looping her arm through her husband's, urging him toward the stairs.

John walked along unsteadily, the stress of the long days since Kate's kidnapping taking its toll. At the foot of the stairs, he let go of his wife, steadied himself on the banister, and turned to his partner. "Thank you again, William. For everything."

"It is my pleasure to help."

Walking from the house to the street, William breathed deeply of the city air. It would be a simple matter to hail a cab to take him to his apartment, but he was so excited that he needed to walk. This was a night to savor, a night of triumph. All of his planning had come to fruition. When he first concocted the plan—hell, when he tried to explain it all to Edwin—he had a few doubts as to whether it could be done. But now, the money safely hidden away, he felt nothing but elation! He couldn't believe how easy it had been!

Before he got too excited, he reminded himself that now was not the time to get careless. This was where lesser minds got caught. He couldn't get complacent, feel like he'd already won. Now was the time to be thorough. Tomorrow he would take a few of the ransom bills to a friend he knew who was an expert on paper money. He would be able to tell him if they had been marked. John had said nothing about marking them, so he doubted that they had been; but he needed to make sure.

Poor, dumb John! If he only knew that he had handed the ransom money over to the man who had masterminded the kidnapping of his daughter . . . and John had been glad to do so! He would be shocked if he knew the truth! *But that will be nothing like the shock he'll experience when I buy out his shares in the company. And that's not all . . . there's still one surprise left for poor, dumb John.*

He hadn't lied to John when he told him that he'd be in the office first thing in the morning. He had work to do. He needed to send another telegram to Edwin, telling him that he'd received the money and that he could do whatever he needed to do with Kate. He knew that his nephew liked the girl, but he didn't share the affection. Throw her to the wolves, for all he cared. Nothing mattered now that he had the money.

Another person who no longer mattered was Edwin. The boy had served his purpose; he'd managed to keep Kate hidden in Texas. Now things had changed. Edwin, the fool, had believed that he would be welcomed back with open arms. He would be silenced. Squirrelly too, for that matter. He was the right kind of thug to get a muscle job done, but he talked too much. This Hayden fellow, though, was the kind of stone-cold killer who would do any job as long as the price was right. Once word reached Texas that the money had been paid, he'd know what to do.

William walked jauntily down the street. He tipped his hat politely to a lady and gentleman that he passed. Even when he was pestered by a raggedy old woman, only one brown tooth clinging to the inside of her mouth as she asked for change he could spare, he walked on smiling. He felt as if he had the world at his feet. Hell, he thought, I've worked long and hard for this. I deserve it. As soon as I hear from my contact in Texas that his man has done away with Kate, Edwin, and Squirrelly, I'll make my move to take control of Tyler-Jacobs Steelworks. Jacobs Steelworks.

Nothing can stop me now!

Chapter 20

KATE WAS SURE IT WAS THE LONGEST NIGHT OF HER LIFE. She hovered over Tate and moved only when she needed to put more wood on the fire. During the night, she heard a coyote howling for its mate and listened to the hooting of owls. The crackle of the burning sticks was a comforting sound. At times, Tate moved restlessly. When she talked to him, it seemed to comfort and quiet him.

"Lie still, honey." She wasn't conscious of the endearment until later. "You don't have to worry about Hayden. Go to sleep. I'll be right here with you." It felt good watching over him, as if he belonged to her. All through the night, she held his head in her lap and stroked his brow. "We've got a good fire going. In case something comes close, I've got the pistol, and the rifle is beside you. I'm not a bit afraid." Kate stretched that last a bit. She *was* afraid. It was so dark and quiet. She looked up at the star-studded sky. It seemed to her that she and Tate were the only two people in the world. "Sleep, my love. Luke will be here in the morning, and we'll get you to a doctor."

During the night, he opened his eyes and looked up at her. His eyes stayed on her face for a long time. She wasn't sure if he was seeing her or not until his lips moved. She cupped his rough cheek with her hand and bent her head to hear what he was saying.

"You're pure hickory," he whispered.

Kate wasn't sure what that meant, but thought it was something nice. "So are you."

She definitely heard what he said next because his voice was stronger. "You're pretty and sweet, too."

"Thank you. I can say the same for you."

That brought a twitching smile to his lips. Kate hoped that the adhesive tape would hold the cut on his chin together. He would have a deep scar if the wound wasn't closed.

"Are you cold?" she asked.

"Not too cold. How about you?"

"I've got my back to the fire. Go to sleep. Birds are chirping in the trees. It will be morning soon."

"Have you slept? I'll stay awake for a while and you lay down and sleep," he murmured.

"You need the sleep more than I do."

"Lay down here beside me for just a little while."

Kate couldn't resist the temptation to close her eyes. Just for ten minutes or so, she told herself. Tate folded back one of the blankets and lifted his head from her lap.

"Come on. Lay down."

Being careful not to bump his arm or his side, she lay down on the blanket. He stretched out his good arm and pulled her head down on it. "Go to sleep," he whispered in her ear.

"I might hurt you."

"No. Go to sleep, you need your rest. We're not sure what will happen tomorrow." Tate moved his knees up behind hers and pulled her against him.

Kate moved slightly away from him, fearing that she would hurt his side. Here she was in the wilderness sleeping beside a man she had known for only a few days, yet she felt that she had known him forever.

When next she opened her eyes, it was near daylight. She lay still for a long time not wanting to move away from the warm body lying so close behind her. Suddenly she realized their fire was only glowing embers. She eased herself out from under the blanket and stood looking down at the man who symbolized all that was good and decent. She realized more than ever before what it took to be a hero.

After feeling his brow and tucking the covers around his shoulders, she moved away to put more sticks on the fire. She waited a minute to make sure it would catch. Soon it was blazing, and the smoke was drifting straight up. She took the canteen back to where Tate lay and lifted his head up to her lap.

"You need water."

Tate took the canteen and shook it. "It's only about half full. You take a drink. We'll have to make it last until Luke gets here."

Kate took a small drink, then lifted his head and put the canteen to his lips. "You need water," she repeated. "And don't argue."

"Yes, ma'am," he said.

"That's better," she replied. "Now drink more." She tilted the canteen again, forcing him to drink. "That's enough for now. I'd like you to eat something. What do we have?"

"More biscuits," he said, looking up at her.

"I don't think I could eat one if I were starving. How about you?"

"They'll be hard as rocks by now. Let's wait for Luke. He should be here soon." He looked away from her. "I'll be all right if you want to go behind the boulders."

"Thank you, I would."

As soon as Kate disappeared, Tate painfully turned on his side and unbuttoned his britches. Hoping she wouldn't see him, he unloaded his bladder out into the grass, then restored his clothing. It was a blessed relief. He could not shock her sensitive ears by telling her he needed to do what she evidently needed to do behind the boulders.

When Kate returned, she had a white cloth in her hand. She knelt down and placed the palm of her hand on his forehead. "No fever yet," she said with relief, "but I need to look at your side and arm."

"What have you got there?"

"You don't need to know."

He reached up and felt the soft, silky material. "It's something of yours, isn't it?"

"It's something I don't need right now. I've already used Luke's shirt and most of yours."

"You've been gutsy through this. You would have made a good pioneer woman."

"It isn't over yet." She smiled down at him. "I might just burst into tears at any minute and blubber all over you."

In spite of the pain it caused him, Tate grinned at her. "I don't think that's likely. If you were going to fall to pieces, you would have done it when Hayden had you."

"Do you think Eddy and Squirrelly are waiting for him back at the cabin?"

"They'll wait for a while. Neither one of them has the sense it would take to survive out here. If you are right that your father's partner is ramrodding this thing, they will have to tell him that they let you get away from them."

"Eddy hinted strongly that his uncle was forcing him to do this. He told me that he agreed so that he could see that no harm came to me. He has tried, but he's not the type to stand up against Hayden and Squirrelly. As soon as we get to town, I'll call my father."

"Yes. We'll head there. I'll call Lyle if he isn't already in Muddy Creek."

"I wish Luke would come. I'm worried about how we are going to get you back to town."

"Luke will build a travois when he gets here."

"What's that?"

"It's a blanket stretched between two poles and dragged by a horse."

"He can't drag you out of here on a blanket. I won't allow it."

"It isn't as rough as it sounds. Leave it to Luke. He'll know what to do."

Tate leaned up on his good elbow and cocked his head to listen. "That's the signal. He's back." He put his fingers between his lips and whistled. A few seconds passed, and Kate heard the whistle repeated.

"How will he know where to find us?"

"He has seen the smoke from the fire. He knows where we are. He whistled so we wouldn't shoot him when he came in."

Kate waited anxiously for the Indian boy to appear. When he did, she was surprised to see that he wasn't alone. Three other Indian boys were with him.

"I'm back," he said. "I send telegram."

"Good."

Luke brushed past her and went to kneel beside Tate. "You hurt? You going to be dead?"

"I sure as hell hope not."

"Of course, he's not going to be dead. We've got to get him down to a doctor."

"We see nothing of Hayden."

"Kate shot him. He's back over there in the bushes."

"Dead?"

"Dead as a doornail."

Luke's face creased in one of his rare grins. "Your woman did it?"

"I'm not his woman," Kate said sternly.

Luke ignored her outburst. "You hurt bad, Tate? You going to be dead?" he asked again.

"No, you muttonhead."

"Then why you lay down and let your woman tend the fire?"

"He's got a hole in his side and one in his arm," Kate said

defensively. "He needs to see a doctor. How will we get him out of here?"

"I know. I no dumb Indian. I build good travois." He turned and spoke rapidly to the three boys with him. One pulled a hatchet out of his belt and took off for a patch of trees; the others followed. "They get poles for travois." Luke turned to Kate. "You done good to shoot Hayden."

"He would have killed me if she hadn't," Tate said. "Hayden was one tough hombre. I'll give him that."

"Tough and mean," Kate said. "Are we going to bury him? We just can't leave him for the animals."

"Why?" Luke said.

"Because we're civilized, that's why."

"What's 'civilized'?"

Tate looked up at Kate. "Explain, Kate, what 'civilized' means."

"Now, don't you be giving me any trouble." She put the palm of her hand on his forehead, then removed the blanket to look at his side. *Thank goodness it's stopped bleeding* Kate quickly and efficiently removed the bandage on his side. She held up the white cloth. "Cut this in two for me, Luke." When he handed the cloth back, she folded one of the pieces and pressed it against the wound, then tucked Tate's shirt down into his pants to hold it in place. The wound on his arm was still bleeding. She wrapped the other half of her petticoat around it and tied it into place. "You have to drink again, Tate." Kate lifted his head and held the canteen to his mouth. She looked up at the Indian boy. "Do you have water?"

"You think I am like silly city boy? Course, I got water."

"Good, because he's going to need it before we get him to town."

The three Indian boys returned with two long poles. They tied the ends together to make an A-frame. Luke quickly set to work building a platform on the end of the poles. After laying two blankets out, he pulled leather thongs out of his pouch, punched holes in the blankets with his knife, and tied the blankets to the poles. He worked swiftly, and soon the blankets were secure. He spread Tate's bedroll on top, then lay down on it to test it. "It'll do," he said. Two of the Indian boys lifted the tied ends of the poles over the horse's rump and secured them to the saddle, while the other boy positioned the poles that would drag.

"Can you move it closer to Tate?" Kate asked. "I don't want him getting up and walking to it."

After moving the travois over to where Tate lay, Luke nodded to the three boys. Each of them picked up a corner of the blanket Tate lay on. The four boys lifted him and placed him on the travois. Tate closed his eyes and gritted his teeth. Kate knew he was in pain. While one of the boys was throwing dirt on the fire, she picked up her bag, the rifle, and the pistol.

"Give me the rifle," Tate said. "It's too heavy for you to carry." She placed it beside him and handed him his hat.

Luke went ahead to pick the smoothest trail. One of the boys led the horse. The other two had disappeared, but Kate knew they were somewhere nearby. She walked along beside Tate, wishing she had something to ease his pain. He never made a sound, not even when the poles bounced over the rough ground. His eyes were closed, and Kate fervently hoped that he could sleep. When he called her name, his voice was weak. He held up his hand. She hurried to him and clasped it in one of hers. "When you get tired, tell Luke," he said. "He'll stop and you can ride on the horse."

"Tate Castle, I'll do no such thing. I wouldn't think of getting on that horse."

"You'll be worn-out by noon."

"Luke will stop and rest the horse. I'll rest then."

The sun, on its way to the zenith, was relentless. Kate trudged along beside the travois that carried Tate. His hat shaded his face, but she could see rivulets of sweat running down from his temples. She hurried ahead and called out to the Indian boy who was leading the horse.

"Stop. Tate needs water."

The boy turned and looked at her, clearly not understanding her words. Kate signaled with her hand toward Tate and from Tate to the canteen that hung over the horse's saddle. The boy got the message and stopped the horse. She carried the canteen back to where Tate lay. "You need water," she said. She unscrewed the lid and held the canteen to his mouth. He lifted his head and took a mouthful of the water.

"You," he said, and pushed the canteen toward her.

"I don't need any yet."

"Drink. You're not used to this heat."

Kate took a handkerchief from her pocket and wet it with water from the canteen. She lifted his hat and spread the handkerchief over his face and patted it down with her hand.

"That feels good," Tate muttered. "But it's a waste of water."

She held the canteen to his lips again. "Take another drink. Luke says we have enough water."

"There's never enough in this country."

Kate didn't answer. She hung the canteen back on the saddle and motioned for the boy to go on. She walked beside the travois. Tate handed her his hat. "Put it on."

She didn't argue. After placing the hat on her head, she clasped the hand Tate held out to her. His fingers tightened around hers with surprising strength.

"When you get tired, I'll whistle for Luke to stop," he told her.

"We should keep going as long as possible. I want to get you to town. You need the care of the doctor."

"You patched me up pretty good with your petticoat."

"How did you know it was my petticoat?"

"Because it smelled like what fell out of your suitcase on the train."

"You're not going to let me forget that, are you?"

"I'm not going to forget it."

"I'll not forget it either. I've never been so embarrassed in all my life."

She looked down to see that his eyes were closed, but he still held tightly to her hand.

"Will Luke stop at noon?" she asked him.

"Indians don't eat three meals a day. They eat when they're hungry. He'll stop soon, or I'll whistle."

"Don't you dare whistle on my account."

Kate turned to see the Indian boy trying to calm the horse. He kept repeating a word she didn't understand.

Tate rose up from the travois. "He's saying the devil steer is near. Devil steer is what the Indians call the longhorns." Tate reached for the rifle at his side and grunted with pain. Kate grabbed it, jacked a bullet into the cylinder, and held it at ready.

"Give me that," Tate said.

"You can't hold it with your bad arm."

Tate called to the boy and spoke rapidly. The boy came back and took hold of Kate's arm and tried to pull her around to the other side of the travois and up a bank to a large tree.

"Go with him," Tate shouted. "Let him help you up the tree."

Kate jerked loose and came back to the travois. "I'm not going to leave you. I'll handle the rifle. You've got the pistol."

It was then she saw the steer. He seemed calm and moved toward them with a swing stride that caused his dewlap to sway like the pendulum on a clock. The steer's tailbone was a peak in the rear, and deep hollows showed between his ribs and hipbone. He picked his way down toward them. The longhorn's coat was not merely shaggy, but rough, patchy. He was still shedding his winter hair. It was the color of sandstone and limestone with highlights and shadows of spotted moss. He was fierce-looking and alert to them. Then he stopped and stood still. His big head sagged far out ahead of his narrow hump. When his back legs spread, Tate shouted a warning to Kate.

Suddenly, so fast it was hard to believe what was happening, the beast charged. The frightened horse reared, almost throwing Tate to the ground. The hooves of the enraged beast pounded on the hard ground as he sped down the hill toward them.

"Go," Tate shouted at Kate.

Chapter 21

Kᴀᴛᴇ'ꜱ ᴇʏᴇꜱ ᴡᴇʀᴇ ꜰᴀꜱᴛᴇɴᴇᴅ ᴏɴ ᴛʜᴇ ꜰɪᴇʀᴄᴇ-ʟᴏᴏᴋɪɴɢ animal coming toward them. She knelt down next to the travois and lifted the rifle. The end of the gun shook slightly, but she tried to hold it steady.

"Give me the gun and go!" Tate commanded.

Kate was so intent on the steer that she didn't hear his words. All of her senses were fixed on the steer. Everything seemed to be happening in slow motion. The animal drew so close that she could see its red-rimmed eyes.

Suddenly the steer stopped within a dozen yards of them. Massive hooves pawed at the rocky ground, sending small clouds of dust into the air. It looked confused, uncertain. Long strands of spittle hung from its mouth. The horns on each side of its head seemed to be a yard wide. Kate had only seen animals this large in a zoo. It seemed even more ferocious than the wildcat they had watched prowl the ledge across from their camp. The steer remained still for a moment, then spun and headed for a gully at the other side of the trail. Kate kept her eyes on the animal, not daring to believe that it was going to leave.

"Now run," Tate hissed.

"I'm not leaving you here," she shouted. "So shut up!"

The animal turned slowly toward them again. For a moment, Kate feared that it had been attracted to the sound of their arguing voices. She gasped and realized that she had been holding her breath. *Oh Lord, what if it charges and the horse bolts? Tate could be dragged along behind and killed!* To lose Tate now would be more than she could endure.

The beast turned so that it was facing them. Kate spoke in low tones to Tate. "Where is the best place to hit him?"

"Between the eyes," Tate answered. "If you get a second chance, aim between its front legs, just below the neck."

Kate pulled the rifle up and sighted on the steer's head. She was wondering how close she should let the animal get when, out of the corner of her eye, she saw Luke run past her toward the steer.

"Stay back, you crazy kid!" Tate shouted.

Luke ignored him, moved close to the steer, and then darted away from it. He ran a short distance up a low hill, pulled the red cloth from around his head, and began to wave his arms and shout, trying to draw the steer's attention away from them. It appeared at first that his ploy would work; the steer turned its massive body and began to move toward him. Then, even as the boy's yelling increased, the animal lost interest, moving back down into the draw. Once again, its attention centered on the horse pulling the travois.

"It's not going to go away, is it?" Kate asked.

"No."

"Will it charge?"

"Don't get panicked," Tate said calmly. "Stay steady. You may only get one good shot, so don't shoot until you're sure."

Kate's hands tightened on the rifle, and she tried to remember everything that her father had taught her about using a gun. She wiped a stray strand of hair from her sweaty brow and drew a deep breath. Calmly she sighted down the barrel, her hands no longer shaking.

It went against her principles to take the life of any living thing, unless she was protecting herself or the man that she loved. She had shot Hayden without a second thought.

Tate's voice came softly to her ear. "I want you to know that I'm proud to know you. You're the spunkiest woman I ever met. I wish we could have met under different circumstances."

"But we have met." She wanted to turn, to look at him, but didn't dare. "That's what's important."

The steer's head moved back and forth. Maybe Luke had only made it angrier. The horse whinnied beside her, and the longhorn fixed its attention on them. This time Kate knew that it was not going to be distracted. As if suddenly making up its mind, it moved toward them, slowly at first, but with each step, it picked up speed.

"Wait," Tate said calmly as Kate lifted one knee and placed the rifle on it to steady it. Sighting down the barrel, she aimed between the steer's eyes, let out her breath, and squeezed the trigger. The sound of the rifle echoed loudly off the rocky hills. The bullet missed, grazing the top of the steer's back. The animal never slowed. Calmly and quickly Kate jacked another bullet into the chamber, aimed, and fired again, this time striking the animal in the neck. It slowed its pace but didn't stop.

Behind her, she heard Tate cock the pistol but did not see him aim it at the back of her head. The thoughts that filled his mind would certainly have surprised her if she had been privy to them.

Oh God! Can I do it? If I have to, I'll shoot her first. I can't let her be gored and die a slow, painful death. I love her enough to do it if it comes to that.

Kate was surprisingly calm. It was up to her to stop the enraged steer. She could hear the longhorn's hooves striking the ground as it barreled toward them. There wasn't much time.

She jacked in another bullet and took careful aim. Slowly she squeezed the trigger, and the rifle bucked in her arms. The bullet struck the animal directly between the eyes. Whether it was from pain or surprise, the steer leaped upward as a bellowing noise came from its mouth. It lowered its head, veered away from them, and staggered. Its legs were suddenly unsure. As she watched the animal, Kate's heart pounded like a jungle drum. Finally the steer fell, its nostrils flaring as it breathed its last. One horn pointed directly toward the sky and the other into the ground.

Cautiously Luke came down from the hillside and approached the longhorn. His eyes were locked on the animal, alert for any sign of life, but the beast lay still in the hot afternoon sun. Looking over the dead animal, Luke grinned at Kate.

"It dead," he announced.

Tate leaned up in the travois and reached for the rifle but found that it was locked in Kate's grasp. She stared ahead at the fallen steer as if she expected it to get up and charge them again.

"Kate," Tate gently prodded. "Kate, give me the rifle." He firmly took hold of the gun but didn't try to take it from her. He waited patiently for her to ease her grip.

Slowly, as if awakening from a heavy sleep, she turned to look at him with dazed eyes. Her body began to relax, and the beginning of a smile calmed her face. Finally she let go of the rifle, and Tate placed it on the travois beside him.

"You did good, honey. More than good. You saved our lives."

"I've only shot at bottles and cans. I even refused to go deer hunting with my father." Her voice faded, and she stared at Tate.

It was amazing to her that the feelings she had for him could be so deep when she had known him for such a short time. Every day that she was with him, every moment, was filled with a joy she had only ever heard about, but never experienced.

Tate tugged on her hand and pulled her down to him. She leaned over the travois to hear his whispered words.

"Kiss me, sweetheart."

For just the briefest of moments, Kate hesitated. With her right hand, she stroked the side of his face. His whiskers felt rough against the smooth skin of her fingers. His steely blue eyes looked up at her with such strength and confidence that she felt as if she would melt. Gently she bent toward him, careful not to touch any of his hurts, and placed her lips against his.

The kiss was soft, sweet, and filled with happiness. *How have I been so lucky as to have met this man?* The realization of all that had happened began to slowly sink in. A single tear ran down her cheek. They were safe for the time being.

When their lips parted, Kate continued to stare down at him.

"I don't think that a woman has ever cried from kissing me before." He winked at her.

"Maybe you're a terrible kisser," she retorted, returning the wink.

"You're an amazing woman, Katherine."

All that Kate wanted to do was to tell him what an amazing man he was. But as she opened her mouth to speak, a voice from behind her interrupted. "Done with the mushy stuff?" Luke asked.

Embarrassed, Kate got to her feet and brushed the dirt from her skirt. She was not ashamed or embarrassed to have been caught kissing Tate. Not wanting to hear any more teasing, she wandered around to the front of the horse and rubbed its nose.

"Kid," Tate said with a chuckle, "you've got terrible timing."

"What I do?"

"Don't try to play the dumb Indian with me," Tate said, and began to laugh.

With the threat from the longhorn steer ended, the group continued its journey across the Texas wilderness toward

Muddy Creek. Before they left the gulch, Kate marveled at the skill of the boys cutting large chunks of flesh from the dead animal. At first, the sight shocked her, but she quickly understood that the steer was a source of food they could not allow to go to waste. When the boys finished, they traveled on much as before, with the Indians spread out around the horse and Kate walking beside Tate.

The sun was high in the sky and blazing hot. Kate was thirsty but didn't want to take any of the water should Tate need it later. She watched anxiously for any sign that he was feverish. For most of the afternoon, even with the bumpy ride of the horse-drawn travois, Tate lay with his eyes closed. The memory of his calling her "sweetheart" and asking her to kiss him kept Kate from thinking about the heat and her weariness.

After a couple of hours, Luke brought the group to a stop next to a stand of scrub oaks. Tate opened his eyes when Luke came and crouched down next to him.

"We eat now. Horse tired."

The three Indian boys appeared, untied the travois, and moved the horse out from under it. One of the boys led the horse away while the rest positioned the travois under the shade of a tall oak tree. Luke built a small fire. In answer to Tate's questioning eyes, Luke said, "Small creek not dry."

"Tate needs more water," Kate said. She took the canteen that Luke had removed from the saddle, uncapped it, and lifted Tate's head. His eyes protested, but once the liquid met his lips, he drank thirstily.

"Now you," he said after he had finished.

Kate took a swallow of water. Nothing had ever tasted so

good. It amazed her how many things she'd taken for granted in her life in New York City: that she would always have something to drink, somewhere to sleep, and clothes to protect her body. The last couple of days had shown her how easy her life had been compared to Tate's and Luke's.

"Kate needs to eat," Tate said.

"I'm fine," Kate protested. "You're the one who needs to eat something."

"Don't try to play tough with me, lady. You're the one walking. I'm just along for the ride."

"Some ride," Kate scoffed.

Luke took a packet out of the saddlebag and placed it on the travois beside Tate. "Both eat."

Tate unwrapped the food pack and gave a folded tortilla to Kate before taking one for himself. Handing the package back to Luke, he said, "Whose kitchen were you in while you were in town?"

"I not tell."

"What will I tell your mother?"

Ignoring Tate's ribbing, Luke joined the other boys, and the four of them spoke in their native tongue. Kate thought that it was a beautiful language, one that contrasted with Luke's halting English. Yet again, she was reminded of the many differences between their two worlds.

After she had finished her food, Kate bent down, unbuttoned Tate's shirt, and inspected his wounds. No fresh blood had seeped onto the bandages. Gently lifting them, she examined the cuts. They didn't look like they had improved, but they didn't look any worse either.

"How much farther do we have to go?" she asked.

"Not far. Shouldn't take but another couple of hours."

"How do you feel?"

"I've come this far." He smiled weakly. "I'll make it."

"I know you will."

After they had all eaten and the horse had been watered, they moved out. A bank of clouds had rolled in from the west, and the sun soon disappeared behind them. The cooler air was a welcome relief. Though she was dog tired, Kate concentrated on putting one foot in front of the other. Her mind drifted ahead to the phone call that she would make to her father. It would be hard to tell him everything that had happened, but she knew that she must. He would be surprised to know that his partner, William Jacobs, had played a role in her kidnapping. She would have liked to forget about Edwin's part in the whole sordid affair, but she couldn't. No matter what he told her back in the cabin, he had still gone along with his uncle's plan and was just as guilty.

Finally, after what had seemed an endless afternoon, the group topped a hill and paused, looking down into a small valley. There, in the scant light of the setting sun, was a town. Wood-framed buildings lined the lone street that split the town in half. A couple of red dirt roads branched out from the main street. They were lined with small houses. Behind each house was a shed or barn, many with a cow staked nearby. What caught Kate's eye was a white church steeple poking skyward on the far side of the town. It seemed out of place in this rough setting.

"Is that Muddy Creek?" Kate asked.

"Such as it is," Tate answered. He rose up on his elbow

and yelled to the boy leading the horse. He spoke in the boy's native language. The boy then called out. Soon Luke came trotting back to the travois.

Kate was confused about why they had stopped. She was anxious to get Tate to town to a doctor.

"We have to be patient," Tate explained. "We don't know if either of your kidnappers is there. For all we know, they've been waiting for us to come in. We're in no condition to defend ourselves against them now, and Lyle hasn't had time to get here."

"I almost hope they *are* there," Kate scowled. Anger was in her voice.

"Don't worry. Their time will come." Turning to Luke, Tate asked, "Did you see a big black car when you went in to send the telegram?"

"Not many cars in town. More horses."

"Were there a couple of men that looked like city folks?"

"No. I not look around. I get hell out of there."

"Your mother wouldn't be pleased to hear you swear like that. You're just a kid," Tate said as he turned his head and winked at Kate.

"I not swear at mother."

If the truth were to be told, Tate didn't much want to go into the town. What he wanted was to go out to the ranch to see how Emily was and to let Jorge and Yelena know that he was all right. But before that happened, Kate needed to phone her father and he needed to see a doctor.

"Luke," he finally said, "someone should go into town and see if the way is clear to the doctor's office."

"I'll write a note and explain," Kate said. She reached for

her bag and took out the envelope that had contained the letter from her uncle. She sat down on a nearby rock and began to write. When she finished, she went over to Tate to read the message.

"I explained that you have knife wounds and need attention as soon as possible. I wrote that I was a nurse and told him what I had done to treat your injuries. I also explained that two men are hunting for us and that we want to come into his office without being seen."

"That's good."

Kate folded the letter and handed it to Luke. Without a word, the boy took off at a trot and was soon lost to sight. Kate squatted down beside the travois and placed her hand on Tate's. Her time with him was almost over. Once he was treated and she had contacted her father, they would part. The two of them sat in silence as the sun began to set behind the western hills.

"Now we wait," she said.

Chapter 22

"How long do we have to wait for that shithead?"

Squirrelly lounged on the bunk. He lay flat on his back, his bent arm under his head. He'd spent the last couple of hours sleeping; his snores had nearly driven Eddy insane.

"Damn, Jacobs," he said with a yawn. "Ain't you 'bout bored out of your skull? This ain't what I signed on to do! That asshole better get back soon."

Eddy looked at Squirrelly with disgust. Even out here in the wilderness, he had washed himself and shaved, which was more than Squirrelly had managed. He'd been wearing the same clothes for days and had done little to better his personal hygiene. Quite frankly he stank. They'd been cooped up in the cabin for nearly a week, patiently waiting for word from Hayden, but none had come. They didn't dare move, for fear that he might return, with or without Kate. Their nerves were becoming frayed.

"I wouldn't call him that to his face," Eddy cautioned.

"Yeah, yeah. You're always tryin' to tell me somethin'." Squirrelly rolled off the bunk and grabbed the bottle of whiskey from the table. He tried to mimic Eddy as he gruffly said, "Don't do this. Don't do that. Don't mess with the girl. Don't talk to Hayden that way. I'm sick of it!"

"Don't drink too much of that." Inside, Eddy felt a bit of satisfaction knowing that he was doing exactly what Squirrelly hated most. "It's not as if you're much good to me sober, but I don't want you getting drunk."

Squirrelly stared at him belligerently for a moment before taking a deep drink straight from the bottle. Some of the dark liquor spilled and rolled down his chin onto his shirt

"That's more like it," Squirrelly said as he wiped his mouth with the back of his hand. "Shitfire! As soon as that crazy man gets back here with that bitch, I'm for gettin' the hell outta here. Muddy Creek ain't much, but there's gotta be a honky-tonk around here somewhere."

"Keep your mind on the job you're getting paid for."

"Ain't but one thing I keep my mind on," Squirrelly said as he waved the bottle around. He took another drink of the whiskey before adding, "Screwin'."

Eddy got up out of his chair and left the cabin. He knew that if he stayed, he would hit the man in his filthy mouth. He'd never met a person like him before—a person who wasn't happy unless he was bitching about something. Let him bitch alone.

Outside, he took a deep breath. The sun was setting in the west, and the night air felt cool. Texas wasn't so bad. For someone raised in New York City, being out in wide-open spaces was a pleasant change. He could see the stars, and he could hear a pin drop; the hustle and bustle of the city was something he didn't miss. Although he had to admit he'd rather go out to a party or visit a club than spend another night cooped up with that stupid son of a bitch.

If everything had gone according to plan, his uncle would have received the money by now. William Jacobs was the kind of man who got what he wanted, and what he wanted more than anything else was money. Soon he'd try to take the steelworks away from Kate's father.

Eddy had been aware from the beginning that Squirrelly was more than an extra hand to help him with the kidnapping. Once William had the money, Eddy was sure that it would be Squirrelly's job to get rid of both him and Kate. His uncle couldn't afford to have either one of them come back. Hell, Hayden was probably hired to get rid of Squirrelly. William Jacobs wasn't the type of man who liked to leave loose ends.

Things were moving quickly. Soon he'd have to go into town to see if there was a telegram. He could only imagine how furious his uncle would be if he found out that Kate had escaped. If she were to make it to a telephone, his goose would be cooked. By the time that happened, Edwin Jacobs intended to be far away in Mexico.

As his thoughts turned to Kate, he hoped that whoever was with her knew how to take care of her. It had been five days since Hayden set out after them. If he caught up with her, would he kill Kate or bring her back? The thought of her being alone with him sent a chill down Eddy's spine. He shook his head. He just had to believe that she would be all right.

"What the hell you doin' out there?"

Eddy turned to see Squirrelly leaning against the door frame, the bottle of whiskey held loosely in one hand.

"None of your business." He could tell that Squirrelly was well on his way to getting drunk. His words were beginning to slur, and his mouth was slack.

"I ain't buyin' that line of bullshit. We're in this together. Everythin' you do is my business."

"If that's the case, then let go of that bottle. We're going to town in the morning, and I won't take you if you have a hangover."

"Shitfire!" Squirrelly shouted. "I'm just gettin' started!"

Eddy walked past the other man to the water bucket, picked it up, and headed for the back door.

"That's what I'm afraid of," he muttered, and went back outside.

"What in the hell, Tate! The lady says you went out and got yourself knifed."

Tate, bare-chested, lay on the cot in Dr. Duval's office. He was bone-tired from the effort it had taken to get from the travois through the back door. Even though Luke and Kate had helped steady him, he'd felt like his legs would fall out from under him at any moment. He had not realized how weak he was. The doctor removed the petticoat that Kate had wrapped around Tate's waist, and nodded his head in approval.

"You did a good job," he said to Kate.

"I had to use what was on hand," she replied.

"Never thought that I'd ever see you wearing a woman's

petticoat, Tate," the doctor said. "Wait till I tell the boys at the billiard parlor."

"You would, you old quack."

"Old?" The doctor raised one eyebrow. "Hell, I'm not much older than you are. Besides, I'm not the one out brawling and getting cut up with a knife. You've never seen me limping back into town in a woman's petticoat."

Patrick Duval came to Muddy Creek three years earlier. A stocky man with curly black hair, a crooked nose, and a constant grin, he couldn't be called handsome, but he wasn't homely either. Unmarried, though there was no shortage of girls who would have been more than happy to land him, he was dedicated to his profession. Tate knew him as a rough but kind man, one he would want on his side in a brawl. He'd been bringing Emily to him ever since he arrived in town, and the little girl had taken an instant liking to him.

"Then hurry it up, sawbones. Quit your jawin' and patch me up."

"Watch yourself. You're in my hands now."

The doctor worked quickly and efficiently. He washed the blood from around the cut in Tate's side. He probed the wound gently with his fingers. At the grimace on Tate's face, he went back to the cabinet.

"Can I help, Doctor?" Kate turned from the sink, where she had been scrubbing her hands. While the doctor's office was smaller than the clinic in which she had worked, she felt comfortable amid the equipment.

"Thankfully it doesn't look like there was any real damage. With the way that the bleeding stopped, I'm still going to have to sew him up. I'll give him a shot of morphine first."

"I can take care of that, Doctor," Kate offered.

While Kate was preparing the shot, Dr. Duval looked at the slash across Tate's chest and at the smaller cut in his arm. "Do you want to keep that dimple in your chin, or do you want me to sew it up?"

Tate smiled. "What do you think, Doc?"

"You'd be awfully pretty with it, just like that Gable fellow in the movies."

"Don't be funny. I'm laying here in pain and you're making jokes. Get on with it so I can get out to the ranch and see about Emily."

"How is Emily doing? Is she walking any better?"

"I'm afraid not. I don't know what to do."

"Does she complain of her hip bothering her?" The doctor spoke as he swabbed the wound.

"It must be. Jorge said that she's been crawling again."

As Kate busied herself preparing the shot, her mind was on the conversation between Tate and the doctor. What was the matter with Tate's daughter? Had she had polio? Kate had learned more about Emily in the last five minutes than she had learned in the five days she had spent with Tate. He was a very private man. He had been at ease with her the night that he told her about his daughter. Evidently he hadn't been comfortable enough to mention any illness or injury.

After the doctor had given Tate the shot of morphine, he prepared to stitch up his cuts.

Kate had watched many times as doctors at the clinic

dressed knife wounds and gunshot wounds, and one time even wounds to a man who had been thrown through a glass window. But this was different. This was Tate. She could hardly bear to see the hurt on his face.

"Will you need my help, Doctor?"

"No. I should be able to handle it from here."

"Are you all right, Kate?" Tate glanced up at her. He was more relaxed than when they had come in. The morphine had helped to ease his pain.

"I'm fine. I just thought it might be a good time for me to call my father."

"I don't want you going out there by yourself," Tate said.

"I won't be alone. Luke's waiting outside."

"What's this all about?" Dr. Duval asked.

"The man who knifed me has two accomplices," Tate explained. "They might have followed us to town." Then to Kate, "Tell Luke to come in."

Luke slipped into the room as soon as Kate opened the door. "Tate dead?"

"He wants to talk to you," Kate told him.

"What you want, Tate?" Luke went to stand beside the cot.

"Take Kate to the telephone office. Take the other boys with you and keep your eyes open."

"I keep your woman safe."

Kate did not protest when Luke called her Tate's woman; she rather liked the sound of it. Turning to Tate, she said, "I'll be back as soon as I've talked to my father."

"Stay close to Luke." He looked like he wanted to say

more, but he only held up his hand. She placed her hand in his and gently squeezed it.

Kate followed Luke to the door, but before she left, she glanced over her shoulder. Even as the doctor bent down to begin his stitching, Tate's eyes were on her.

Chapter 23

K ATE SLIPPED OUT INTO THE DARKNESS behind the Indian boy. Her legs were tired. She couldn't remember another time when her feet hurt so badly, but the anticipated call to her father practically overcame her discomfort. She had to hurry to keep alongside Luke, not wanting him to get ahead of her.

Muddy Creek was quiet. Most of the stores that fronted the boardwalk were dark. Light shone from the mercantile, the barbershop, and the billiard parlor. Kate could hear laughter and loud voices coming from the parlor, where men were shooting pool and drinking. Although Prohibition had been repealed the year before, some counties remained dry, and some only allowed the drinking of 3.2 percent beer. Two horses were tied to a hitching post in front of the parlor. Very few cars were parked along the street. Kate was relieved not to see the big black sedan. Overall, the town looked terribly primitive. It reminded Kate of a scene from a western movie.

A cowboy came down the boardwalk toward them, the heels of his boots making a hollow sound on the wooden planks. As he drew near, he put his hand to the tip of his hat and nodded politely. If he wondered what a woman was doing with an Indian boy, it didn't show on his expressionless face.

Suddenly Kate remembered her shabby appearance. Her hair was dirty and stuck to her cheeks with sweat. She had washed her hands at the doctor's office, but she wasn't sure if her face was clean. She longed for a full bath, not having had one since she left New Orleans. Her clothing was worse. Tate had split her skirt, and although she had it held together with safety pins, a good part of her legs still showed. The bloodstains on her blouse had dried to a dark brown. She was certain she looked like a bum who had just come in on the freight train. But there were many things more important to her now than how she looked.

Luke stepped off the boardwalk and into the darkness. He crossed the street and turned a corner, stopping at a modest two-story house that was set behind the board fence. When he started up the walk toward the door, Kate held back.

"Where are we going?"

"Telephone," Luke said impatiently.

"Here?"

"Tate say telephone. This," he said as he pointed, "where telephone at."

"This looks like someone's house."

"Woman here has telephone."

"Well . . . all right. I thought that we were going to an office."

"What an office?" Luke asked, but she knew he was teasing her.

"Never mind," she said, and followed him up the steps.

After Luke had knocked, the door was opened by a short, middle-aged woman wearing an apron. Her eyes were magnified by the thickest pair of spectacles that Kate had ever seen. She smiled pleasantly as she looked first at Kate, then at Luke, and then back at Kate again. The smell of fresh-baked bread wafted from inside the house. Kate's stomach growled. She ignored it and said, "I need to use a telephone."

"Come in." Kate took Luke by the hand and pulled him into the house behind her. The woman looked skeptically at the Indian boy but kept on smiling at Kate.

"Can I make a long-distance call from here?" Kate asked.

"Where to?" the woman said.

"New York City."

"I've never called New York before, but there has to be a first time for everything." Kate followed her into the living room where a switchboard had been set up. The large wooden frame that held the contraption stood along one wall next to a picture of a girl on a swinging gate. A dozen wires were plugged into the board. Lights blinked from several more outlets. The woman sat down in front of the board on a well-padded chair and put on a headset. "Do you know the number?"

Kate scribbled it on a pad that lay next to the board. "I'd like to reverse the charges." She stood back and waited, her heart pounding with anticipation of hearing her father's voice.

"Operator," the woman said into the mouthpiece, "this is Merna at Muddy Creek. Connect me with Central. I'm making a call to New York City." After a brief pause, she added, "Thank you. I'll wait."

Turning to Kate, she said, "First we have to go through Dallas, and then Chicago, before we can get to New York." She turned back to the switchboard when a blinking light drew her attention.

"Operator. Hello, Mrs. Bishop. Yes . . . I'll ring Marcia." She plugged another line into the switchboard.

With each passing moment, Kate's excitement increased as she came closer to speaking with her father. It was so long since she had heard his voice. She knew that he would be gravely disappointed when she told him about his trusted friend, William Jacobs, being involved in her kidnapping. She was anxious to tell him about the man who had rescued her.

Out of the corner of her eye, she saw Luke move toward the picture that was hanging next to the switchboard. He peered intently at the image of the little girl on the gate. She heard him mutter, "Silly woman."

A hand on her arm drew her back to the telephone operator. She was holding out a headset like the one that she was wearing. "If you want privacy, honey, I'll go to the other room."

Kate accepted the headset, slipped it over her head, and adjusted it for her ears. "Thank you."

As the woman left, she called back, "Let me know when you're finished."

Through the headset, Kate heard the phone ringing, then Malcolm's voice saying, "Tyler residence."

"Malcolm, this is Katherine," she nearly shouted. It felt wonderful to hear a familiar voice, even if it was the butler's. "I want to speak to my father."

"Miss Katherine?"

"Yes, Malcolm, it's me. Please get my father."

"At once!" Through the earpiece, she heard the usually calm butler shouting excitedly, "Mr. Tyler! Mr. Tyler! It's Miss Katherine on the telephone!" Back into the mouthpiece, he said, "He's coming, miss."

Kate glanced at the clock that hung behind the switchboard. It was late in the evening, and it was even later in New York City. She imagined that her father had retired to his room for the night. There was a loud click as he lifted the telephone and bellowed, "Kate! Kate! Is it you?"

"Yes, it's me, Daddy! I'm all right!" At the sound of his voice, tears began to well in the corners of Kate's eyes. She swallowed the sob in her throat. "Oh, Daddy! I've got so much to tell you."

"Honey, I've been so worried. Where are you?"

"I'm in Texas. In a town called Muddy Creek."

"Did the bastards hurt you?" he yelled.

"No, no! Your friend in the Texas Rangers sent a man to find me. He got me away from them and brought me to town. He kept me safe."

"Oh, thank God!" her father exclaimed. "I've been worried sick. Those goddamn bastards! I did everything they asked of me. They said they would let you go."

"Did you pay the ransom?"

"I paid it, every damn dime! I've been waiting for the last twenty-four hours for them to call me and tell me where to find you. I hadn't received the call and was afraid that I'd never see you again."

"Daddy, you won't get a call. There's something that I need to tell you." Kate paused and took a deep breath. She knew that what she had to say would be difficult for him to hear. "One of the kidnappers was Edwin Jacobs."

"What in the hell?" he shouted.

"It's true. He and two other men took me from the train and drove me to a cabin out in the wilderness. They kept me there while they waited to get the ransom money."

"That son of a bitch! What will I tell his uncle?"

"Wait, Daddy," Kate said as she drew another deep breath. "Eddy was blackmailed into kidnapping me. He didn't want to do it, but he was following someone else's orders. In the end, he decided to go along, thinking he could protect me, and he did to a certain extent."

"Whose orders?"

Kate hesitated before she answered. "His uncle's, William Jacobs."

Silence was all that she received from the other end of the line. She knew that her father would believe her but that he would be in shock that the man who had helped him to build Tyler-Jacobs Steelworks had betrayed him.

John Tyler asked hoarsely, "Are you sure?"

"One of the men with Eddy was a lowlife named Squirrelly. Do you know him?"

"I've heard of him. He's Felerri's kid. His father's a bigtime crook here in the city."

"Several times, Squirrelly mentioned something about William. From that, and a couple of other things that Eddy said, I learned that William was behind it. He had me kidnapped to get your money."

"I can't believe it!"

"It's true, Daddy."

"I'm so glad that Lila and Susie aren't here. They're at another one of those god-awful parties for Senator Forrest. They'll both be devastated when they find out William and Eddy are involved."

"You need to be careful, Daddy," Kate warned. "William never planned for me to come back."

"Oh my God!"

"He won't hesitate to hurt you. Don't tell anyone else unless you have to."

"You're right," John agreed. "But I'm more worried about you. I'm going to call my friend Lyle Holmgaard in Waco and let him know you're in Muddy Creek."

"We've sent him a wire."

"Then stay right there until he arrives. I'm coming to see you too. Where can we find you?"

"I'll be with the man who rescued me. His name is Tate Castle. The Ranger will know where to find us."

"You can trust Lyle. When you see him, tell him I want these men prosecuted to the fullest extent of the law."

"I will. Daddy, I need to go," Kate said. "The man who rescued me was badly hurt and I need to tend to him." As happy as she was to speak with her father, she worried about Tate and wanted to go back to him.

"I understand. It's wonderful to know that you're safe."

"I love you, Daddy. I'll call again as soon as I can."

"I love you too, honey."

"Use your head, Tate. You know that I can't let you go home tonight. I just sewed you up. You won't be doing Emily any good if you bust open your stitches and bleed to death." Dr. Duval stood back from the cot, put his hands on his hips, and shook his head.

"I need to let her and the Gomezes know that I'm all right," Tate complained. "They were expecting me back home days ago. I need to get the horses ready that I've sold to the army. They'll be here by the first of the month to get them. I'm leaving tonight."

"Do you want to head home only to have to turn around and come right back? That's what will happen if you're foolish enough to leave here tonight."

"I'm telling you . . ." A loud knocking on the door interrupted Tate. "Wait and find out who it is before you open the door, Doc. Could be those men looking for us."

Dr. Duval nodded and called out, "Who is it?"

"It's me—Kate."

After letting Kate and Luke into the office, the doctor closed the door and turned the key in the lock. Kate immediately went to where Tate lay and placed her palm on his forehead. She lifted it and looked at the doctor.

"Have you taken his temperature? He feels feverish."

"I'm not feverish," Tate insisted. "I'm just sweating. It's almost July, you know."

"Doesn't feel like sweat to me," she countered.

The doctor pulled a thermometer from a drawer and

handed it to Kate. She looked down at the man on the cot with a frown on her face. "Open your mouth and don't fuss."

Tate stared at her silently for a moment. She wasn't sure if he would cooperate. Finally he opened his mouth, and she slipped the thermometer under his tongue. With her finger and thumb, she pinched his lips together.

"Mmm mm mmm."

"Don't talk," Kate ordered him. She looked at the doctor and winked.

"He bucks me every step of the way," Dr. Duval said. "He follows your instructions better than mine."

Kate pulled the thermometer from Tate's mouth, held it up, and then handed it over to the doctor. Dr. Duval looked at it closely and frowned. "Your temp is up a degree. No reason to be alarmed. At least not yet."

"You're only saying that because you don't want me to go home."

"Now that I know you have a temperature, I insist that you stay here for the night. End of conversation." Dr. Duval turned his back and began to sterilize the thermometer.

"You should listen to what the doctor says. You're in no condition to be moved."

"I'm needed at home," he protested.

"What you need is to get some rest. We can go out to your ranch in the morning."

"But if I stay here, I'll have to find somewhere for you to stay."

"She can stay right here," the doctor offered. "There's a little room with a cot just off this one."

"Would I hear him if he needed me?" Kate asked.

"It's right here." The doctor opened a door that was connected to the surgery. A small cot stood against one wall. It was no more than ten feet from where Tate lay. "If he starts moaning in pain in the middle of the night," Dr. Duval said with a grin, "it's because he wants you to come keep him company."

Kate smoothed the hair from Tate's forehead, then left her hand lying gently against his ear. "That solves that problem. Now there's no reason for you not to stay the night."

Tate was reluctant but, with a sigh, gave in. "All right. But I'm leaving first thing in the morning, even if I have to steal a wagon to do it."

"Then you'd be in jail instead of at home." Kate rolled her eyes at the doctor. "I swear, he's the most bullheaded man I've ever met!"

"What 'bullheaded' mean?" Luke asked. "Tate don't have bull head."

Chapter 24

INSIDE THE SMALL ROOM IN DR. DUVAL'S OFFICE, Kate prepared for bed. The doctor considerately provided a teakettle of warm water, a towel, and an old flannel nightshirt.

"This isn't very fancy, but it's clean," the doctor said.

"It's fine. I'm eager to get out of these filthy clothes."

"If you need anything, my room is just beyond the office. Just call out. I'm a light sleeper."

"Thank you for everything, Doctor. I'll check on Tate during the night. If his temperature is up, I'll wake you."

After the doctor had left, Kate washed herself from head to foot and slipped the nightshirt over her head. It was large, covered her from shoulders to knees, and was much better than her torn skirt and bloodstained blouse.

She opened the door a crack and looked out. The doctor had left a dim light on. She could see Tate on the cot. His head was turned toward her, his eyes open. She glanced down to be sure that she was covered with the big night-shirt, then pushed the door open and walked barefoot into the room. She made her way to the cot, knelt down, and placed her palm on Tate's forehead.

"Are you hurting? Is that why you're not asleep?"

"I hurt in places I didn't even know I had."

"Aren't you glad that we didn't try to leave tonight?" Before Tate could argue the point, she said, "Let me go and get the doctor. He'll give you something for the pain."

"No, I don't want anything that'll make me sleep."

"Then what can I do? Do you want me to tell you a bedtime story?"

"I've always been partial to the story of the three bears."

"I thought you might like Sleeping Beauty." She laughed softly.

"You'd better go to bed. You've had a rough day."

"Not any worse than the four or five days before this one. I'm starting to get used to it."

"It isn't every day that someone saves a man's life. You did it two days in a row. If it weren't for you, I wouldn't be here in this bed complaining about how much I hurt. You were as calm as anyone I ever knew."

"What did you expect me to do?"

"What I'd wanted was for you to do as I told you. When Hayden attacked us, I told you to run." Smiling, he added, "I suppose I should be glad that you didn't."

"I don't always do what people tell me to do."

"I'm beginning to find that out." Tate's hand dropped down and covered hers where it lay on the cot. He held it tightly. "You're a woman to ride the river with, Katherine."

In an imitation of Luke's voice, she said, "What that mean?"

Tate pulled her hand up and held it on his chest. She could feel his heartbeat through his shirt. "Cracking jokes? You must be feeling better. It's either that or you're getting sassy."

"I do feel better after talking to my father."

"Did you tell him about his business partner?"

"I did. It was hard for him to believe that William would do such a thing, but he'll think about what I told him and he'll know what to do. Unfortunately he's already paid the ransom, and the one thing that really bothers my father is to have someone take something from him. First William took me, and then he took my father's money. You can bet one thing: He'll see that William Jacobs gets what he deserves."

"Did he say anything about calling Lyle?"

"He said that he would. I told him to tell his Ranger friend that I would be with you, so that he would know where to find me."

"You're coming home with me. You'll be safer with me than if you stay here in town waiting for Lyle." At these words, Kate's heart fluttered. She'd hoped that she wouldn't be left behind in Muddy Creek when Tate went home. She tried to hide a smile as Tate continued. "We don't know what the other two polecats are up to. I don't think they'd just leave the area without finding out what had happened to you and Hayden."

"They were afraid of Hayden."

"They should've been. He was a dangerous man. If you had hesitated, he would have killed me and then you." Tate squeezed her hand. "I'm thinking it was in the plan all along to get rid of you and the other two."

"Really?"

"Your father's partner wouldn't have allowed you and his nephew to come back. He could be sent to the chair. Since what happened to the Lindbergh baby, kidnapping's a federal offense and punishable by death. Hayden would have made sure that you never left Texas alive."

Kate knew he was right. Even now that Hayden was dead, the vision of him drawing his knife frightened her. He would have killed them all. "It shocks me to think that William was behind all of this. He always insisted that my sister, Susan, and I call him 'uncle.' He was so nice to us, bringing us presents and taking us to lunch when Daddy was away."

"He sounds like a good con man."

"I've not had much experience with con men."

"I've dealt with a few," he said with a frown. "You'd better get some sleep. I want to leave as early in the morning as I can. I'm hoping the doc can help me find a way to get to the ranch. If not, I'll send Luke out to get Jorge. The two of them can come in with the truck to take me home."

Kate placed her palm on his brow. It was warm, but not any more so than when they had taken his temperature. She did not want to leave him. This might be the last time that she would be alone with him. Tate seemed reluctant to let go of her hand.

"I'll have to go so you can get your rest," Kate murmured.

"Sit down here," Tate said, and patted a spot on the bed

next to him. "We couldn't decide on a bedtime story, so why don't you tell me about your life back in New York."

"It all seems so ordinary and boring now. You're the one that's had the exciting life. Tell me something about you. Tell me when you first met Hayden."

"You don't want to hear about that."

The last thing that she wanted was for him to stop talking, so she quickly said, "Then tell me about your daughter and your ranch. What about Jorge? Does he work for you?"

"Yes. He and Yelena, his wife, are a Mexican couple who live with us. They're more like family than hired help. I don't know what I would have done without them after Hazel left."

"Hazel is your wife?" Kate asked tentatively.

"Was. Now she's my ex-wife. We divorced a few months after she left."

"Does she ever come back to see Emily?"

"No, she hasn't been back once since the day she left. Emily wouldn't know her if they met walking down the street. Hazel left when she was only a few months old. Yelena's the only mother she's ever known. There's a part of me that will always hate Hazel for what she did."

"You shouldn't hate her too much. She gave you Emily."

"I suppose you're right. For that, I am grateful. Emily is the most important thing in my life. I only wish that I had the means to take her to a hospital where they could fix her leg."

Kate picked up his hand in both of hers and held it in her lap. This was a difficult subject for Tate. She was reminded of the conversation that he had had with Dr. Duval and wondered if it was a topic that he could talk to her about. After a moment's pause, she decided to ask, "What's wrong with her?"

Tate's eyes met hers, and she saw them soften. "One of her legs is shorter than the other."

"How much shorter?"

"A little more than four inches. When she walks for too long, her hips hurt."

"Have you tried a shoe with a built-up sole?"

"We had one, but it was too heavy."

"That's too bad. With the right shoe and practice, she'd be able to move around easily."

"The biggest problem is that we've spoiled her. She knows that when she cries, Yelena will carry her. She's getting too big for Yelena to carry, and at some point, it'll have to stop. I want her to be as much like other children as possible."

Tate had never talked so frankly with a woman before. The only person he had discussed Emily with, outside of the family and the doctors, was Lyle. He didn't feel awkward or uncomfortable talking with Kate about his daughter.

"I'm eager to meet her," Kate said softly.

"You like kids?"

"Of course, I do. Who doesn't?"

"Hazel didn't. She was angry from the day she found out she was pregnant, all the way until the day she left. Besides not wanting a child, when she had Emily and saw her deformity, Hazel couldn't pack her bags fast enough."

"It isn't normal for a mother not to love her child."

"Hazel wasn't normal," Tate said matter-of-factly.

"Then Emily is better off without her."

"I know. But will Emily understand when she's older?"

"All I had was my father when I was a small child. He had to be both my parents, but I don't recall feeling deprived because I didn't have a mother. I know that Daddy felt guilty about it. I'm sure that's the reason he married Lila, my stepmother. While she and I have had our disagreements, she was good to me when I was little."

The thought entered Tate's mind before he could stop it. *You'd make a good stepmother, Katherine.* As soon as he considered it, he began to argue in his mind against the idea. He could not envision Kate Tyler, a woman from New York City, pulling water from a well, canning beans, or baking bread. He was sure she was eager to get on the train and be on her way to California. He would have only a couple more days, at the most, with her.

He looked away from her, then back. When he did, his eyes caught hers. He tugged on her hand and pulled her down toward him.

"I will always remember the time I've spent with you, Katherine."

"It isn't over yet, is it?"

"It will be as soon as Lyle gets here. He'll put you on a train, take you back to Waco, or stay with you in Muddy Creek until your father arrives to get you or you continue your trip. Either way, you'll have to go."

"I—I don't want to go yet. I want to get to know Emily."

"And me?"

The question hung heavy in the air. Staring into his eyes, Kate answered, "Yes, you too."

"I wish we could have met under different circumstances. If I could go back to that platform in Simon, I would have walked over to you and introduced myself. I would have done something—hell, anything—to make sure you noticed me."

"But I did notice you that night. You may not be aware of it, but, Tate Castle, you're a very handsome man. When I spoke to you, your blue eyes looked right through me. I was scared to be on that dark platform, but I was thankful you were there."

"I thought you were too pretty to be real. Untouchable."

"And now?" Kate laughed reflexively. "I can't be very pretty after all we've been through. My nose is blistered, my hair hasn't been washed in two weeks, and I'm sure I smell as bad as that longhorn steer."

"You're prettier now that I've gotten to know you; prettier than you were on the train." He slid his hand up behind her neck and pulled her head down to his. It only took the slightest pressure. Their lips met in a soft, tentative kiss. He pulled her tighter to him, and the kiss became deeper and more passionate. It seemed to go on forever.

Kate floated in a sensuous haze. She didn't want the kiss to end, but it did. She lifted her head and looked down at him. He was so handsome.

"I don't want you to go yet," he said huskily.

"I won't be leaving for a few days."

"That's not what I mean. I don't want you to go to that other room. I want you to stay here with me."

A small excited laugh escaped her. "What would the doctor think? I'm supposed to be a professional. Nurses don't sleep with their patients."

"I doubt that we'd do much sleeping."

"Why, Tate Castle! Are you having lewd thoughts?"

Tate grinned up at her and said, "What 'lewd' mean?"

" 'Lewd' means—ah—that you have something other than sleeping on your mind."

"What man wouldn't have lewd thoughts with a beautiful woman sitting on his bed in a nightshirt?"

"Maybe I'd better go back to my own bed."

"I think you'd better stay. My fever may go up in the night."

Kate laughed softly. "You would make a good con man."

"Just a little while longer?"

There was nothing she would rather do than spend the night with Tate. To feel his arms around her and his breath on her face would be heavenly. But she wasn't ready to take that step and was fearful he could reopen his wounds. Instead, she tried to compromise. "I guess I can stay a minute or two more."

"That isn't long enough for even one kiss."

"Then we'd better get started." She leaned over and kissed him gently and sweetly on the forehead. When she leaned back and looked at him, a frown creased his face.

"I like the other kind better," Tate grumbled.

"Complaints, complaints. I can tell you're on the mend."

He lifted his head from the cot and moved toward her. Hungrily his eyes slid over her face. Their breaths mingled for an instant before she lowered her face and covered his mouth with hers. When their passionate kiss ended, he pressed his cheek to hers.

"Sweetheart," he murmured, his hand stroking the nape of her neck. "I'll never get enough of kissing you now that I've had a taste. I hate to say it, but I'm almost glad you were kidnapped. Otherwise I never would have met you."

She lifted his knuckles to her lips. There had been no words of love spoken, but something wonderful throbbed between them. Her lips touched his, and she was filled by feelings of sweet intimacy.

A stirring in the room beyond jarred her out of her contentment. "I must go," she whispered.

"See you in the morning, honey."

After she had returned to her room, she lay in the tiny bed and replayed their conversation in her head. It was as if her heart would burst from her chest! *Honey. Sweetheart.* Kate closed her eyes and prayed that what had happened was real. She prayed that he really meant the endearments.

Chapter 25

THE CONVERTED SEDAN THAT DR. DUVAL used to transfer patients to the Alpine hospital was parked outside the back door. Tate lay on a canvas sling that had been rigged in the back of the vehicle. Kate sat beside him as the car was started and began to glide slowly down Muddy Creek's main street.

The small town was quiet in the early morning hours; few cars and even fewer people moved along the boardwalks. At the end of the block, Tate called out for the driver to stop and then asked Kate to go into the mercantile and get a present to take to Emily.

"What shall I get?"

"She likes good-smelling things. Get my wallet out of my pocket."

"I have a few dollars in my bag."

Kate knew she was a spectacle in her split skirt and dirty blouse, but she held her head high and entered the store. When she returned, she carried a small bottle of Blue Waltz perfume. She climbed into the back of the car and handed it to Tate "Do you think she'll like this?"

"I'm sure she will. It smells good."

Kate noticed that people on the sidewalk were stopping to watch as Dr. Duval's car went past. The car must be well known, and they would be wondering who was going to the hospital. A small girl, her stark white dress bright in the morning sun, stood in the drive of the Phillips 66 filling station and waved. Reflexively Kate waved back, and the little girl smiled before disappearing from view.

In the light of day, Kate noticed things about the town that she hadn't seen in her nighttime trip to the telephone office. Muddy Creek must have been a wild and woolly place in its heyday. A few unpainted buildings on the main street still showed signs of dull lettering. One said "SALOON" and another said "TONSORIAL." Smaller letters underneath the latter sign read "HAIRCUT AND BATH." A group of men were constructing a building at the end of the street. They stopped to watch the doctor's car pass, wiping their brows with the backs of their hands.

"What did Luke say about being left behind?" Kate asked.

"Nothing. He'll be fine."

Tate had assured Luke that Jorge would come back to town to bring him and the other Indian boys out to the ranch. They were going to help get the horses ready for their delivery to the patrol.

Kate looked down the flat road that stretched to the horizon. The Texas sun sent shimmering heat waves over the grassy plain. Dried grass rolled back on each side of the road. No trees grew along this stretch. Kate thought they might as well be traveling across a space as empty and limitless as the sky. They were alone except for a small herd of cattle and a windmill that was silhouetted against the blue sky. It was a harsh but fascinating country.

When she noticed Tate straining to look out the window, she lifted his head. "We're almost there," he said. The car turned down a narrow lane at the end of which was a weathered plank house with a porch that spanned the two front doors. At the side of the house was a pole-fence corral. A number of horses were eating from large piles of hay.

Tate lay back in the sling. The car came to a stop between a shed and the house. A Mexican man came hurrying toward the car as the driver got out and opened the back doors. A woman carrying a little girl in her arms stood on the porch.

"Señor Castle!" the Mexican man called.

"Hello, Jorge. Don't worry, I'm not badly hurt," Tate hastened to say. Kate knew he didn't want them to see him this way. "Just some stitches in my side. Dr. Duval insisted that I come home in this contraption."

Kate climbed out of the car and stood near the back. She'd had him to herself for the last several days, but now she had to share him with his family.

"Is Emily on the porch?" Tate asked.

"Sí, señor."

"Can you bring her down here to the car? I don't want her to be frightened when they pull me out of this thing."

Jorge went to the porch and took Emily from Yelena. As

they approached the car, the little girl called out, "Daddy! Daddy!"

Tate held out his arms, and Jorge raised the girl up into the car. She looked tiny in her father's embrace. Emily threw her little arms around Tate's neck and held him tightly. "I missed you, Daddy!"

"I missed you too, sweetheart."

"Did you bring me something?"

"Sure did." Tate reached down and handed her the bottle of perfume. "Smell it, honey."

"Oh, Daddy," Emily shouted as she took a whiff of the bottle. "It smells good!"

"Have you been a good girl for Yelena?"

"Sometimes," the child muttered as she looked away from him. As her eyes tried to avoid her father's gaze, they suddenly landed on Kate standing at the back of the car. For a moment, the little girl stared. "Who's that?"

"That lady is a nurse, honey. Her name is Miss Tyler."

"Is she gonna stay here?" A look of distaste crossed Emily's face. The strength of the child's reaction was surprising.

"For a little while."

"I don't like her."

"You should. She's helping to get me well."

"I can help you. Tell her to go away!"

"Emily," he chided. "Be nice."

Jorge reached into the back of the car and lifted the child up in his arms. Emily began to whine and kick her feet out in frustration at being taken away from her father.

Kate's eyes were drawn to the girl's legs. One was considerably shorter than the other.

Jorge walked away with the child and handed her to Yelena. "Stay with Yelena, *niña*. I help get your papa in the house." As she was taken to the door, Emily's eyes stayed locked onto the strange woman.

Kate moved into the car to look at Tate's wounds. She lifted the sheet and inspected the bandages. There was no fresh blood staining them. She'd been concerned that the drive, or having Emily against him, might have caused them to open.

"Your little girl is beautiful."

Tate ignored the compliment. "I'm sorry for what she said."

"I understand her anxiety."

Tate sighed. "I've been away too much lately. I need to stay home and use a stronger hand with her. I'd hate for her to grow up and be like her mother."

Before Kate could answer, Jorge came back to the car. He looked surprised to see her bending over Tate. She straightened and pulled the blanket back up to cover his chest.

"Jorge," Tate said from the car, "this is Miss Tyler. She's the lady that Lyle wanted me to find. She's a nurse and will be staying here with us for a while."

A wide grin split Jorge's face. "*Hola,* señorita."

"How do you do?" The friendly smile on the man's face eased a bit of Kate's apprehension.

Jorge climbed into the car as Kate exited. The driver took hold of one end of the stretcher-sling and unfastened the chains that held it in place. Jorge did the same on the other end, and they eased Tate down onto the floor of the car.

"Can you handle that end?" the driver asked.

"Sí."

Kate held the car door open. She was nervous about how they were going to get Tate into the house. The driver, however, seemed confident. Jorge lifted his end of the litter, and they easily moved Tate out. Kate went ahead of them and opened the door of the house.

As they entered the kitchen, Yelena was setting Emily down on the table.

"Why are they carrying Daddy?" The child's voice was shrill.

"He has a little hurt in his side," Kate explained. "But don't worry. He'll be all right in a few days." She followed the men until they reached a room at the front of the house and set Tate gently onto the bed. When Jorge and the driver left the room, carrying the empty litter, Kate went in.

"Wasn't an easy ride, huh?" she said as she wiped beads of perspiration from Tate's brow.

"I sure as hell wouldn't want to do it every day."

"Rest awhile. Later I'll change your bandages."

Yelena came into the room carrying Emily. She set her down on the edge of the bed next to her father. Tate introduced the two women. "Pleased to meet you," Kate said, and held out her hand. Yelena took it and smiled warmly.

"Emily cry for her daddy. Want to see him."

"Be careful and not hurt your daddy," Kate said kindly.

"I won't." Resentment was in the child's voice.

"I'm sure you wouldn't do it on purpose, sweetie. Let

your daddy rest for a bit, and later I'll show you where he's hurt."

"You go. Me and Yelena will take care of Daddy."

"Emily," Tate said firmly. He rose up on one elbow and fixed a stern look on his daughter. "Miss Tyler will be here for a few days. I expect you to treat her nicely." Sensing that this was a conversation that would be better if she weren't in the room, Kate glanced at Yelena and slipped out the door.

"I don't like her." Emily's voice reached every corner of the small house.

Tate frowned, his patience stretched to the breaking point. "I have never spanked you, but I just might do it if you're not nice to a guest in our home. She saved me from a bad man."

Emily's face crumbled, and tears began to roll down her cheeks. "I don't want the present," she sobbed, and reached into her pocket for the bottle of perfume. "You don't like me!"

"Of course, I like you. That's why I'm telling you this. I want you to be nice so other people will like you too."

Yelena, who had heard this conversation several times before, said, "I get dinner ready," and left father and daughter alone in the room.

When she reached the kitchen, Kate was standing at the window watching the doctor's vehicle head back down the lane. She turned when she heard Yelena enter the room and said, "I'm sorry if my being here is a bother. Tate insisted I stay with him until his friend Lyle gets here. Besides, the doctor wanted me to tend to his injuries. He has three deep knife wounds."

"You are nurse?" Yelena asked.

"Yes. I worked in a clinic in New York City."

"Who do this, señorita?" Kate's head turned at the sound of another voice. Jorge stood at the far end of the kitchen. She hadn't heard him enter the room.

"A man named Hayden tried to kill him."

"Ah, no. That one again. He not give up."

"He will now. He's dead."

"*Madre de Dios!*" Jorge exclaimed. "That good. He bad man."

"Hayden and two other men kidnapped me. Even though Hayden is dead, the other men are still out there somewhere."

"You safe here."

Yelena left the room and came back a minute later with a skirt and blouse thrown over her arm. "Señor say you will want bath. He say your clothes stay on train. I bring you clean ones to wear while I wash others."

"Thank you very much." Simply washing herself with a towel at the doctor's office had been welcome, but a full bath with clean clothes to wear would be wonderful.

The Mexican woman handed Kate the clothes, a towel, and a cake of good-smelling soap. "Señor bring this for little one."

"Are you sure I should use it?"

"Use it and smell nice. Go with Jorge. He show you bath."

Kate followed the short Mexican man out to the barn. It was built out of the same wood as the main ranch house and painted to match. Jorge proudly showed her to a lean-to built on to the side of it. It was small with a wooden slat floor. A rope hung down from the ceiling. Grinning, Jorge said, "Pull the rope, the water come down."

"Is it cold?" Kate asked as she laid her towel and clean clothes down on a small bench to one side of the lean-to.

"Not cold. Sun warm the water."

Bidding her to enjoy her bath, Jorge went out and closed the door behind him. Kate looked to see if there was a bar or latch, but there was none. *Oh, well! They take public baths in Europe, don't they?* She giggled at the thought.

She stripped quickly. Standing under the shower, she pulled the rope and a splash of water came down. It felt wonderful! She soaped her wet head and then the rest of her body. She pulled the rope again to release more water. After several bucketfuls had poured over her, she got out from under the contraption. Kate had taken many a wonderful bath in her day, but none had been as refreshing as this one. She rubbed the towel vigorously over her head before slipping on the skirt Yelena had given her. It was too big in the waist and came only to her knees, but it was clean. The blouse, with a deep scoop neck and puffed sleeves, was plenty large, but too short to tuck into the waistband of her skirt. The neck was so big that she wondered if it should hang off one shoulder. She put on her moccasins and left the lean-to.

In the yard, between the barn and the house, was a clothesline. Kate hung up her towel, stepped up onto the porch, and went into the kitchen. Yelena was at the stove. She turned to smile when Kate entered.

"That was wonderful. Thank you for the clean clothes. I've been wearing those dirty ones for more than a week."

"I will wash them, señorita."

"I don't want to be any trouble." Kate smiled. "I'll rinse out the blouse."

Kate spent the rest of the afternoon working around the kitchen with Yelena. She was hesitant about going into Tate's room, since Emily was still in there with him. The little girl was very possessive of her father. Children usually liked Kate, but this one didn't. It would be a challenge to win her over.

After the evening meal, Yelena showed her to a cot in Emily's room. Kate's handbag and newly cleaned clothes sat on the cot. While Yelena washed the little girl and got her ready for bed, Kate went to Tate's room to change his bandages. She carried with her the supplies that Dr. Duval had sent with them. When she entered, Tate leaned up on one elbow and grinned.

"That's quite a contraption you have out there for taking a bath." She sat down on the edge of his bed. It felt wonderful to be near him again.

"It serves its purpose." He lifted his hand to her head and ran his forked fingers through her damp hair. His touch was even better than the bath had been. "It feels nice."

"I never enjoyed a bath so much."

"I'm looking forward to one of my own." He slid his hand down from her hair and rubbed the fabric of the blouse between his fingers. "I see that Yelena found you some clean clothes."

"She did." She plucked at the blouse neck, suddenly self-conscious. "I didn't know what to do with the neck. Do they pull it down over one shoulder?"

"Only if you're at a cantina."

"What's that?"

Tate's grin widened. "I guess you could call it a poor man's nightclub."

"Then I guess I'll keep it on both shoulders."

"I don't know." Tate chuckled. "You'd look pretty nice to me."

"I wouldn't suggest teasing me, Tate Castle."

"And why's that? What'll you do to me?"

"There are any number of things that I could do to you as soon as I take those bandages off. I might decide to wash your wounds with whiskey. Or if you make me really mad, I'll drink the whiskey and pour vinegar on your wounds."

"I wouldn't like that."

Both of them laughed at their playful banter. Kate was suddenly struck by the thought that this was one of the few times they'd been able to be completely at ease with each other since they met. It was nice to be able to relax. Then, just as she was about to comment on her thought, Tate frowned.

"I'm sorry for what Emily said to you today."

"About her wanting me to go?"

"Yes." Before continuing, Tate took one of Kate's hands and gave it a gentle squeeze. "She doesn't want to share me with anyone."

"That's understandable. I felt somewhat the same about my own father."

"What did he do about it?"

Kate thought for a minute. "I think he made me feel that

no matter who else was around, I was still his favorite. I was still his little girl and nothing would change that."

Tate nodded his head and said, "There haven't been many women around since Hazel left. Emily knew that those who did come here weren't going to stay. For some reason, it's different with you. Even when I tried to explain that you'd be here for just a few days, she was still upset."

"Why is she upset if she knows I'm leaving?"

"Emily doesn't understand time. To her, a few days seems like forever."

There was a knock at the door, and Yelena entered. "Emily in bed. She want you to see her."

"Tell her I can't come to her tonight," Tate explained.

"She want story, señor."

"How would she feel about my telling her a story?" Kate asked. "I know a few that could entertain her. It might be a chance for us to get to know each other."

Yelena shrugged and left the doorway.

Tate gave Kate's hand another squeeze. "She may not be nice to you."

"I've handled children who weren't nice. I won't be hurt by anything she says. Let me give it a try."

"You'll come back?"

"You want me to?"

"I do."

As Kate got up and left the room, she looked back over her shoulder to see Tate watching her go and felt her heart stumble. *Careful,* she cautioned herself. *You're out of your element here. You could very well leave with a broken heart.*

Before going into Emily's room, Kate stood in the hallway and took a deep breath. She was confident that she'd be able to get Emily to like her; it would just take some effort. When she entered, the little girl was lying in bed, her eyes fixed on the doorway.

"Emily," she said gently, "your daddy can't get out of bed to come see you. He asked me to tell you a story for him."

"But I want my daddy," she fussed. Looking at her, Kate could see the ways she resembled her father. Their eyes were the same clear blue, with dark brows and lashes. They both had the same wild black hair.

"I'm sorry, sweetheart. But it would hurt your daddy terribly to get up."

"No, it wouldn't. Daddy never hurts."

"He does, but he just doesn't tell you." Kate knew she needed to change the subject from Tate. If they kept talking about him, Emily would want to see him more and more. "Have you heard the story of Cinderella?"

"I don't like it."

"Well, how about the story of the naughty little girl who wouldn't stop saying, 'I don't like it,' and refused to eat her supper?"

"I don't know that one." Kate saw a flicker of curiosity in Emily's face. "Is it in a storybook?"

"Oh, yes. Where I live, everyone knows this story."

"Where do you live?"

"A place called New York City."

Emily stared at her for a moment before saying, "I'll listen to your story."

"May I sit down next to you?"

"Uh-huh."

Kate sat down on the edge of the bed and folded her hands in her lap. She smiled gently before starting her story. "In a kingdom far, far away, there lived a little girl named Elizabeth, who was six years old."

"I'm six," Emily said.

"Elizabeth had pretty dark hair, just like yours. She was always saying, 'I don't like it.' When her father bought her a new dress, she said, 'I don't like it.' When a friend of her mother painted her a picture, she said, 'I don't like it.' One day her father brought her a beautiful birthday cake. Without thinking, she said, 'I don't like it,' and her father took the birthday cake away. That night a fairy princess came and asked Elizabeth if she had liked the beautiful dolly that she had put inside the cake. The next morning the little girl ran to find her father. 'I want my cake! I want my cake!' Her father frowned as he said, 'Sorry, honey. You said you didn't like it, so I gave your cake to Sally, the washerwoman's little girl. She wanted the cake and was very happy.' "

"But the dolly," Emily said.

Without answering, Kate continued. "Elizabeth sat under a tree in the garden and cried. She didn't like Sally because she had the dolly that was meant for her. 'I want it back! I want it back!' she cried. Suddenly she opened her eyes, and the fairy princess was standing before her."

"What did she say?" Emily asked. She looked anxiously at Kate.

"She said, 'You told your father you didn't like it before you even knew what was inside. You tell people you don't like them before you get to know them. You say you don't like food before you taste it or music before you hear it.'

Elizabeth cried because she knew the fairy was right. 'I won't do it anymore.' The fairy princess touched her on the head with her wand and said kindly, 'If you treat people nicely, they will be nice to you.' The end."

With the story finished, Kate unfolded her hands and looked down at Emily. The little girl's eyes were wide and fastened to her face. "Was Elizabeth nice after that?"

"She was so nice that everybody in the entire kingdom loved her. She grew up to be a beautiful princess, married a prince, and lived happily ever after."

Emily was quiet, looking at Kate with the same expression on her face that she had seen on Tate's when they discussed Emily's behavior. Finally she asked, "Will you tell me a story tomorrow night?"

"If you'd like me to."

"I do."

Kate stood, reached over, and tucked the bedcovers around Emily's shoulders. She leaned down and placed a kiss on the girl's forehead. "Good night. Sleep tight."

"You won't forget the story?"

"I won't. I promise."

Emily's eyes followed her out of the room. At the door, Kate turned and waved. Emily lifted a hand off the bed and waved back.

Chapter 26

KATE PUSHED THE DOOR OPEN A FEW INCHES and peered into the room. A kerosene lamp gave out a dim light, but it was bright enough for her to see Tate. He lay on the bed, arms crossed over his chest, looking at her. Kate went into the room, leaving the door ajar.

"Well?" he said. "How did it go?"

"Fine," Kate said with an easy smile. "She's a bright little girl."

"She didn't give you any sass?"

"Just a little bit." Kate crossed the room until she stood next to Tate's bed. He looked tired, haggard.

He reached out, grasped hold of her hand, and pulled until she was sitting on the edge of the bed.

"Emily must have liked it because she asked me to tell her a story tomorrow night. I think she's reconciled to the idea that I'll be here for another day."

"I wish it would be longer."

His words made Kate a little breathless, but she managed to say, "I told the doctor I'd stay a few days in case you developed an infection and came down with a fever. It will take that long for your friend to come for me." Kate paused. There was so much she wanted to say, so many things she wanted to tell him. "I hope you know how much I appreciate your coming to get me. If not for you, I'd be dead."

"Don't talk like that. Sometimes a man is given a gift in the most unexpected way." His eyes held hers.

"What do you mean?" she whispered.

"By doing a favor for my friend, I met a most unusual woman, who could come to mean a great deal to me." While Tate was talking, he slowly raised his hand toward her face, touched her, then began to caress her cheek with his knuckles. "Beautiful Katherine," he said softly. "I know that nothing can come of this, but it makes me happy to dream that you're mine. Are you shocked to hear that?"

"Why do you think I'd be shocked?"

"We live in different worlds, you and me."

"And that makes me unfit to live in yours? Not all of the women who come from the city are like your wife."

"My ex-wife," Tate interjected. He looked at her steadily before adding, "I suppose you're right. It's just that we're used to different things. What I have here wouldn't make you happy."

"Tate . . ." She said his name softly.

"I wish I could get up." His voice was raspy with frustration. "I'd hate to think I'll spend the whole time you're in my home trapped in this bed."

Kate brought her finger to Tate's mouth and pressed gently against his lips. At that moment, sitting on the edge of his bed, all she wanted was to be with him.

A flood of tenderness overwhelmed her as she turned his

face to hers. She kissed him with a lingering softness. As their lips touched, she found his mouth sweet, his breath warm, and his cheeks pleasantly rough against her face. At first, the kiss was hesitant, but then became more demanding.

As the kiss lengthened, her fingers began to move, slowly at first. They roamed over the firm muscles on his shoulders and into the silky down on his chest. She wanted to touch him, instinctively knowing that it was what he wanted too. He drew his lips away and buried his face in her throat. His body answered the movement with a violent trembling.

He groaned against her neck. "Is this all there is for us?"

"Is this all you want?"

"Someday I'll show you what I want," he said, his lips pressed to her cheek. His arms pulled her tightly against him, until her head rested on the pillow next to his. Their mouths touched, their breaths coming as one. He captured one of her hands and pressed its palm against his bare chest. Her fingertips slid across his chest and then up and over his smooth shoulders to his neck. Rough stubble scratched against her skin before she plunged her hand into his thick black hair.

"Your hair smells like spice," he said as he took a deep breath, drawing in the scent of her. "I've dreamt of being with you like this every night. Now at last, you're here in my arms."

He pulled her closer, their bodies pressing together. Kate's arm moved over his body, but as she ran her fingers down his side, Tate's face winced in pain.

"I'm sorry," she said quickly. "I didn't mean to hurt you."

"This is worth a lot of hurt," he whispered reassuringly.

She wanted to tell him how she was feeling, to open up and pour out these new thoughts, but she couldn't find the words. Her heart hammered in her chest, and there was a fluttering in the pit of her stomach.

In the stillness that enclosed them, she could see his face in the faint light from the lamp. His eyes searched hers. He swallowed the tightness in his throat. Never had he wanted anything as much as he wanted to hold this wondrous sweet woman. He wanted to gather her up and carry her away where there would be just the two of them. He'd work, he'd slave, sweat, and fight to provide for her. *You fool,* he groaned inwardly. *If you jump the gun, she'll shy away.*

"I've not kissed a man as many times as I've kissed you. I suppose you've kissed lots of girls lots of times." Her words broke into his thoughts. Her voice shook with uncertainty.

"I've kissed a few. But I've never wanted to do it as much as I want to do it now." He laughed in relief. She lay relaxed against him. Her soft breasts were against his chest. He wanted more than anything to caress them, strip away her blouse, and let the rough hair on his chest arouse her nipples to rock-hardness. Fighting down his desire for her, he stroked her hair. Her breathing was quiet, and he wondered if she had drifted off to sleep. He closed his own eyes, but they wouldn't stay closed. He wanted to be aware of every moment he held her. He wanted to fill his mind with an indelible memory of her.

Footsteps sounded on the wooden floor outside the

door. She stirred. Her lips brushed against his ear. "I should go."

Quickly she sat up, smoothed her hair down, and pulled up the neck of the blouse.

"Embarrassed?" His eyes teased her.

"I don't want Jorge and Yelena to think I'm taking advantage of you."

"They might think I'm taking advantage of you," he said, chuckling.

Tate pulled her back down to him and held her chin firmly. She felt a flutter of excitement rush through her as he brought his face close to hers. Again, their lips touched. Their kiss began firmly, but then softened as their passion rose. She moaned as his lips began to roam to her chin, her cheek, and her neck. Her breath came in fits, and she found it hard to move.

When her arms slid around his neck, a low groaning sound came from his throat. Kate felt a sweet singing in her blood as she lifted her head and looked down at him. He was looking at her with such a yearning that, for a moment, she was speechless. When she finally spoke, it was low and breathless.

"You do strange things to me."

"I've never met another woman who could make me feel like I do when I'm with you," he murmured. "You're so beautiful."

Tears came to her eyes. They weren't tears of sadness, far from it; she was overwhelmed with joy. Tate was surprised to see the shimmer of tears in her eyes.

"Why are you crying?"

"I'm not," she lied.

"Yes, you are," he said firmly. "You didn't cry when I took you from the cabin, and you didn't cry when you shot Hayden or the longhorn. Why are you crying now?"

"I . . . am not . . . crying." A sob racked her body.

"Look at me." With one hand, Tate turned her face toward him. Through wet eyes, she could see the concerned look on his face. "I'll never hurt you. Don't you know that?"

"It's too late. You already have," she answered as another large tear ran down her cheek. "Ever since you came for me, everything that you've done has made me care for you, but it's not enough. Soon you'll make me leave."

"Why do you say that? I won't make you leave. Sweetheart, a few more days here on the ranch, and you won't be able to get out of here fast enough."

"How can you say that? How do you know how I'll feel?" A flare of anger rose in Kate. She started for the doorway, but before she could reach it, Tate called out.

"I don't want you to jump into something you'll be sorry for later."

Scarcely pausing to answer, Kate said, "I think we've both said enough for tonight. If you need me for anything, call out." She left the room.

For a long while, Tate stared at the closed door, fearing he'd ruined his chance with her.

His concerns were real: Her life in the city was too different from life in Muddy Creek. Conflict raged within him. After Hazel had left, he convinced himself that he would never marry again. Meeting Kate had changed all that. He wanted her to stay. What they had could be wonderful.

*   *   *

"Let's go back to town."

Squirrelly stood in the doorway, oblivious to the beautiful scenery spread out in front of him. The sun had begun to rise in the east, and the tops of all the trees were bathed in the early morning light. "I'm gettin' so sick of this place. Hayden's probably killed her anyhow. If he hasn't, it ain't any skin off our nose. If someone's pissed about it, we'll just blame the whole damn mess on him."

Eddy got up from the table, where he had been looking at a map. "Stop complaining," he barked. "You don't have anyone to blame for your boredom but yourself. If you hadn't gotten as randy as a goat and pulled your pants down around your knees, things would be different now. You had your mind on one thing. That's why we lost her."

"She'll pay for that," Squirrelly groused, choosing to ignore the blame that Eddy was placing on his shoulders. "The damn high-and-mighty bitch."

Eddy grunted with disgust. "Don't talk about Kate like that."

"I don't wanna be here any longer!" Squirrelly strode across the room and snatched the empty booze bottle off the floor next to his bunk. "Damn! If the old man's got the money, then I'm gonna get my share no matter what Hayden does to that bitch. I got enough in my pocket for a train ticket out of here. I'm going home to get my money from Jacobs."

"You're welcome to go anytime."

"I want to go now!" Squirrelly shouted, and tossed the

empty bottle into the corner of the room. It exploded in a shower of glass. "Take me to town!"

"All right, goddamn it! I'm sick of your whining and bitching. Get your stuff together, and I'll take you. Don't think you're going to fill your father's shoes with that attitude."

"You think I can't do it?" Squirrelly said confrontationally. "You think I can't deal with men like William Jacobs? Hell, guys like him will be working for me before long!"

Eddy ignored the boasting and headed for the door. The sooner he was rid of the whiner, the better. "Come on. I'll drop you off at the station in Muddy Creek."

Not much was said between them on the drive to town. As they approached the depot, Squirrelly turned in his seat and said, "You better hope that split tail don't make it back here. Her old man'll be on us like stink on shit. My father will protect me, but ain't nobody gonna look after you. Your uncle sure as shit won't do nothin'."

"What happens to me isn't any of your business. But I'll tell you one thing: If Hayden's done anything to Kate, there's nowhere he'll be able to hide. He'll pay with his life." The only response he got out of Squirrelly was a laughing fit.

They drove slowly into town. Eddy glanced at his watch: a quarter after one. Muddy Creek was active in the early afternoon. Men and women walked along the boardwalks and moved in and out of the shops. He hated to be visible as a stranger in town, but if it meant getting rid of Squirrelly, he'd take the chance. Eddy stopped the car beside the depot.

"I'll see if there's another wire. Stay here."

"I'm not sittin' in the car," Squirrelly growled. He got

out of the vehicle, slammed the door with a bang, and followed Eddy into the depot.

"Keep your mouth shut," Eddy warned as he walked up to the counter. The same agent who had been there on each of their previous visits looked up from his newspaper as they approached. "Hello, again," Eddy said.

"You fellas still here?"

"Just for a few more days." Eddy smiled easily. "Anything for me?"

The agent placed a yellow envelope on the counter. "It's a good time for you two to come to town, what with all the excitement we've had around here today."

"What kinda excitement?" Squirrelly asked, his ears perking up.

"Haven't you heard about the woman that was kidnapped from the train?"

"You don't say?" Squirrelly said. "Now, what kinda dirty, low-down skunk would do a thing like that?" Before he could continue, one of Eddy's elbows found his rib cage and silenced him.

"Has she been found?" Eddy asked the agent.

The agent grinned. "Yep. Tate Castle, a fella that sometimes works with the Texas Rangers, found her and brought her back to town last night. From what I heard," the agent whispered as if he were telling a secret of the utmost importance, "they went out to his ranch this morning. Couple of people in here earlier said they saw the doctor's car headed that way."

"I'm glad she was found." Eddy picked up the envelope from the counter and started for the door. When he realized

Squirrelly was lingering behind, he called over his shoulder, "Better come on. We're late enough as it is."

"Late for what?" Squirrelly asked as he followed Eddy to the car. Once they were both inside, Squirrelly reached for the telegram. Eddy jerked it out of his reach and opened it. He scanned the message before handing it to Squirrelly.

THINGS COMPLETE ON THIS END. STOP. DO WHAT YOU'RE SUPPOSED TO DO. STOP.

"Hot dog!" Squirrelly whooped. "The old man paid up! We're rich!"

"Hush your mouth, you stupid fool," Eddy hissed. "Do you want everyone in town to hear you?" He glanced up and down the street, looking for anyone within earshot. An old woman was making her way down the boardwalk toward them but gave no sign that she'd heard anything.

"You know what we gotta do now, don't you?" Squirrelly said.

"What are you talking about?"

"We gotta get rid of the girl." The look in Squirrelly's eyes was disturbing. Even voicing the thought of killing Kate had excited him. "We know where she is. I bet that Castle fella is the one that knocked me out! All we gotta do is find out where his ranch is and we'll get 'em both!"

Eddy folded the telegram and put it in his pocket. For a moment, he seriously considered just driving out of town, shooting Squirrelly, and dumping the body. The thought surprised him; killing was completely abhorrent to him. He'd never thought about killing anyone, even a low-down, worthless piece of trash like Squirrelly. Would he even be able to do it? He supposed that he could if either his or Kate's life were threatened, but to kill someone in cold blood was an entirely different matter.

A crowd of thoughts raced through Squirrelly's mind. Any plans now of getting on the train were forgotten. The girl was still alive! If she were to testify against him, he'd be sure to get the chair or, at minimum, life in prison. He couldn't leave until she was taken care of. Hell, he just might have to get rid of Hayden and Jacobs too. That son of a bitch Hayden, supposed to be so tough, but he hadn't even managed to find one girl, let alone get rid of her!

Well . . . I'll show them what it means to be tough!

Chapter 27

JOHN AWOKE FROM A FITFUL SLEEP. The turmoil filling his mind had allowed him to sleep for only a few hours. He'd spent the entire night thinking about Kate and how he was going to settle matters with William Jacobs. God! It was a relief to know that she was all right. He hoped he would never have to go through an experience like that one again!

He'd had a long talk on the telephone with Lyle Holmgaard in Waco. His friend had assured him that Tate Castle, the man who found Kate, was honorable and that Kate would be perfectly safe with him. Lyle also said one of the men involved in taking Kate from the train had been killed, but he didn't know any of the particulars. Further, there had been no sign of Edwin and Squirrelly. John gave descriptions of the two, and Lyle said he would send a couple of agents to Muddy Creek.

Later that morning, he had a meeting with Detective Michael O'Malley, a man who had been of considerable help to him in the past. John was anxious to have his confrontation with William over. He wasn't sure how he was going to proceed, but one thing was certain: He would make sure William Jacobs got what was coming to him.

Neither Lila nor Susan was up when John went down for his breakfast. They were still resting from yet another party they attended the night before. There was a smile on Malcolm's face when he greeted him in the dining room.

"Morning, sir. I'm so happy Miss Katherine will be coming home."

"So am I, Malcolm."

"Do you know when she will be returning, sir? We thought it would be nice to have a homecoming celebration. Cook will make her favorite dinner."

"Good idea. She will be pleased," John said. "Have you seen Mrs. Tyler this morning?"

"No, sir."

"After breakfast, I'll be leaving. You can tell Mrs. Tyler I'll be going out of town and won't be back until noon tomorrow. Will you have Jamison bring the car around?"

"Certainly, sir."

John hurried through his breakfast and was soon headed through the early morning traffic toward Tony's restaurant, where he would be meeting the detective. He hadn't wanted to talk to his wife this morning. He didn't want Lila to know anything about what had happened until it was over. He had cautioned Malcolm not to tell her.

Shortly after John had been seated in the restaurant, Detective Michael O'Malley came through the door, cautiously looked around, then walked over and took a seat at the table where John was sitting. Placing his hat on the empty seat next to him, he said, "This is a good place for us to talk. Not many customers here this time of the morning."

O'Malley was a short, brawny man with a head of thick brown hair, a squat neck, and broad shoulders. His suit coat was wrinkled, and there were a couple of spots on his tie. He was much younger than John, though there were already deep lines in his face and sprinkles of gray in his hair. Despite his appearance, O'Malley was considered a meticulous police officer.

"Thank you for coming down so early, Mike."

"What's on your mind?"

"It's a long story." John waited until after the waiter had filled their coffee cups and walked away before he continued. "My daughter was kidnapped."

Mike nodded and lifted his coffee cup, his sharp brown eyes on John's face. He listened intently for the next ten minutes while John spoke in detail about the events of the past week. "I can't tell you, Mike, how disappointed I was when Kate told me that my partner, William Jacobs, planned this whole thing in order to get money from me. I need help in finding out the truth. I am determined to see that those responsible are punished for what they've done."

"You gave Jacobs the hundred thousand dollars to deliver?"

"I did. He insisted he should be the one to deliver it. He said it would be too dangerous for me. I was supposed to stay home and wait for a phone call from the kidnappers, but the call never came."

"Clever."

"Not as clever as he thinks. I had the bank mark the

bills. It's a new process they have. It takes an X-ray machine to detect the markings."

"If we're going to convict him, we'll have to get some of those bills. Do you have any idea where he might have hidden the cash?"

"I've been thinking about this ever since Kate told me William was involved. He'd want the money to be secure. He has a safe in his office, but I doubt that he would be foolish enough to hide it there. The next place would be his apartment."

"Where does he live?"

"The Asbury House on Park Avenue."

Mike took a notebook out of his jacket pocket and wrote down the address. "I'll take this to a judge to get a search warrant. Do you know what his schedule is? I'll want him to be home when we get there."

"He's involved in a lot of social activities and is usually gone most evenings. He should be back before midnight."

"Sounds good."

"I want to be there, O'Malley."

The detective nodded his head. "I can understand how you feel, John. Where can I get in touch with you?"

"Call here and leave a message with Tony. He'll get it to me."

The detective placed his hat back on his head, got up, and went to the door without a backward glance. John sat at the table for a few minutes more, then slipped a bill under his coffee cup and walked out the door. He melted into the heavy sidewalk traffic.

*   *   *

John Tyler sat in the car in front of William Jacobs' apartment house next to a uniformed police officer. It was eleven-thirty in the evening. Detective O'Malley had gone in to talk to the doorman. When he returned, he climbed into the backseat of the car. "Jacobs is in his apartment. The doorman said that he and a lady went up about an hour and a half ago. That doesn't make any difference, John. The wheels are in motion. Are you ready?"

"As ready as I'll ever be."

They got out of the car and stood on the sidewalk.

"Let's get up there in case he decides to leave." O'Malley went through the front door. He paused and spoke briefly with the doorman. "Don't let anyone go up to the apartment until we come down."

The doorman nodded as he crammed the bill John handed him into his pocket. John, O'Malley, and the policeman stepped into the elevator. On the ride up to William's floor, John tried to tamp down his rage. He had to stay calm and control his anger. Manipulating him through the kidnapping of his daughter had been easy for William. The bastard had played him for a fool. He had laughed up his sleeve when the ransom was handed over, John thought bitterly. The man had placed his daughter's life in jeopardy! If it took him the rest of his life, he would see that William Jacobs paid for what he had done.

Getting off on the twelfth floor, the three men walked down the hall to William's door. They heard music coming from inside. The detective motioned John forward and then rang the bell.

A moment later William opened the door. At the sight of

his partner, his mouth dropped. "John!" he exclaimed. "Has something happened? Have you heard from Kate?" William looked beyond John to see the detective and the uniformed policeman standing in the hall.

"I've heard from her," John said dryly as he pushed open the door, forcing William to step back. The other two men crowded in behind John and closed the door.

The spacious apartment was decorated in brown and maroon. Velvet drapes hung from the tall windows. The pattern in the Persian carpet repeated the maroon in the upholstery of the two chairs; the couch was a luxurious brown. Priceless paintings hung on the wall. A collection of clocks stood on the mantel above the marble fireplace. On a small table near the two chairs were two half-filled wineglasses. William was wearing a chocolate-brown smoking jacket over his pajamas. His gray hair was tousled as if he had just gotten out of bed.

"What *is* this, John?" William asked indignantly.

The detective stepped forward with a paper in his hand. "This is a search warrant, Mr. Jacobs."

"Search warrant? My God, what's this all about?"

"I think you know, Mr. Jacobs," the detective said calmly.

It was all John could do to remain calm and not plant his fist in the man's face. How dare Jacobs stand there and act like he didn't know why they were here!

"Do you have a safe?" Detective O'Malley asked.

"I've got a little one that I keep papers in." William unfolded the warrant and started to read it. His eyes scanned the printed words. John watched his face turn pale. "Are you behind this, John? Do you actually believe that I had something to do with what happened to Kate?"

"I do, William." John stepped back. He didn't want to speak to the son of a bitch unless he had to.

"Where's the safe?" Detective O'Malley asked, stepping between the two men.

"I'll show you. I have nothing to hide," William said defiantly. He strode across the Persian carpet to the wall to the right of the fireplace. He removed a picture, revealing a small safe set in the wall. With a few twists of the metal dial, the safe was opened. William stepped back with a smug look on his face.

Detective O'Malley pulled out a handful of papers from the small safe and began to look through them. John joined him and scanned the papers; most of them were documents relating to the business property William owned.

William snorted. "You have no right to come into my home and make such an accusation!"

"Is this the only safe you have here?" Detective O'Malley asked, cramming the handful of papers back into the safe.

"Yes. I keep everything else at the office."

"Search the rest of the apartment," O'Malley ordered the uniformed officer, ignoring Jacobs' denial. Leaving the safe door open, he began to look behind the books on a nearby shelf.

"Suit yourself. Look through the whole damn place. There's nothing here." John stared at his partner, and for just a moment, he saw a look of unease settle over his features. He wasn't as confident as the words he spoke suggested.

For the next hour, the two police officers searched through the contents of the main room. They pulled books from shelves and rifled through their pages. They opened the drawers of an antique writing desk and spread out their contents on top. They even lifted each of the clocks off the mantel and looked underneath. Through it all, William stood with his hands in the pockets of his smoking jacket, John watching him.

Finally Detective O'Malley said, "We'll need to look in the other rooms."

"I must protest!" William argued. "Hasn't this gone on quite long enough? You've ransacked my home!"

O'Malley ignored Jacobs' protests and motioned the uniformed policeman toward the bedroom.

The two cops stepped into the room, John behind them. It was as lavish as the rest of the apartment. The four-poster mahogany bed on the far side of the room was covered with red satin. The bed's sheets were of the same color but were bunched up at the foot of the bed, one large throw pillow on top of them. A large bureau with an equally large mirror sat in one corner. John walked over and picked up a woman's brassiere.

"Company this evening?" he asked.

"Earlier tonight. She left an hour before you arrived."

"Where do these doors go?" O'Malley asked, pointing at two doors to the left of the one that they had entered.

"One goes to my bathroom, the other to my closet."

Detective O'Malley opened the door to the closet. The

small space was stuffed full of clothing. He began to separate the items by sliding them along the clothes rod. Other random pieces of clothing littered the floor.

O'Malley nodded to the uniformed officer, who then went to work searching the room. Each of the bureau's drawers was checked and rechecked. William looked incredulous when the officer got down on his hands and knees and looked underneath the bed.

Ten minutes later, when John was beginning to lose a little of his hope, O'Malley called from the closet, "Over here!"

The uniformed officer, with O'Malley's help, began to throw blankets out into the room. Finally the two men stepped back to reveal another, much larger safe set in the back of the closet.

"I thought you said you only had one safe in the house," John said bitterly.

"I seldom use it," William said belligerently. "I haven't opened it in years."

"Open it," O'Malley ordered. "Now!"

"I'm afraid I can't." William sank his hands into the pockets of his smoking jacket. "I can't remember the combination."

With those words, John lost control of the anger he'd been trying to restrain. Grabbing William by the front of his jacket, he slammed the man hard into the bedroom wall.

"Open it!"

William's face was sweaty and white as he nervously stared at his old friend. John's face was cold and hard. Veins stood up across his forehead, and his lips curled with hatred. Caught in a lie, William was still defiant.

"John, I swear . . . I know nothing about this," William stammered.

"You no-good, lying son of a bitch! Open that goddamn safe, or I swear I'll kill you!" John slammed him repeatedly against the wall. "Do it."

"All right. All right."

William knelt before the safe and with trembling fingers, turned the dial back and forth several times and then tried the handle. It refused to open. He whirled the dial again. After Jacobs had made several attempts, Detective O'Malley said, "Quit stalling."

William looked up at him with hate-filled eyes but kept trying to open the safe.

A minute later the safe door swung wide. John reached in and pulled out a paper sack. The bag was filled with money—the ransom money he had given William to take to the kidnappers. Detective O'Malley produced a pair of handcuffs. When William was cuffed, the detective grabbed him by the arm and pulled him to his feet.

"I'm placing you under arrest for your involvement in the kidnapping of Katherine Tyler."

"I want to talk to my lawyer," William said defiantly. He opened his mouth to say more, but before he could speak, the sound of a crash came from the closed door to the bathroom.

"I thought you said you were alone," Detective O'Malley said angrily. He pulled his revolver from his shoulder holster and moved to the door. "Come out of there!"

The men heard a click as the door was unlocked and then swung open. John stood as if rooted to the floor. He was speechless. Lila, his wife, in a flimsy gown and peignoir, came from the bathroom. Her beautiful head was held high. Not a hair was out of place. Diamond earrings hung from her ears.

"Lila!" John exclaimed. "What are you doing here?"

"What do you think she's doing?" William sneered. "You think you're so smart. You can't even hold on to your wife!"

"Lila, what is the meaning of this?" John demanded. He felt as if his world had been turned upside down and shaken. He'd imagined many ways in which his confrontation with William could go, but not one of them included his wife coming out of the man's bathroom.

Lila looked down her nose at her husband as if he were far beneath her. "William and I were discussing a fundraiser for Senator Forrest. You frightened me when you came in, so I ran into the bathroom."

"What?" John said in disbelief.

In that moment, John saw his wife in a different light. The little physical touches she and William had exchanged over the years suddenly took on new meaning. But what surprised John was that he wasn't particularly hurt by her infidelity. Instead, he was rapidly piecing things together, arriving at a truth that nearly knocked him to the floor. "You were in on Kate's kidnapping!" he blurted.

"What are you talking about?" she said.

"He knows, love." William took a step toward her and was pulled back by the officer. "No point in trying to pull the wool over his eyes. Your little plan backfired."

As if a light switch had been turned, the expression on Lila's face changed. Gone was the innocent dignified wife caught in a simple misunderstanding. In her place was a sneering witch whose cat was out of the bag. "My little plan!" she shouted. "You had as much to do with it as I did."

"Hush, love," William warned. "Everything you say can be held against you."

John didn't want to hear any more. "Go home, Lila," he said, "and start packing your clothes. I want you out of my house by noon tomorrow."

"Your house?" She laughed. Her voice sounded different, harsher. "Don't think that you can just throw me out! I've put up with you for twenty years. I deserve half of what you have."

"Try and get it! You've lived pretty well these last twenty years. But enough of this. We won't air our marital problems in front of the police and this so-called friend of mine."

"Believe it or not, I *am* a friend of yours," William said. "You've got to believe me, John. The only reason I was in on this scheme of hers was to keep Kate from being hurt."

John balled up his fist and stepped toward his partner. As his arm swung, another, stronger arm grabbed him and brought his hand to a stop. John looked over to see O'Malley shaking his head. "Just hold your temper, John."

"You lying son of a bitch!" John yelled. He knew O'Malley was right and that he shouldn't strike William, but he had to let his anger out somehow. "You're not wiggling out of this by telling that cock-and-bull story! I've talked to

Kate and she told me everything. You would have had her killed if not for the Texas Rangers!"

"We've had our problems, John, but you have to believe William was behind this scheme." Lila moved closer. "He will try to put the blame on me to keep his neck out of the noose."

John glared at her. "Shut up, Lila. I don't think I can stand to listen to one more lie coming from your mouth."

"You know I've always loved you, John," she pleaded. Like a chameleon, she'd again changed her skin. Now she was back to the loving wife. Her hand lightly brushed against John's. Her touch made him sick.

"Is she under arrest?" he asked O'Malley.

"Not yet."

"Go home, Lila," John said. "Unless you want to go to jail with your lover."

She stared at him for a couple of seconds, and he saw the chameleon change once more. She left the room with her head held up proudly. She wasn't the least bit shamed by what she had done. The only emotional reaction he had was to wonder what all of this would do to Susan and to Kate.

Detective O'Malley took William by the arm and handed him over to the uniformed officer. "Take him down to the station and book him. John and I will be along soon." William said nothing further as he left.

Once they were alone, O'Malley turned to John and said, "We'll determine shortly if this is the money you gave to Jacobs. Once we get a match, he'll be charged."

O'Malley picked the sack up off the bed, tucked it under

his arm, and led the way to the elevator. In the lobby, the detective asked the doorman to hail a taxi.

As the two men stood on the curb in front of the building, waiting for the cab to arrive, O'Malley took a cigar from his pocket. He stuck it in his mouth but made no attempt to light it. "I'm sorry you had to find out about your wife this way."

"I suppose I shouldn't be surprised. She'd been going out a lot. The shock of it was that it was William she was meeting." He shook his head before adding, "More than that was the thought of her being involved in Kate's kidnapping."

The men were so intent on their conversation they didn't see the car until it was almost on top of them. With only a second to spare, John shoved the police detective back. They both fell to the sidewalk as the car roared past, nearly clipping John's legs. Whipping his head to the side, John saw Lila's black Lincoln speed off down the street without its lights. He picked himself up and extended a hand to the detective.

"Jesus Christ, that was close!" O'Malley exclaimed. "Son of a bitch didn't even have his lights on! Was he trying to run us down?"

"I think it was a she."

"What are you saying?"

"It was my wife behind the wheel. It was one of my cars."

The detective picked his hat up off the ground and slapped it against his pant leg. "I guess there's more to Mrs. Tyler's scheming than I thought. Did she think that with you out of the way, she'd have it all?"

"Then she would have been disappointed. I've made out a will leaving the bulk of my estate to Kate and just enough for Lila and Susan to live comfortably, but not richly. Even that will needs to be changed." John shook his head. "I can't believe she would try to kill me."

"Well, it sure looks like she did. I guess she realizes that we can charge her as an accessory to the kidnapping."

"She knows I'm going to divorce her now that I've caught her with William. At the very least, she'll lose her place in society because of the scandal. That's all that really matters to her anyway."

The taxi pulled up in front of the building. Still shaken by what had happened both men tensed as the car approached. They climbed into the back, and O'Malley told the driver to take them to the 87th Precinct.

"After we have the money examined, we can file kidnapping charges against Jacobs," the detective explained during the drive. "All we're holding him for now is suspicion of kidnapping. The bigger question is your wife. Do you want to file charges against her for trying to run us down?"

John thought about it for a moment. There was a part of him that wanted Lila to be punished, to make her pay for her part in Kate's kidnapping. She'd even tried to kill him. It would be easy to do, but in the end he realized that she'd lost enough. "I don't, but what about you?"

O'Malley shook his head. "The kidnapping charges will be easier to prove."

The cab pulled up in front of a big square building. Police cars lined the streets, and officers milled about. After they had stepped out of the cab and onto the sidewalk, John handed the driver some bills.

He followed O'Malley into the building. He wanted to get this over and done with. Both his life at home and his business had been turned upside down in a matter of hours. Things needed to be settled with both Lila and William. He would never forgive either of them for their part in Kate's kidnapping. The sooner they were out of his life, the better. First thing in the morning, he would call his lawyer and start the ball rolling.

Chapter 28

As Kate went into the kitchen for breakfast the next morning, the hope that Emily was going to accept her as a friend was just that—a hope. The little girl sat at the table in a light blue dress, her dark hair pulled back. She would have looked like an angel if not for the frown on her face.

"Good morning," Kate said cheerfully.

The only answer that the child gave her was to start banging a spoon against the table. "More sugar," she ordered.

"You have two spoonfuls. That enough," the Mexican woman said.

"I want more sugar! I'll tell my daddy on you." With that, the spoon-banging intensified. Yelena ignored her. Kate could only wonder if this sort of thing happened often.

Kate sat down at the table opposite Emily, then buttered a biscuit and reached for the jelly jar. Using her spoon, Emily moved the jar out of Kate's reach. "I don't like you," she said.

Kate looked surprised. "I like you."

"No, you don't. You only like my daddy."

"Can't I like both of you?"

"When are you going?" the girl said quickly. It surprised Kate that there was so much anger, so much frustration, in the child's voice. Maybe Tate was right. She had been spoiled.

Yelena turned from the stove and scolded, "That not nice, *niña.*"

"It is, too, nice," the child blurted.

"Eat your Toasties, and after a while we cut out paper dolls."

"I don't like your old paper dolls."

"What *do* you like?" Kate asked.

"I want you to go away," she said loudly, and dropped the spoon on the table with a clang. She folded her arms across her chest and pursed her lips, all the while glaring at Kate.

"I'm not going until your daddy is well again," Kate said.

"I'm gonna go tell him to get well." Emily climbed down from the chair, held on to it for a minute to steady herself, then walked with her awkward gait out of the kitchen.

Yelena looked at Kate and shook her head.

"Should I help her?" Kate asked.

"She not want it, señorita."

"I'll check on her just the same." Kate got up, left the room, and watched Emily go down the hallway. Kate thought about following her into Tate's bedroom but decided to leave her alone with him for a while and instead went back to the kitchen and sat down at the table again.

The Mexican woman started to prepare a piece of beef

for dinner. Not wanting to be useless, Kate asked, "Is there anything I can do to help?"

"No, señorita."

"I could take Tate some warm water to wash in."

"Jorge take him water this morning."

"Has he had breakfast?"

"At first light." Yelena turned and smiled easily. Kate found her to be a very likable woman. "Jorge take him food and they talk about horses. Luke and boys help to ready them. Army men come today."

Both women turned at the sound of Emily crying. Tate's voice floated down the hallway after the sobs, trying to soothe the little girl. Knowing that she was the cause of the anguish, Kate said, "I'm sorry that by being here I'm upsetting her. Is she like this with all women, or is it just me?"

"It not you. Emily not have a mother. Her own mother leave her. She not like any women who come here. She not like Miss Sophie when she come."

"Is she a friend?"

"She live near. She Señor Wilbur's daughter."

"Kate," Tate shouted from his room "Will you come in here?"

When she got to the room, Emily was sitting on the side of her father's bed crying. Her eyes were red, and teardrops rolled down her cheeks and dampened the fabric of her blue dress.

"Emily has something to say to you."

"There's no need."

"I think there is. Say what you're supposed to say, Emily," Tate prodded.

"I'm sorry," the child spoke between sobs.

"I accept your apology, Emily. Will you take me out onto the porch so I can see the horses?" Kate held out her hand. Emily put hers into it, slid off the bed, and stood tentatively, trying to balance herself.

"I can walk," she said as she wiped her eyes on the back of her hand.

"I can see that." Kate wasn't sure how much help she was supposed to give her. Tate had said that walking sometimes hurt Emily's hips. She looked at Tate for reassurance. His face was expressionless, but he nodded his head. Kate and the small girl walked slowly out of the room.

"Which way?" Kate asked.

Emily tugged her toward the kitchen and out the back door onto the porch.

Outside, the day was beautiful. The sun shone down from a cloudless sky. In the sunlight, the colors of the surrounding trees and flowers jumped out at her. Yellows, reds, and oranges. Jorge was throwing hay over the fence for the horses. A couple of the hungrier animals were already eating. He looked up and waved.

"Shall we sit down here for a minute?" Kate pointed at the long bench on the porch.

"All right."

Kate sat down and reached for the child to help her sit on the bench. After they'd settled, a big shaggy dog came out from under the porch. "Old Bob," Emily called cheerfully. "Come here, boy!"

The old dog painfully climbed the steps to the porch and made his way toward them. His shaggy tail wagged with excitement, and his tongue hung out the side of his mouth. He went right to Emily, and she rubbed his head. "Want to pet him?" Emily asked.

"Sure." Kate scratched the side of Old Bob's face. He gave her a long, wet lick on her hand as a way of saying thanks. "I had a dog when I was a little girl."

"Was your dog pretty like Old Bob?"

"He had big spots on his coat."

"What was his name?"

"Guess. What would you name a dog who had spots?"

"I don't know," Emily said with a quizzical look on her face.

"Think about it for a minute."

Emily looked up and grinned. "I'd call him 'Spot.'"

"That was his name. You're a very smart little girl."

Emily seemed happy with herself. They sat silently on the porch, and both scratched Old Bob with the tips of their shoes. The dog lay on his side and basked in the attention, his thick tail banging against the wooden planks when he wagged it.

"Are you going to tell me a story tonight?" Emily suddenly asked.

"Do you want me to?"

"Yes."

"Then I'll tell you a really good one."

Kate looked up to see two riders coming down the lane toward the house. Emily also saw them, and a grimace spread across her face. "Is it someone you know?" Kate asked.

"It's that old Sophie and Mr. Wilbur. She likes my daddy."

"Maybe we should tell Yelena someone's coming."

Old Bob had finally noticed the approaching riders, roused himself, and began to bark. Yelena came to the door and said, "I tell the señor."

Kate helped Emily off the bench. The little girl held her arms out for Kate to pick her up. Kate lifted the child to straddle her hip. Yelena held open the door, and they went inside, through the kitchen, and on to Tate's room. He lay on his bed with arms at his side. He frowned when he saw Kate carrying Emily. "She's too heavy for you."

"I'm fine." Kate smiled. "You have company."

"Yelena told me." Pointing at the rocking chair in the corner of the room under the window, Tate added, "Come. Sit down." Kate took a seat and held Emily on her lap. The little girl snuggled tightly against her. Leaning up on one elbow, Tate said, "I don't intend to tell Wilbur you're the woman who was missing from the train."

"Why not?"

"Because he's so damn nosy. Besides that, he's shirttail kin to Hayden."

"Oh my," Kate said worriedly.

They could hear their guests' steps echo across the porch, followed by their greetings to Yelena. Another minute passed before Yelena led them through the door to Tate's room. "Got company, señor."

"Come in, Wilbur, Sophie," Tate said.

Sophie wasn't a particularly pretty girl, but she wasn't ugly either. She was slightly overweight with mousy-brown hair. As she came into the room, her eyes were on Tate. She wore a pale yellow blouse with a dark blue riding skirt.

Small golden earrings hung from her earlobes. She had spent time on her appearance this morning.

"We just heard that you'd been injured." Sophie hovered over the bed. "Are you going to be all right?"

"I'm fine, Sophie."

"How can you say that? Look at you." She was so busy fawning over Tate that she hadn't looked at either Kate or Emily. She placed her hand on Tate's arm. "I'll stay and help Yelena."

"I've already got a nurse." Drawing the woman's attention to the rocking chair, he introduced them. "Miss Tyler, this is my neighbor Wilbur and his daughter, Sophie."

Kate nodded politely. "How do you do?"

Sophie looked her up and down but said nothing. Kate knew that Sophie immediately regarded her as a rival. The look in her eyes reminded Kate of the wildcat they'd seen on the ledge. Finally Sophie spoke. "Hello, Emily. My, but you look pretty today."

Emily frowned. "You always say that."

Wilbur cleared his throat. A rotund man, he was obviously Sophie's father; most of their facial features were the same. Instead of his daughter's long, mousy hair, Wilbur's was white and very short. Instinctively Kate didn't like the man. He carried an air of superiority. "I see that a patrol is camped down by the river. Are they here to get your horses?" he asked.

"Yes. They should be gone in a day or two," Tate answered.

"What about the wild stallion? Seen any sign of him?"

"The Indian boys told me the herd had moved farther

west," Tate lied. The thought of Wilbur's capturing that horse chapped him. Truthfully, the last he saw of the herd led him to believe they were going in the opposite direction.

"Damn Indians would steal the shirt off your back."

Tate gritted his teeth and remained silent.

After another twenty minutes of small talk, most of it about horses and Tate's condition, Sophie and Wilbur left. As Sophie went out the door of the bedroom, she gave Kate a killing glance. Kate could only smile in return. As soon as she heard the back door slam, she said to Tate, "She thinks I'm trespassing on her territory."

"Then she's mistaken. She doesn't have any territory here."

"I don't like her," Emily offered.

Tate grinned. "I don't like her either."

Later in the morning, as Kate was about to change the bandages on Tate's wounds, he caught her hand and brought it to his cheek. It felt pleasantly rough. Kate's mouth curved into a wanton little smile that in turn grew into a throaty laugh. "How long has it been since you've shaved?" she asked.

He pulled her down to him, a low laugh escaping him, and locked his arms around her. He felt her hand on his face and was slowly filled with warmth. Their lips met in an innocent kiss that was equal parts soft, generous, uninhibited, and sweet. "Katherine," he whispered.

His feeling for this woman had been growing steadily since the day he first saw her, standing on the platform. Now it nearly consumed him. She was so open, so giving.

When she responded to his kisses, she was as unrestrained as a summer breeze.

Tate had saved his love. He had stored it away, bestowing it only on Emily and those who shared his confined life. Now all the love that he had to give was Kate's. His heart was drumming hard. His breathing was shallow. He burrowed his face into the fragrance of her hair and felt himself harden and tremble.

Kate abandoned herself to the heavenly feeling of being in his arms. Her fingers touched his hair and his nape and then felt along the hard line of his jawbone. A low moan escaped her when her lips parted from his, and she clung to him as if she were trying to merge her body with his.

"I didn't know kisses were like this," she sighed.

His lips traced a line along the side of her face, culminating in a gentle kiss to her trembling mouth. Moving down the other cheek, he whispered into her ear, "I've never felt like this before. I'm so damn scared that you'll leave and that we'll never get to know how wonderful our lives together could have been."

Kate pulled back and cradled his face with her hands. She could feel light tremors rippling through his body. "I'm scared too. I didn't even know if I should come in here again, afraid that I'd read too much in the kisses that we shared last night. We have the power to hurt each other, Tate, simply because we care so much."

As he looked into her soft, tender eyes, fear left him. Seeing her smile, the flash of a dimple forming in her cheek, made Tate feel as if he could take on the whole world. Love surged through him like a river. How was it possible that this woman, with her gentle smile and calm words, could make him feel like this?

"We'd better change your bandages," Kate said when their lips parted.

"Your cheeks are pink," he teased. His eyes, shining silver between hedges of thick, dark lashes, danced over her face. "Everyone will know it was my rough whiskers that scratched your face."

"I don't care if the whole world knows you kissed me."

At that, Tate said a silent prayer. *Please, God, help me to keep this woman with me!*

Shortly after the noon meal, the patrol rode into the yard. Jorge met them and showed them the horses. The sergeant and two other men dismounted, and as the Indian boys drove the horses through a chute into the corral, they carefully examined each horse. It was a quick process; the sun was still high overhead when they finished.

Jorge brought the army officer into the house and back to the bedroom where Tate lay. There the men conducted their business. The sergeant accepted the bill of sale on behalf of the government, shook hands with Tate, and left. Jorge and the Indian boys assisted the patrol in getting the horses bunched together and ready to move out.

Tate could hear the shouting and whistling as the horses left the ranch. It was strange for him to be lying in bed while others did his work. As the last sounds of the horses vanished in the distance, Luke appeared in the bedroom doorway. Tate smiled. "How did it go?"

"It go. Horses gone."

"Did Jorge cut out the mares I wanted to keep?"

"Jorge did."

"Good. I'm depending on those mares to be carrying the wild stallion's foals. All we need to do is find him." Tate rose up in bed and leaned against the headboard. "I won't be able to ride for a while. I'll need you to keep an eye on that herd, Luke."

"While you keep eye on city woman?" Luke grinned.

Tate frowned. "She does have a name, you know. It's Kate."

"Kate," Luke repeated. "What kind of name is Kate?"

"It's short for 'Katherine.'"

"Why not say 'Katherine'?"

"You and your damn questions."

"If I don't ask, I don't know," the boy said with a shrug.

When Tate first met Luke, the youngster was quiet, not wanting to speak or interact with people outside of his tribe. It was with pride that Tate looked upon this young man, the kind of pride that a man might feel when looking at his growing son. "There's no reason for you to go. There will be plenty of work around here if you'd want to hire out."

"I think about it."

"Well, don't think too long. I'll hire somebody else."

Luke laughed. "Nobody good as me."

"Or as modest," Tate joked back.

"What 'modest' mean?"

Luke and the other boys left a few hours later. Tate knew better than to offer them a monetary payment for helping him get back to town and for helping with the horses; Luke was too proud for that. Jorge had given them some meat from the smokehouse, and they'd been on their way.

The sun was high in the western sky when Kate slipped into Tate's room. Laughter came from the kitchen, where Emily and Yelena had settled down to cut paper dolls out of the Sears catalog.

"It's been a busy day around here," Kate sighed.

"I half expected Lyle to come for you today."

"He might be waiting for my father to arrive."

"He'd come all the way from New York?"

"He might come by airplane. He's made several trips to Chicago that way."

"What a time we live in." Tate grabbed hold of her hand, caressing it with his fingers. "But when your father arrives, you'll go."

"When I was trapped in that cabin, I would have been overjoyed to know my father was coming to get me. But now . . . ," she started, but couldn't finish.

"But now?" Tate prodded.

She reached down and smoothed the hair back from his forehead. She could see what he wanted her to say written on his face. "I don't want to go yet," she finished.

"Then don't go," he said.

"Are you asking me to stay?"

"Yes and no. Hell, I'm so damn mixed up I don't know what I should say. I want you to be here with me, yet I know that if you do stay, it'll just bring more heartache for both of us."

"How do you know that?"

"You couldn't be happy here, Kate."

"I'd be happy wherever you are."

"You can say that now, but how would you feel after a blazing hot summer here on the ranch? How about a lonely winter? Could you really give up the life you've known for this?" The strength of his words told Kate he was convinced that what he was saying was the truth.

"Then you don't even want to give us a chance?"

"All that I'm trying to do is what's best for us, but especially what's best for Emily. She might be a stubborn little thing, but I can see that she'd learn to love you. If you were to leave, she'd be heartbroken. She's been abandoned once already . . . I don't want to make it twice."

Katherine looked down at him, her eyes bright with tears. His words had hurt her, and she lashed out. "Maybe we're not right for each other, then. Love is more than physical attraction. Love is trust, confidence, and respect. Evidently you feel none of those things for me."

"That's not what I meant . . ." Tate's words faltered. Kate was about to ask him what he had meant when Yelena ran into the room.

"Señor! A car is coming. It coming fast!" she said breathlessly.

"Take Kate and Emily with you to the cellar," Tate ordered.

"What's going on?" Kate asked. The sudden explosion of movement confused her. Yelena dashed from the room toward the kitchen to retrieve Emily while Tate tried to rise up in the bed.

"Someone's coming that we don't know." Once his back was up against the headboard, Tate said, "Get me the rifle, then go with Yelena."

"Do you think it's Eddy and Squirrelly?"

"Maybe. I described the car to Jorge and Yelena. She must think it's the car, or she wouldn't have alerted me. Now, go on to the cellar!"

Kate ignored his command and instead peered out the bedroom window trying to get a look at the car, but didn't see it. Snatching the rifle from the corner, Kate checked the load. She laid the gun down on the bed beside Tate. "Where's your handgun?"

"The top shelf in the wardrobe."

Kate opened the doors, pulled out the gun and box of shells. After checking to see if the weapon was loaded, she took extra ammunition and put it in her pocket.

"What in the hell do you think you're doing?" Tate said disbelievingly.

Once again choosing to ignore him, Kate went back to the window, but still saw no sign of the car.

"Damn it, Kate! I mean it!" Tate continued his tirade. He'd swung one of his legs to the floor and was struggling to rise. Sweat beaded his brow from the effort. "I don't want you here! If it's who we think it is, they're gunning for you! Go to the damn cellar!"

"Hush up, Tate!" Kate scolded. "If you think I'm going to go away and leave you here to face them alone, you're crazy! Besides, Eddy won't hurt me."

"Then you're a fool," Tate spat. "Your testimony could put both him and that other guy in the chair. They'll do whatever it takes in order to get rid of you."

Suddenly Kate heard the car and then doors slamming. This was followed by the sound of chickens squawking. They were in turn joined by Old Bob's barking.

With the revolver in her hand, Kate started for the back door. She turned and kissed Tate softly on the lips, then hurried toward the kitchen. Through the window she saw the familiar black car that had been there the day she was taken from the train. The two men were even more familiar; Squirrelly and Eddy stood in front of the car looking at the ranch house.

Fear coursed through Kate. How had they managed to find her? Steeling herself, she moved far enough away from the window so that she'd still be able to see them coming without being an easy target herself.

As the two men walked up to the back porch, movement to their left startled them. From his spot beneath the house, Old Bob charged. The dog's teeth were bared as he ran toward Squirrelly.

"Get back, you son of a bitch!" Squirrelly snarled. He yanked his gun from the belt of his pants and fired. The sound of the shot rang out like a thunderclap. Old Bob yelped loudly before he dropped to the ground, unmoving.

"What the hell did you do that for?" Eddy demanded.

"Damn barking dog," Squirrelly muttered.

"Idiot! That shot could bring the hired help back to the house!"

"Then we'd better get our asses in there and get it over with."

Seconds later the two men entered the kitchen without as much as a knock. Both of them stopped in their tracks at the sight of Kate looking back at them down the barrel of the handgun.

Chapter 29

"WELL! IF IT AIN'T THE SPLIT TAIL!"

Squirrelly's loose-lipped grin showed the gap between his two front teeth. He hadn't shaved and looked even more despicable than when she last saw him. His shirt was stained, his hair, face, and hands dirty. He swung the pistol around wildly, not even bothering to level it on her. He looked like a wild man, ready to pounce and kill. "I owe you one, girlie," he snarled.

"And I owe you one, you low-down, slimy toad. It takes a real man to shoot a dog." Hatred burned in her. The gun barrel shook slightly as she aimed at his chest.

"Sister, you ain't had a real man yet, but ya will! I was about to show you one when you hit me. I owe you one for that and another for takin' off. Shit, Hayden was as mad as a goat with his pecker caught in the fence!"

Kate ignored the reference to Hayden and instead looked at Eddy. He seemed a bit the worse for wear. Their eyes met.

"I've already talked to my father, Eddy," Kate said. "I

told him everything. He'll take care of your uncle, and the Texas Rangers will take care of the two of you."

"That's if I let you live, bitch!" Squirrelly shouted.

"Calm down, Squirrelly," Eddy said.

"To hell with that!" Even with her gun pointed at him, Squirrelly began to move around the kitchen. He craned his neck to look down the hallway behind Kate. "Where you hidin' that son of a bitch you left with? You ain't smart enough to get all the way out here by yourself. Someone helped ya! Is he hiding behind your skirt?"

"He's gone," Kate answered calmly.

"Gone?" Squirrelly laughed incredulously. "This is his ranch, ain't it? The depot agent told us that he'd been to the doc and that you'd been with him." Squirrelly kept looking around. "Who else is here?"

"Nobody."

"Ain't there no cowboys? All ranches have cowboys."

"Not this one." Kate tried to look at Eddy again, but the moment that their eyes met, he looked away. "Are you here for the same reason that this pile of filth is, Eddy? Are you going to get rid of me so I can't testify against you?"

Still looking away, Eddy answered, "You know I wouldn't harm a hair on your head."

"He wants to kill me, Eddy!" Kate shouted.

Slowly Eddy's eyes rose from the floor. But instead of settling on Kate, they bore a hole in Squirrelly. "He won't. I promised he wouldn't hurt you. I came to make sure of it."

"What the hell are you talking about, Jacobs? That's what we're here for." Squirrelly moved toward the far side of the kitchen. He was only a couple of feet from where

Kate stood. Cocking his ear toward the open door, he asked, "Who's in there? I heard something."

"The dog you killed had puppies. Are you going to shoot them too?"

What happened next only took an instant. Kate's eyes darted from Squirrelly to Eddy, but in that split second, Squirrelly covered the distance between them to stand behind her. She could feel the barrel of his gun in her back.

"Drop the gun, slut!" he ordered.

To emphasize his words, he gave her a hard poke in the back. She thought about trying to turn around quickly or to point the gun at Eddy, but she knew that either would be useless. He'd simply kill her. Defeated, Kate let the gun slip out of her hand, and it clattered on the kitchen floor.

"Gonna have me some fun with ya before ya die," Squirrelly whooped.

Kate spun around to spit in his face, but what she saw over Squirrelly's shoulder nearly caused her heart to stop. Tate was leaning against the doorjamb, his feet unsteady beneath him. The rifle was in his hand.

"Get away from her," Tate growled.

Squirrelly turned quickly at the sound of Tate's voice. "Thought you said no one was here," he barked at Kate. "Who the hell's that? Santa Claus?"

"If you don't get away from her, I swear I'll blow your head off!" Tate lifted the rifle and attempted to hold it steady. The barrel made lazy circles in the air. Roughly Squirrelly jerked Kate in front of him.

"Go ahead and shoot, cowboy! It'll save me the trouble."

Kate watched in horror as Tate tried to steady the rifle.

Sweat covered his face. Simply trying to stand was taking what little strength he had left after having made the trip down the hallway. It would only be a matter of moments before Squirrelly tired of playing with him and shot him. But before she could act, she caught a sudden movement to her side as Eddy rushed toward Tate.

"Eddy! Don't!" she shouted.

But Eddy yanked the rifle from Tate's grasp. The cowboy offered no resistance. All that he could do was glare at the man as he struggled to maintain his balance. "Goddamn it!" His legs buckled beneath him, and he slumped to the floor. From where she stood, Kate could see a fresh red stain on Tate's bandage.

A crazy, unnatural laugh came from Squirrelly. For once, he was the one in charge. He had the upper hand and he knew it. What was more, he liked it. "You don't look so tough now, Santa!" he chortled.

Yanking Kate by the arm, his fingers digging deeply into her flesh, he started across the room toward Tate. When he was near the prone man, he flung Kate toward Eddy. She crashed into the other man hard, but stayed standing. "Hold on to the bitch while I take care of the cowboy," he snarled. With that, he swung his leg and kicked Tate in the side.

A scream of pain poured out of Tate's mouth and echoed around the room. Instinctively he rolled over on his side to protect the wound. His face instantly drained of color. Blood appeared and spread rapidly in the binding that was wrapped around his waist. Through clenched teeth, Tate threatened, "I'm going to kill you!"

"Leave him alone!" Kate screamed. Watching Squirrelly attack Tate was horrifying! But there was nothing that she could do, no way to protect the man that she loved. She turned frantically to Eddy, her eyes wet and pleading. "Make him stop!"

Eddy was nearly as disgusted by what he was seeing as Kate. *Mother of Christ! The man is a lunatic!*

Squirrelly was still laughing hysterically, his breath coming in fits. From the look in his pinched, dark face, he was enjoying himself immensely. His eyes had an unnatural glitter, and his mouth was slick with saliva. He readied himself to deliver another kick but stopped when Eddy prodded him in the back with the rifle he'd taken from Tate.

"Stop it, you stupid fool!" Eddy warned. "If you kill him, the Texas Rangers will never give up until they've tracked us down."

"Who the hell's gonna tell 'em?! Her?" Squirrelly jerked his head toward Kate while simultaneously stomping on Tate's hand. Another yell came from Tate. Squirrelly just giggled and lifted his revolver. "That bitch ain't gonna be around to tell anyone nothin'! We're gonna do what we came here to do!"

Ignoring the gun in Squirrelly's hand, Kate broke free of Eddy's grip and ran to kneel over Tate. His head leaned against the doorjamb, and blood ran down his sleeve to the hand that Squirrelly had stomped. Pain covered his face, and his eyelids fluttered in their struggle to stay open. She leaned down to whisper in his ear. "Hold on, sweetheart. Jorge will come."

Tate turned his head, and his lips brushed her cheek. "I love you," he whispered.

"And I love you." It tore her apart to see him in such a state. She was afraid he would lose consciousness. No matter what happened to her, she was determined to protect him. She stood and turned on the two men. "Kill me. It's what you came to do!"

Quick as a snake, Squirrelly reached out and grabbed a fistful of Kate's hair. With a yank, he jerked her toward him until their faces were only inches apart. "Gladly, sweetheart."

"Let her go," Eddy said calmly.

Squirrelly's eyes latched onto Eddy's angry face. With a grunt, he tossed Kate to the floor next to Tate and turned to face him. "What the hell's the matter with you, Jacobs? You ain't goin' soft on me, are ya? I told you that I planned on screwin' this bitch's eyeballs out before I killed her, and I aim to do it!"

"I don't think so. I told you before that I wouldn't let you hurt her, Squirrelly," Eddy sneered. "Or should I call you 'Bartholomew'?"

Squirrelly's eyes went wide as he shouted, "Don't call me that!"

"What's wrong?" Eddy said sarcastically. "That's your name, isn't it?"

" 'Squirrelly' suits him better," Kate said.

"Shut your mouths!" Squirrelly yelled. "Shut your fuckin' mouths!" Spittle formed on his lips as he whipped the gun back and forth. He was becoming more agitated. Kate was sure that he would kill them all, Eddy included.

Kate glanced at Eddy. He was watching Squirrelly.

Squirrelly grabbed her by the elbow and yanked her back to her feet. "Which way to the bedroom?" he asked. After another laugh, he shoved her toward the kitchen table. Her ribs bounced off the edge, and she crumpled to the floor, trying to regain her breath. "To hell with it! I'll just screw her here. This way, her hero can watch a real man at work!" With that, Squirrelly started to fumble with his belt.

"Touch her, and I'll stomp out your guts," Tate said, his voice faint.

"You don't look like you could stomp a fly!" Squirrelly bent down until his face was inches from Tate's, and then slapped the man hard across the face. Tate struggled to keep from sliding into the black void.

"Stop it," Eddy shouted.

"Screw you!"

Squirrelly strode over to Kate and started to lift her from the floor. She raised her foot and kicked backward, hitting him squarely on the shin. At the same time, her elbow struck a blow to his stomach.

"Bitch!" he snarled.

He dropped his hold on her, and she fell to the floor again. "Damn it, you slut! We coulda done this the easy way, but you ruined that chance. I told you that I'd screw you whether you were dead or alive, and I meant it! But first I'm gonna kill your man to teach you some manners."

As he turned, Kate came up off the floor, fighting like a wildcat. She kicked and scratched at the man with all of the strength she had left. Her fingers dug into his skin and grasped at his hair, but it wasn't enough. With a shove, Squirrelly drove her to the floor again and leveled the gun.

A thunderous blast filled the kitchen. The noise was so deafening that Kate's head throbbed with pain. Reacting instinctively, her hands went out to ward off the shot. Confused, she turned her head to see Squirrelly falling on top of her.

With a scream, she shoved him away. He was too heavy to roll, so his body merely slid across hers until he lay face-down on the floor. His blood was on her arm and chest. *What happened?*

"Get up, Kate. It's over."

Looking up, she saw Eddy standing over her, the rifle in his hand. He reached down and turned Squirrelly over onto his back. His eyes were open and staring.

Quickly Kate crawled across the room to where Tate lay, and hovered over him protectively. "You'll have to kill me first!" she yelled.

"I'm not going to kill you." To demonstrate his intentions, Eddy placed the rifle on the kitchen table. "I never wanted it to come to this. All I wanted was to keep them from hurting you."

Their eyes met, and in that moment, Kate understood that Eddy was telling the truth. She lifted Tate's head and held it in her lap. She kissed his forehead lightly. "He needs to be in bed. Help me, Eddy. Help me get him back in bed."

"I think it would be better not to move him."

"Then get me a pillow, some blankets, and whatever cloth you can find. I need to stop the bleeding before he bleeds to death."

For the next ten minutes, the two of them worked to stop the bleeding in Tate's side. He moved in and out of consciousness; the only sound he made was a low moaning. Eddy worked right alongside her, fetching anything that she needed.

Eddy's hand touched her lightly on the shoulder. "I need to go, Kate."

"Why did you do this, Eddy? Why did you go along with your uncle?"

"There are lots of reasons, one of which is that I'm a fool." He flashed the easy smile she had seen him use many times before. He'd dazzled rooms full of New York society with that smile.

"You're no fool, Edwin Jacobs."

"If only you were right, Kate." He got up and went to the window. With his back to her, he continued. "The main reason I came was that I wanted to be able to protect you. Uncle William had given orders to kill you after your father had paid the ransom. Men like Hayden and Squirrelly are the type who kill without asking why. I couldn't let them do that to you."

"But why go along with it at all?" Kate asked. "Why not turn your uncle in to the police?"

Eddy turned from the window and stared at her intently. "Because Uncle would have managed to throw all the blame on me, and this was my chance to escape."

"I don't understand."

"I've wanted to get away from my uncle for years. He's a conniving bastard who would burn an orphanage to the ground if he thought he could profit from it. When he told me of his scheme, I realized it was my chance to get out from under his thumb. We're close to Mexico. I could lose myself down there, live off what I've stashed away. I can be my own man."

Listening to what Eddy was saying, Kate felt a close affinity for the man. What had happened to her wasn't all that different from his experiences. She, too, had "escaped" from the life she had known. What she had found with Tate was a chance to start anew.

"I think I understand," Kate said.

"I want you to know I am sincerely sorry for all you had to endure. I wish I could have . . ." A sound from outside startled them. Eddy listened closely for a moment before adding, "I've got to leave, Kate."

"What about Susan?"

"Your sister doesn't love me. She cares far more for the parties I take her to and the people I can introduce her to. Your father will be thrilled to have me out of the picture, I suppose. Speaking of John, be sure to warn him that his partner is a dangerous man. He's the type who will do away with whoever gets in his way."

"I've already told my father about William. He'll know how to handle it."

Eddy came over and stood next to her. His gaze moved from her to Tate. "Are you in love with him?" he asked.

"Yes. I am. I want to spend my life with him."

"Then be sure to tell him that Hayden is still out there looking for you."

"No, he's not," Kate said as she shook her head. "I killed him."

"You what?!" Eddy said, a look of genuine surprise on his face.

"I'm not proud of it, but it was something that had to be done. He would have killed us if I hadn't. This way, you won't have to worry about him popping up to implicate you in your uncle's scheme."

"That's a relief."

"Will I ever see you again?" Kate asked.

"No." Eddy turned to her and slowly shook his head. His eyes looked wet as he said, "Good-bye, Kate."

"Good-bye, Eddy." She reached up and kissed him on the cheek. "I hope you find someone to love and you can be as happy as I am."

The car left the ranch and was swallowed up by the vast Texas prairie.

Kate was sitting on the floor beside Tate when the pickup truck drove in and Jorge and Luke rushed into the house. They had been in the south pasture when they heard the shot.

"Senor!" Jorge exclaimed. "*Madre de Dios!* What has happened?" He looked from Kate to Squirrelly's motionless body and back again. "Are you all right, señorita?"

"I am now, Jorge." Kate got to her feet, the realization of what had happened now pressing down on her. Her legs trembled. She kept one hand on the doorjamb to help steady herself.

Luke was peering down at Squirrelly. "He dead. Who shoot?"

Ignoring the question, Kate said, "Help me get Tate back to the bedroom."

Luke grunted, stepped over Squirrelly's body, and helped Jorge lift Tate from the floor. Gently they carried him down the hall. Tate never regained consciousness as they placed him in his bed. Despite what she and Eddy had done, the wound in his side had reopened. Jorge came in with a basin of water and a stack of clean cloths. He moved Tate so that Kate could rebind the cut. Finally, after they had done all that they could for him, they left him to rest.

"What we do with this one?" Jorge asked as they once again stood over Squirrelly's body.

"Before you go to fetch the doctor, we should move him out of kitchen," Kate answered. "I don't want Emily to see him."

"Sí, señorita."

Jorge and Luke lifted Squirrelly's lifeless body and carried it out of the kitchen, across the porch, and into the barn. When Jorge returned to the truck to go after the doctor, Kate ran out to him.

"Tell the doctor he'll need to put in more stitches. He'll know what to bring." Jorge nodded solemnly, jumped into the vehicle, and sped down the lane.

For the next hour, Yelena kept Emily away from the house. Kate went to Tate's room and sat down in the rocking chair. The long days of uncertainty and fear had finally caught up with her. As she held her head in her hands, tears ran from her closed eyes. A small sob escaped from her lips at the thought of what Tate had endured. She was thankful they were both still alive, but she still couldn't stop crying.

Suddenly Kate heard a child's shout from outside. "Old Bob!"

She got quickly to her feet, wiped the tears from her cheeks with the back of her hands, and hurried out the door. Emily knelt on the ground beside the still dog, crying as if her heart would break.

"Old Bob!" she sobbed, her hands in his fur. "Old Bob, get up!"

Kate ran over and knelt down beside her. With all that had happened, she'd forgotten that Squirrelly had shot the brave dog. "Let me look at him, Emily. I need to know where he's hurt." Immediately she saw the dog was still alive, but panting shallowly. Looking closely, she found that the bullet had creased the dog's head, taking off part of his ear.

Gently scooping up the limp dog, Kate carried him toward the porch as Emily followed along behind. Yelena met them there and folded an old blanket to lay him on. After cleaning the wound and smearing it with pine tar, Kate wound a bandage around Old Bob's head.

"Don't cry, Emily," Kate said comfortingly. "He'll be all right in a few days."

When Emily settled down beside the dog, Kate hurried back to Tate.

Her heart lurched; he was lying so still and pale. She placed her hand on his chest and felt a steady beating. Relieved, she kissed his face again and again. Taking his hand in both of hers, she hoped the doctor would arrive before he awakened. He would be in terrible pain.

Silently she prayed.

Chapter 30

Time crawled by as Kate waited for the doctor. Tate moaned occasionally but never regained full consciousness. Luke came silently to the door, looked in, and just as silently left. Yelena kept Emily on the back porch near Old Bob and amused her by showing her how to make a chain with a piece of yarn and a crochet hook.

Jorge returned and came immediately to Tate's room. Kate was upset that the doctor was not with him.

"Woman have baby," Jorge explained. "Doctor come soon."

"Did you tell him what happened? Did you tell him Tate needs more stitches in his side?" Kate worried that the message she had sent hadn't been properly relayed. Fear gnawed at her gut that the delay in receiving medical attention might mean Tate would die.

"I tell him all you say, señorita. He come soon."

"All right," Kate sighed. "I guess that's all we can do."

Jorge moved slowly toward the bed, his hat in his hands. He looked intently at the crimson stain that seeped from the white bandages on Tate's side. "Señor bleed plenty."

"I've done all I can do. We need the doctor to sew it up again."

Jorge nodded solemnly and headed for the door. Before he left, he turned and said, "Talk in town about Hayden. Hunters saw buzzards circling in sky and found body." Without waiting for a reply, he left.

For the next hour, Kate was alone with Tate. She felt tired, worn-out from all that had happened, and struggled to keep from falling asleep. Then, when she glanced over at him, she saw that his eyes were open. Quickly she went to kneel down beside the bed. His lips moved, but she had to put her ear close to his mouth to hear what he was saying.

"Are you all right?" he whispered.

She smiled. "I'm fine. Eddy killed Squirrelly to keep him from hurting us." Kate bent over and kissed him softly on the brow. She cupped his rough cheeks with her palms. "Sweetheart, I know you're hurting. Jorge went for the doctor. He'll be here soon."

"He didn't hurt you, did he?"

"Not much."

"I've never wanted to kill anyone that bad. Damn rifle was too heavy, wouldn't stay steady."

"How did you manage to get out of the bed?"

"I knew that I had to. I could hear what those bastards were saying and that they were going to hurt you. I couldn't let that happen."

The image of Tate standing at the end of the hallway was burned into her thoughts. The pain must have been excruciating! "It's all over now. Just lie still until the doctor gets here."

"What about Emily?" Tate asked weakly.

"She's all right. The only thing she saw was Old Bob. Squirrelly shot him when they arrived, but I think he'll be fine. He'll just be missing part of his ear."

"Thank God everyone's all right."

Hot tears began to well in Kate's eyes. Even as badly hurt as Tate was, his first thoughts were for the safety of those he loved. "I died a thousand times when Squirrelly kicked you. I thought he was going to take you from me."

Tate brought Kate's hand to his lips and kissed it, his eyes on her face. "Did I dream you told me that you loved me?"

"It wasn't a dream," Kate said as a tear broke free and rolled down her cheek. Tate wiped it away with a finger. "You said you loved me too."

"What about us?" he asked.

"Now that I've found you, I don't want to give you up."

Before Tate could reply, the sound of a car turning into the drive drew her attention. She rushed to the window and looked out. Dr. Duval was getting out of his car and running toward the house.

"Thank God!" Kate exclaimed. "The doctor's here!"

For the next hour, Kate assisted as the doctor restitched all of Tate's wounds. Kate worried that he'd lost too much blood. Dr. Duval worked confidently. By the time he was applying the last bandage, Tate was asleep.

"He'll be sore, but he'll live," Dr. Duval said after they'd retreated to the kitchen.

"Did you bring anything to help ease the pain?"

"I can leave morphine. I'll write out the dosage. Make sure

you don't give him even one drop more. After a couple of days of rest, he won't need it anymore."

"Thank you, Doctor."

"He's not out of the woods yet." Dr. Duval gathered up his medical bag. "He isn't running a temperature, but if one spikes, send Jorge to fetch me. We might need to take him to the hospital in Alpine."

After the doctor had left, Kate went back to Tate's room. She was surprised to see that he was awake. "You should try to rest," Kate advised. "You've been through a lot."

"You'll stay with me?" he whispered as he closed his eyes.

"A team of mules couldn't drag me away."

The next morning, Yelena was pulling a pan of biscuits from the oven when a car drove in and stopped at the back of the house.

Kate entered the kitchen carrying the wash pan from Tate's bedroom. She had washed his face and smoothed back his hair. After a full night's rest, he was much improved. "Is someone here?" she asked.

"It Señor Lyle," Jorge said from the window. "Someone with him."

She went to the kitchen door. "Daddy!" she exclaimed, and dashed out of the door and across the porch, throwing her arms around the big, dark-haired man. "How did you get here so quickly?"

"I flew in an airplane, honey. I had to be sure you were all right."

"So much has happened. It will take me all day to tell you."

"I've got a few things to tell you too, but first I want to introduce you to someone." John indicated the man who had been driving the car. "Kate, this is Lyle Holmgaard, my Texas Ranger friend."

"It's very nice to meet you, Mr. Holmgaard."

"Nice to meet you, ma'am," the man said with a tip of his hat. He struck her as an easygoing man that most people would find instantly likable; he had a smile that reminded Kate of a preacher.

"I suppose I have you to thank for sending Tate after me?"

"How is he?" Lyle asked, his smile changing to a look of concern.

"He's resting now. The doctor came last night. He left us with some morphine for the pain. It will take time and plenty of rest, but he should be fine."

"That's good to hear. Tate Castle is one tough son of a gun."

"I owe him my life," Kate said softly.

"And I owe him a lot. The man is a hero," John said.

"What about you, Daddy? What happened in New York City? Did the police arrest William?"

"He's sitting in a jail cell right now, sweetheart. The police went to his apartment and found the ransom money hidden in his safe. He'll get everything that's coming to him."

Their reunion was interrupted as Yelena came out onto the porch. "*Hola*, Señor Lyle."

"Yelena, this is my father," Kate said, introducing them.

"*Bienvenido*, señor. Come in, come in. Biscuits out of oven."

"Come on, John," Lyle said as he slapped the other man

on the shoulder. "All this talking can wait until after breakfast. Yelena's biscuits are the best in Texas, and that's saying a lot."

John seemed completely at ease in the ranch kitchen. At first, Emily was quiet with the stranger, but after she found out the man was Kate's father, she warmed up to him. As they sat down for breakfast, she surprised everyone by asking, "Can I sit on your lap?"

"Of course, you can, little honey." John had a pleased grin on his face when he lifted Emily and set her on his leg.

"Kate told me a story," she said proudly.

"I used to tell her stories when she was a little girl, just like you."

"My daddy hurts."

"I'm sure he'll be all right, honey. He just needs to rest, and before long, he'll be up and telling you stories."

"Kate's stories are better." The little girl smiled, and everyone laughed.

Once breakfast was finished, Kate excused herself and went to Tate's room. He was awake but didn't seem to be in the best of spirits. "Your Ranger friend and my father are here. Do you feel like talking to them?"

"Did your father come to take you home?" Tate asked gruffly. The tone of his voice surprised her; he sounded angry.

Kate didn't answer. "He's eager to meet you. He'd like to thank you for all that you've done for me."

"I don't need his thanks," he muttered.

A light knock on the door frame ended their conversation. Lyle eased into the room. "I see that Hayden finally caught up with you," he said with a grin.

"Bastard would have killed me if Kate hadn't shot him."

"That so? Some hunters found his body and brought it into Muddy Creek. Everyone in the whole darn county's talking about it. The buzzards had a turn with him, but it was definitely him."

"He could have lain out there and rotted as far as I'm concerned . . ."

Tate fell silent as another man stepped into the room. He looked the stranger up and down before grabbing hold of Kate's hand and holding it tightly. Kate felt confused at his reaction but smiled and introduced them.

"This is my father, John Tyler," Kate said. "Daddy, this is Tate, the man who saved my life. He rescued me from the cabin and brought me all the way to Muddy Creek."

John Tyler walked to the bed and extended a hand the size of a ham. "Pleased to meet you."

"Likewise," Tate murmured.

Tate's eyes went from the big man to Kate. He could see no resemblance between the two. John Tyler was as big as an ox and had rough features, but his daughter was small-boned and dainty. Even his eyes were a darker blue than hers. Kate stood by while her father and Tate assessed each other.

"Saying thank you seems insufficient after all you've done for my daughter. There's no way for me to adequately repay you."

"It was my job," Tate said.

Kate looked down at him. *My job?* She held her tongue to keep from voicing the question. "Here's a chair, Daddy. I'll go get another one for Mr. Holmgaard. I know you all have a lot to talk about, so I'll leave you for a while."

A half hour later the men were still talking in Tate's room. Kate had tried to busy herself helping Yelena in the kitchen, but her thoughts were never far from what was happening in the other room. Finally she could stay away no longer. She knocked gently on the door and entered the room. "Are you all right, Tate?" she asked.

"I'm fine."

"How about you, Daddy?"

"Splendid, but I will be leaving soon. My plane is waiting in Alpine."

"Can't you stay longer?"

"No, sweetheart, I can't. There are many things that still need to be settled at home. I'm sorry to have to tell you this, but I'm afraid that your stepmother had a part in the kidnapping scheme."

"Oh, no!" The shock of her father's words felt like a blow to the chest. She couldn't believe what she was hearing. "But why? How could she have done something like that?"

"For money, I would suppose. We found her in William's apartment when we went to search for the ransom money. I was shocked myself, but what's done is done. I haven't pressed charges against her, but I've already asked my lawyer to file for a divorce. The sooner that I am free from her, the better. She's moved out of the house. Sorry to say, Susan has chosen to go with her."

"Why would Susan do that? Was she involved in what happened?"

"I don't think so, but your sister is terribly confused. She'll want what is comfortable. She belongs more in Lila's world than in mine."

"I'm sorry, Daddy," Kate said, and sincerely meant it.

"This whole ordeal has been difficult for everyone. They've made their choices, and they're the ones that will have to live with them." Kate knew that what her father was saying applied to her as well. She had her own choices to make.

"Lyle," John said, turning to the Texas Ranger, "did you remember to bring that train schedule with you?"

"I did." Lyle pulled a small pamphlet from the breast pocket of his shirt. He handed it to Kate.

"What is this?"

"It's a listing of arrival and departure times for the Southern Pacific Railroad. I'm not even going to try to talk you into coming back to New York with me." John chuckled. "But your uncle is still expecting you to join him in San Francisco in a week's time."

"San Francisco," Kate repeated, her voice trailing off. She looked up from the pamphlet to see Tate staring at her. This was it, the moment that had been destined to come. This was the time for her to make her decision and to live with it. She knew what she wanted to do; she wanted to be with Tate. *But what does he want?*

"Kate?" The voice came softly from the bed. Tate had pushed himself up onto one elbow. He trembled from the effort. The hand that Squirrelly had stomped on was stretched out to her. She crossed the room and took it in her own hand, holding it gently. "Are you going to leave?" he asked.

"Do you want me to?"

"You know I don't, but as your father said, you have to make a choice you can live with. We've talked about this before. Our lives are as different as night and day. I can only be what I am, and you can only be what you are. You've seen my home. This is all I can provide for you at the present. I won't ask you to give up your dreams and the life your father has given you."

"Do you love me?" she whispered. Her whole world hinged on the answer.

"With all my heart. If you stay with me, I'll never let you go."

"What's going to make me happy is to be with you. You and Emily. This isn't what I thought would happen, but I can't change the fact that it did. You came into my life, and I don't want to leave you."

"Sweetheart, you've got to decide right now, before your father goes."

She bent down and kissed Tate's lips, then looked up at her father, her eyes bright with happiness. "I want to stay with Tate, Daddy. I love him and he loves me!"

"Is this what you truly want?" John asked.

"Yes. This is what I want."

He smiled brightly. "Then I'm happy for you." He held out his hand to Tate and said, "Happy for both of you. Welcome to the family."

After the two men had shaken hands, Kate looked down at Tate. He had never been more handsome to her. Her heart soared with elation at the thought of them spending the rest of their lives together. All she wanted was to kiss him. As she bent down and their lips touched, she heard her father chuckle behind them.

"I guess this means that I have a granddaughter."

Epilogue

September 1937

It was evening. Kate and Tate sat on the porch swing and watched Emily come from the side of the house, Old Bob at her heels. She walked easily on the shoe that Grandpa John had sent from New York.

"Hello, Mama. Hello, Daddy."

Tate had his arm around his wife. "Look at the smile on her face. That shoe has done wonders for her."

"Why are you always kissing Mama, Daddy?"

"Because I like to kiss her."

"She's prettier than Patty May's mama."

"Really? I was thinking about trading her for Patty May's mama."

"No," Emily screeched.

"Stop teasing her, Tate. She'll wake up John Amos."

"He's already awake and wanting his dinner."

Emily came up onto the porch and leaned against Kate's knee. Kate hugged the little girl. "Your daddy's a tease."

Emily grinned. "I know."

Kate had not dreamed that her life could be so complete or that she could be this happy.

Tate had not been intimidated one bit by John Tyler and his wealth. Kate's father came to visit them several times. The man had become very fond of his son-in-law and knew better than to suggest financial assistance. The only help Tate had accepted was John's offer to find a shoemaker to make Emily a special shoe. The results had been amazing. It had changed the child's life. She adored her Grandpa John.

From inside the house, they heard their son crying.

"He wants his mama, but so do I. I'm getting tired of playing second fiddle to a three-month-old cowboy."

"Oh, you. You're so terribly neglected."

"I'm not used to sharing."

"You shared me with Emily before John Amos was born."

"That's different," Tate countered. "Emily has changed since she got her shoe and the baby came. She can go see why he's fussing." Tate laughed.

"Let me go in and check on him." Kate got up off the porch swing and went into the house. She marveled at how much her life had changed from the time Tate rescued her. Much had happened.

William Jacobs had been convicted and sentenced to life in prison for his role in the kidnapping. The trial had front-page coverage in the *New York Times*. However, all throughout the trial, nothing was ever mentioned about Lila Tyler; John Tyler had managed to keep her name out of the whole sordid affair. Lila and Susan had moved to Chicago, where

Lila married a millionaire twice her age. Susan came to Pittsburgh occasionally to visit her father and to New York to see old friends.

Kate's father was a doting grandfather to both Emily and John Amos. The baby had been named for both grandfathers, a fact in which John Tyler took great pride. He often called on the new telephone that had been installed at the ranch to see how his grandson was doing and to speak to Emily. He'd returned to the steelworks and worked hard to repair the damage William had done to the company's reputation. Whenever they spoke, he sounded happy to be back at the mill in Pittsburgh.

Tate followed Kate into the house. "He's either soaking wet or hungry," he said as he picked up the crying child. He held him carefully against his shoulder and patted his back. "He must have wet a bucketful."

"This is a joint venture, partner. I'll feed him, and you change his diaper."

"Fair enough, I'll go first."

After he had changed the wet diaper, he handed the child to Kate. Sometimes he had to pinch himself to be sure he was awake and not dreaming. All of this happiness had come unexpectedly.

While Kate was nursing the baby, she gazed lovingly at her husband. He and the children were her life, and she couldn't imagine what it would be like without them. She kept her dream of being a nurse and worked part-time with Dr. Duval at his office in Muddy Creek, often giving medical advice when the doctor was at the hospital in Alpine. Kate had been accepted by the town's population and was never thought of as an outsider. Living on the ranch with her family, Jorge, and Yelena was all she dreamed it would be.

Tate took the baby from Kate's arms and returned him to the cradle. They both stood by and gazed at this child they had made together. "Isn't he beautiful?" Kate said.

"Just like his mother." Tate held her in a loving embrace. "Now it's my time to be with you."

"You're spoiled, Tate Castle."

"That I am, Mrs. Castle."

"Oh!" she exclaimed. "I forgot to tell you I got another card from Eddy today! I picked it up at the post office. He said he'd found a girl and that she might be the one who will share his life. I'm glad for him, and I hope he will be happy." Eddy had sent a card two or three times a year since he'd left for Mexico. They were all signed "E."

"He redeemed himself in the end by saving our lives."

Later that evening, after they had settled in for the night, Tate pulled her close to him. "Luke's coming tomorrow. He doesn't really like that school he's going to, but he knows that he needs to get an education if he's going to help his people. When he finishes school, he wants to have a horse ranch of his own. Maybe we can help him get a start."

They shared a few kisses, and then Tate said, "You know, I'm beginning to hate Dr. Duval. You spend more time with him than you do with me."

"That is not true and you know it."

"I know it"—he chuckled—"but I'm jealous of every man who looks at you."

"That's just silly."

"I love you." He moved his face until it was only inches from hers. His nose brushed her cheek as she laid her head on his shoulder. She smelled a tangy odor and realized he had shaved before coming to bed.

Tate's hand worked beneath her hair; his fingers stroked the nape of her neck. It felt so good that Kate almost purred.

"You've had a busy day." The words were murmured as he crossed a leg over hers.

"No busier than other days."

"I'd hoped to keep you so busy you wouldn't have time to miss your life in New York." He leaned over her.

"I haven't missed it at all."

He lowered his head and whispered in her ear. "I'm glad." Tate took a deep breath. "I love you more every day. I'll love you when you're old and gray and without teeth."

Kate giggled. "I'll be a sight without teeth."

"You'll be beautiful."

"When we're alone like this in the dark, it reminds me of the nights that we spent on our way from the cabin to Muddy Creek. Then I felt like we were the only two people in the whole world. Even now, lying in our bed, I feel like we're all there is." She could feel the warmth of his breath against her neck and savored being close to him.

"For me too, sweetheart. With you, I feel like I have the world in my hand. I know you're tired, but I want to love you."

The sincerity in his voice touched her heart in a way his words did not. She remembered the pain in his eyes the day he thought she would leave with her father. She would not have guessed how much she would love the man with the gruff voice, wild hair, and silver-blue eyes.

She turned her face to his, angled her nose alongside his, and caressed his lips with her own. Nibbling, stroking with her tongue, deepening the kiss, and withdrawing. All the adoration in her heart was given to him now. She murmured his name as her lips glided over his straight brows, short thick lashes, and cheeks to his waiting mouth. Her hand slid over his chest and down over his flat stomach to the aroused length of him captured between their bellies.

"Ah, love. Don't stop." His voice came huskily, tickling her ear. His hands kneaded her rounded bottom and pressed her tightly to him. He pulled her leg up between his thighs. "I can't get enough of you."

"I'm glad."

His legs glided off of hers, and his hand moved to spread her thighs. He lifted with strong hands at her waist, and when he settled her on him, she made a purring sound like that of a pleased kitten.

"Just be still, sweetheart. Just be still." His hands glided up over her hips to the sides of her breasts, which were flattened against his chest. He grasped her head and turned it so his lips could reach her mouth. "We fit perfectly, my love. We're perfect together," he said, breathing deeply. His voice was a shivering whisper that touched her very soul.

Much later as she lay quietly beside him, he turned and buried his face in the curve of her neck. She held him, stroking his thick dark hair back from his forehead, loving him, wanting him to feel loved.

In spite of the hazards, the hardships, and the dangers, she would be forever thankful that she had taken the train from Marietta. Because of it, she had met the man who made her life complete.

About the Author

DOROTHY GARLOCK is one of America's—and the world's—favorite novelists. Her work has appeared on national best-seller lists, including the *New York Times* extended list, and there are over fifteen million copies of her books in print translated into eighteen languages. She has won more than twenty writing awards, including five Silver Pen Awards from *Affaire de Coeur* and three Silver Certificate Awards, and in 1998 she was selected a finalist for the National Writer's Club Best Long Historical Book Award.

After retiring as a news reporter and bookkeeper in 1978, she began her career as a novelist with the publication of *Love and Cherish*. She lives in Clear Lake, Iowa. You can visit her Web site at www.dorothygarlock.com.